Civic Center Corpse

A Ken Knoll Architectural Mystery

by

Christian Belz

For information, email **Cozy Cat Press**, cozycatpress@aol.com or visit our website at: www.cozycatpress.com

COZY CAT PRESS

ISBN: 978-1-939816-30-6
Printed in the United States of America

Cover design by Karri Klawiter
http://artbykarri.com

1 2 3 4 5 6 7 8 9 10

To Iris Lee Underwood and the Leapers
Thanks for years of support
and those wonderful Monday nights

Chapter 1

Surprises may pummel us without warning. I was driving down I-75 one Saturday evening headed for metro Detroit after leaving a business meeting in Gaylord. My firm had designed the client's home when he retired to that Alpine community. I hit the road later than planned—the client was a conversationalist and his wife had made a delicious meatloaf dinner—and now there was a back-up outside of Brighton. My friend Steve's anniversary party would be gathering momentum miles south of me. I planned to shave time by skipping my customary peach cobbler stop at Millie's on Grand River but it was already past nine o'clock.

I kicked myself. He asked me a couple of times about making it. I ought to have finished working last night and been on my way back home this morning. But yesterday afternoon, the client's son requested another meeting. If I'd known the summit would include 18 holes of golf and a homey dinner, I might have reconsidered.

Traffic cleared and we were moving again. My phone sounded. *Mighty Mouse*. Edison, my intern.

"Hey pal," I said.

"There's a man dead. I think you should get over here."

"What? Where are you?"

"Um, sorry. I know you're at the party and everything, but this is probably important. You should be here. The sign fell and—"

"Wait, I'm not at Steve's yet. Slow down. What sign?"

"At the civic center. Jeanelle and I attended the poetry reading. You know, it's one of the inaugural events. By the way, the building looks great. Love that grand stairwell. Anyway, in the middle of the program, the sign fell off the building. The Neumann Auditorium sign."

"Whoa. The big sign? Off the roof?"

"Exactly, this is what I'm telling you. And it killed somebody."

Our building. Recently completed. What the hell?

Edison continued. "You better get here. This isn't good."

"Yeah, yeah. I'm about forty minutes away."

I hung up and punched the accelerator.

How could the sign fall? It was secured to the metal framework atop the building, bolted to the steel frame. Did Steve, our structural engineer, make a mistake? Not likely. Of course there was that time in Traverse City, when he had indulged in too much partying. But it was just once and he was so appalled at his own failure I doubted he would make an error like that again.

My phone chirped. Robert, the boss.

"Cannoli—we've got trouble. Are you watching the news?" Robert's voice had more of an edge than usual. The dash clock said 10:09. "Cannoli?"

The nickname annoyed me. Wally, one of our rambunctious project managers coined the label, alluding to my pronounced pot belly and six-foot-three-inch frame. It was an easy transition from Ken Knoll.

"No, Robert. I'm on the freeway, heading back from the Gaylord meeting with Walter Gruen."

"Oh, yeah. I hope you have good notes. I want to hear about that later. Right now, a crisis has reared its ugly head, and I need you on this. How quick can you be at the civic center?"

I resented his tone. "Robert, I've been on the road for hours after a difficult meeting. Can you—"

"I don't care what you've been through. Jerome Neumann is dead. The sign has just fallen off the Neumann Auditorium and squashed him flat. Unlucky bastard. It's all over the news."

Jerome Neumann?

Robert continued his rant. "How the hell could this happen? Did the contractor blow it, or did you guys screw up the design? Get hold of Steve Dickerson and survey the conditions A-S-A-P. I want photos, measurements, the works. What a predicament! I'll track down our insurance agent Sue what's-her-name and get her down there too."

"Robert, that assembly couldn't have failed. Those connections were tested and certified. But what about Motor City Sign?" I said.

"Humpf. What?"

"Do we know where the failure occurred? Have you called the sign company? Maybe it's in the attachment of their sign to our framework, not in the framework we designed."

"Christ, Cannoli, do I have to do everything? Call Paul Larkin and get him out there too. Meanwhile, you guys document every nut, bolt and weld. I want to know what went wrong before we end up in court."

"On my way." I hung up. I dreaded the long night ahead of me.

Ever since last month's liability seminar, Robert had been acting particularly prudent. What a switch. I guess those lawyers scared the bejesus out of him. Document everything. And don't rely on the police or the insurance people or anyone else. Sad. He was thinking about repercussions to the firm, and a man was dead. Priorities.

I pictured Jerome Neumann chuckling, brown plaid vest over a pale yellow shirt, freckled skin stretched taught over the bony head beneath his thinning strawberry hair. He never left my office without a golf joke, or asking about me personally. Sweet man. Not to mention the $3 million he donated to the library that prompted the auditorium project to come to fruition.

Edison phoned again to fill me in on the identity of the dead man.

"I know, Robert just called me. Listen, he wants me to bring Steve and survey the place."

"I don't know how you're going to do that. The police are all over."

"We'll figure something out. Are you going to be there for a while?"

"We'll hang until we see what the police do."

"What about Nicole? Is she there?" I wondered how Neumann's wife was faring.

"She was here earlier. I don't know, now."

I disconnected and dialed Steve, our structural engineer du jour. The firm changed consultants every couple of years. You're only as good as your last job, the saying goes. If Dickerson was responsible for today's catastrophe, he would be out the door too.

"Hey, Ken. Are you coming over? We're having a blast." I heard a muddle of conversation and giggles in the background, the distinctive strains of AC-DC's *Dirty Deeds Done Dirt Cheap* blaring.

"No, Steve. Sorry to ruin your party. Robert wants us down at the auditorium project."

"No, can't go now, Ken. What's Robert's problem? It's Saturday night." His voice was raised over the ruckus behind him.

"There's been an accident. Jerome Neumann was killed."

"Huh, what'd you say?" He must have moved, as the

background noise muffled somewhat. "Killed? Oh my god. How?"

"Apparently he was, ur, ahh... felled by the 'Neumann Auditorium' sign."

"What? The sign killed him?"

"Uh-huh."

Silence stretched on, until I thought I'd lost the line.

"Ken, that's impossible. The connections—"

"Were tested, I know."

* * *

The Neumann Auditorium was a recent annex to the Southfield City Library. After weeks of interviewing, presenting concept sketches and battling it out with eleven other firms, BPW Architects was awarded the project. As much as I detest Robert Westin, one of the partners, I believe his lobbying helped tip the scales in our favor. Robert had returned to the firm a few months before the project came along, after being away for almost a year on a personal leave of absence.

Our plans called for demolition of a large portion of the old Fitzgerald Reading Room, a ton of modifications to what remained, and the addition of a new two-hundred seat auditorium, with integrated technology updates. At the roof we designed a circular screen, sheathed with a standing seam copper roof on a sixty-degree angle. The simple addition of a metal roof screen would change the appearance of the entire building. Along the Evergreen Road elevation, we placed a sign panel above the parapet: the words "NEUMANN AUDITORIUM" in three-foot high letters, attached with metal framework to the roof, the text backlit by four rows of T-5 fluorescent lamps. Against the night sky, the dark letters appeared outlined in white.

* * *

Steve and I approached the building. The aluminum

"Auditorium" letters remained at the parapet, though no longer lit. It appeared cold against the sky.

We encountered a hub of commotion on the front lawn along Evergreen. News trucks from Fox2, News-4 and Channel 7 lined the drive, glaring lights on enormous poles illuminating the lawn like a football field. A crowd in formal attire was crammed up against the yellow police tape. We approached the accident scene, fitted with cameras, tape measure, and clip boards. Steve Dickerson was dressed in casual slacks and a sport shirt, but I had on the grungy jeans and a t-shirt I had changed into for the drive home. I was not expecting this failure investigation to be a formal event.

The crowd looked out as if this were a spectator sport. Pushing our way to the front of the group, our eyes were drawn to a point twenty feet away. The trussed metal carcass lay face down, the letter "M" squarely on a sprawled-out tuxedo-clad torso, the leading leg of the "A" across the back of his head. I was relieved to see there was little blood.

Sergeant Gilmore, who I had met during the course of the auditorium project, moved toward us. As he approached, I noted that the lines on the forehead of his oval face appeared deeper, and the scantiness of his thinning salt-and-pepper hair more meager in the harsh light.

"Sargent Gilmore, Ken Knoll, we met—"

"Yeah, yeah." Mouth tight, eyes hard.

We explained our mission.

"No," Sergeant Gilmore grimaced. "You'll have to stand clear. Access is restricted to our investigators. No private investigation. No cameras, no measurements. Tomorrow, maybe." He turned away.

"But it will be helpful to determine the cause—" I called after him.

Sargent Gilmore jerked a thumb at an officer, who

headed our way. We weren't going to make any headway here. We took in what we could see from that vantage point, then drew back.

FOX2's reporter was off to the side, microphone in hand, every line of her plum suit immaculate. She interviewed a woman in her early forties, the subject gesturing emphatically. A cocky smirk on her pale, wide face, she pointed up to where the sign had stood, jabbing her finger in the air like a mad-woman. Her actions spelled jocularity despite her professional attire, a form- fitting teal suit over an ivory blouse. The skirt ended just above the knees, strappy black heels polished off shapely legs.

Could it be my raven-haired nemesis, Shirley Hanson?

Chapter 2

"Quite an act, isn't she?" Steve said. "Nice stems though."

"I don't believe it. Wherever she goes, trouble follows." Like watching a wreck on the freeway, I couldn't take my eyes off her exaggerated motions. "Let's get to work before she sees us."

Ignoring Sergeant Gilmore's mandate prohibiting us from investigating the scene, I led the way. Entering the building from the east, I was intent on getting to the roof. One of the utility rooms on the mezzanine level provided access to a steel ladder which would take us to the roof hatch. We crossed the polished black-and-white marble flooring and hoofed up the carpeted grand stairway. At the top, we found a police sentry blocking the doorway to the utility rooms.

No dice.

We back-tracked down the stairs and surveyed the reception hall. I was surprised to see new widow Nicole Neumann at the scene, slouched against a table in the corner. Her auburn hair and canary yellow dress against her milk chocolate complexion would have been striking under other circumstances, but given the tragedy, it cried out in irony. With the red in her eyes and moisture on her cheeks, the effect was grim. Three women of equally glamorous attire were at her side, obviously lavishing comfort.

I was struck by the fragility of life. Not a month ago, the couple, Jerome and Nicole Neumann, rife with enthusiasm and vitality, had come by the office to express their pleasure at the new building.

How quickly our circumstances can change.

On the walls, well-crafted posters identified the evening's event as honoring Michigan's unofficial poet laureate, Gwendolyn something-or-another. In the abutting hallway I noticed placards for the annual used book sale, and next week's blood drive.

"Steve, we've got to get up higher than the roof level in order to check those sign supports."

He nodded.

We exited the lobby through the glass vestibule. Though the sun had set, people congregated outside in their formal evening wear, some of the ladies in backless attire in the unseasonably warm evening. The yellow police tape provided a somber backdrop.

Here we go again. Rumblings from the past fed a growing knot in my stomach. Fifteen months earlier two deaths plagued our firm, including the murder of my secretary, the bodies found on one of my construction sites. That was a time, and those were emotions I ached to forget, shut in a forged steel vault and destroy the key. Why did death seem to follow me around?

We looked to the neighboring structures. The three story library/media center was set back to the left, the one-story city offices to the right. Both buildings were dark, the occupants long gone and certainly the doors locked.

"What'cha doing here, Ken? Protecting your butt?" Shirley Hansen's voice fell on my ear drums like a squealing water pipe.

I spun around and was struck by her blazing blue eyes. "Shirley Hansen! Why the last time I saw you... Oh, that's right, you didn't show. And now you're a sensationalist. What a waste of intelligence. Here to dig some dirt? A man is dead. Have you no sense of dignity?"

Shirley smiled, giving Steve the once-over.

"Listen," she said. "I saw you looking around. Trying to get to the roof, huh? I may be able to help. I have a friend, lives in the apartments over there." She pointed to the fifteen-story Towne Center apartments immediately on the other side of Evergreen.

"Shut up, Shirley. I'm not going anywhere with—"

"She's a dentist. Has a telescope. Twelfth floor. I bet you could see plenty."

I wasn't inclined to allow her the satisfaction of helping me.

Steve turned first to the apartments, then back to the auditorium, gauging the distance. "Ken, I think that might work."

His optimistic glance held no sway against Shirley's know-it-all smile. "Forget it, we'll find—"

"Good riddance! The guy was a bum," a man's husky voice boomed from my right.

Our heads pivoted in unison.

The man standing at his elbow said, "You can't mean that! Shut your mouth. No one deserves to die."

"Hell yes, I mean it. The guy was the most mean-spirited S.O.B. I've met in my life. Treated people like dirt! Thought he could walk all over everybody. I should know. And what he did to his wife!"

I recognized the speaker as Matt Lance, a member of the city's planning board, a group I knew well. When I returned my attention to Shirley, she was barreling toward the men on four inch heels.

"Thank God. I was afraid we weren't going to get rid of her," I mumbled.

Steve nodded. "She *is* kind of annoying."

"Listen, Steve, we've got to get up high to get a view of the roof. Ideas?"

"Two. There's a truck-mounted boom crane on site,

on the far side of the golf center. If only we could find a way to commandeer it. Do you know anyone at Andover Construction?"

"Not bad, but I haven't worked with Andover. What else do you have?"

"Check out those TV news trucks. I bet we could see the roof from the top of those towers." He pointed in the direction of the white news vans, fitted with camera towers which must have risen thirty feet above the ground. The trussed, triangular framework certainly would be scalable.

My phone rang. Robert. "Well? What did you find out?"

"Sergeant Gilmore is in charge of the site. He's not letting us on the roof, or anywhere near the fallen structure," I said.

"This is critical. It's imperative you find a way up there and take those pictures!"

"We're trying," I said flatly and signed off. "Steve, let's look around the other side of the building. There must be a way to climb up on that roof." We shuffled along the side of the structure, noting the two story brick wall. Mullions on the glass and aluminum curtainwall were not close enough together, or of adequate depth, to scale. No trees. No site furnishings. This side of the building was quiet, away from the crowd, the noise and the news lights. We continued around the building to the trash enclosure, opened the wooden gates and noted the overflowing dumpsters, piled high with stuffed black garbage bags, the dumpster lids open, leaning back against the building wall. Even if we stood on them we would not be able to reach the top of the building's wall. I hated to say it. "It doesn't look like we're going to be able to get up high enough from here."

As we pondered the situation, movement in my

peripheral vision caught my eye. I shifted to see a blue Genie ambling in our direction. What was it doing outside? I was accustomed to seeing maintenance people use that kind of lift to change lamps in gymnasiums, or contractors putting up drywall in a two-story lobby. The articulating boom was in its lowered position, the tuxedo-clad operator wobbling on the tiny-wheeled machine. Or was he dancing? His kinky dark hair flew in all directions. Edison! My common-sense challenged intern.

He waved a chubby hand in our direction. As he neared our position, he said, "Hey guys, need a lift?"

Chapter 3

"Hey!" I said. "You're appearance is timely! But what—? How?"

He climbed off the machine. "Yeah, Ken, well, like I said: Jeanelle and I were here for the poetry thing. Did you know she's a poet, too? Last week on that shoot with Steven Meisel in Bangkok—did I tell you about that? His office called her at absolutely the last nano-second. I guess one of his girls came down with the flu. What a great opportunity for—"

I sighed. My normal tolerance for Edison's rambles had been eroded by my keyed-up nerves. I wanted nothing more than to finish our task and go home to bed. My impatience must have registered on his side, as he stopped mid-sentence.

"Ah, well, anyway, we were in the auditorium, when we heard this insidious metallic clattering. The program ground to a halt, and everyone ran outside. We—"

"Wait. You could hear it from inside?"

"Yeah, yeah. Jeanelle and I, we had seats in the third row. You know Li-Young Lee read a couple of pieces. I never followed him much, except his poem 'Furious Versions,' with the line *I lay dismantled*. I think about that sometimes in bed after an exhausting day. He's captured exactly how I feel. Nailed it. But what's with the first and last names being the same? I more preferred the—"

"Edison!"

Steve looked on silently.

"Oh, yeah. Obviously the sign had fallen off. We

exited from the doors beside the stage. The wreckage loomed big as a dinosaur. We noticed the guy's arm sticking out from beneath the belly of the beast. Everyone became frantic, checking to see who was missing. Of course, the police were there stat—they just walked over from the station next door—and kept everyone back. Channel 4 was set-up here covering the readings and set their cameras up outside. The guy had to be dead, unless he was the Hulk or something.

"It didn't take long for Nicole Neumann to start screaming and go hysterical. The ladies in her group took her inside. A while later I noticed the police had sought her out. Apparently Neumann had gone outside during the intermission and never popped back into his seat."

"What time was the intermission?" I said.

Edison screwed up his face, as if pondering calculus. "We broke about eight-thirty for twenty minutes."

Steve joined in. "What time did the sign fall?"

"Once they returned to the program, a couple of Michigan's top poets read some pieces, before they introduced Gwendolyn Darmus, the main event. She'd just barely started...I'd say about nine-twenty-five."

Steve raised his eyebrows. "Wonder what occupied Neumann's time for half an hour?"

We stared at each other for a moment. I scanned over the clunky machine before me. "Edison, when did you get the Genie?"

"When I saw you guys pull up with your clip boards, I realized we'd have to find a way to the roof to check out the sign supports."

"So where did you requisition this from?" Steve said.

Edison smiled. "I thought of the Community Center. Remember last year? Work sent me to the Construction Trades Show here in Southfield; thought I could learn something. During the building codes seminar the guys were out on the floor with this Genie, replacing burnt-out light bulbs. Our first break, I talked to the maintenance guys, Paul and Lester. They showed me how to run the thing, and I changed a few bulbs. Getting up high is so much fun, they should have these at Cedar Point. Maybe set up a beefed-up game of dodge-em cars. Anyway, I thought you guys could use some leverage getting up to roof level. For sure, the cops would have it locked off."

"So, you and Jeanelle came out to the poetry reading," Steve accused.

Edison affected his sheepish look. "Yeah, I know you had your party tonight, but Jeanelle was so geeked by the poetry response. I didn't finish telling you. In Bangkok she shared a couple of her sonnets with Meisel. He absolutely flipped! I heard later he called Maki Justine— you know, she's that hot fashion designer, born in Detroit by the way—making a splash all over the world."

As if I would know these things.

"Maki Justine was so impressed with Jeanelle's poetry, she's entertaining the idea of printing her poems on silk camisoles."

Yes, Edison's latest girl was a model. High fashion. I was agog. How did an ordinary guy, I mean plain average Joe, manage to charm celebrities and models? It was beyond my comprehension. Maybe if I spent more time with him, some of it would rub off on me.

Early in his adulthood, Edison was what you might call a kept man. At the tender age of eighteen, he caught the eye of Motown hip hop queen QDevine. She was hot stuff. Her "Pop the Top" single crashed into the Billboard Top 10 and stayed there for twelve weeks. Follow-up hits made her a household name and earned her enough money to build a recording studio in her eight-thousand square foot Detroit mansion, a grand affair in Detroit's Palmer Park district. Edison met her at a concert at Meadowbrook Theater, where she welcomed the public in a "meet and greet event." They began hanging out, and soon she invited him to live with her.

QDevine introduced Edison to half the world of celebrity. They turned the city upside down, throwing lavish parties and attending all of the premier social events, until Q kicked him out. Reasons remain unexplained, at least to me. Rumor has it that QDevine's hit "Hurt Nobody" recounts the story of their breakup.

It was Edison's time in that part of town, I understand, with its richly detailed homes, that turned him on to architecture.

Edison climbed back on the Genie. "So, where shall I set up?"

A big-eyed gazelle in a silky black number with a scalloped skirt floated in. With her olive skin, I likened her to a dusky mermaid.

"Hi, Baby." She ran her fingertips along Edison's upper arm.

Edison's chunky lips smiled. "Hey. Decide to come outside again?"

"I missed you." Small and high-pitched, her voice fell easily on my ears. "And I'm queasy from all this unpleasantness."

"Well, Sweetie, let me lift these guys up to the roof, and then I'll take you for tea."

She offered up her lips, which he happily bussed. Then she turned on her heels and sashayed away.

"Ok, guys, let's get this going."

Steve and I led the way to a position below where the sign had stood. Edison maneuvered the Genie into place on the sidewalk.

"Edison, can you lock this contraption down?" Steve said. "We'll have to hang the boom over the roof edge so I can get close enough."

"And what have we here?" erupted a voice behind us. "If it isn't Laurel and Hardy at the Auditorium."

I recognized the baritone before seeing Sergeant Gilmore. "You're interfering with a police scene."

"But, Sergeant, we need to—" I began.

"What you need, gentlemen, is to move this apparatus out of this area immediately."

So close.

"Yes, sir," I said. Back to square one. "Thanks for trying, Edison. Would you mind scooting the Genie back to where you found it?"

He nodded, and wheeled the gizmo about.

The Sergeant turned back to us, "Don't go too far, gentlemen. I'm going to want to speak to you in a bit."

We nodded and he walked away. Steve and I looked at each other. "What now?" he said. "Are you thinking of taking Shirley up on her offer?"

"I can't stand that woman. But Robert—"

A woman's voice interjected. "Robert what?" *Shirley again.* "Not Robert Westin? I was under the impression that he blew town after those murders at your Flamingo Shores project last year." Though her expression was one of concern, her voice betrayed her excitement.

I hid my shock at her knowledge of the firm's dark past.

"Oh, thought that had escaped me, huh? True, I was away in Brazil covering that Estah Apartment project at the time, but I heard about it later." What was the deal with her pink frosted lipstick? She wasn't twenty anymore.

Ignoring her, I said to Steve, "Let's get out of here."

"What about your work?" Shirley flashed her eyes at

me sideways. "What about Robert? Leaving your job unfinished?"

I started walking toward the car, away from Shirley. "I need a break." Steve kept up with my long stride.

"Uh-huh."

"Let's grab a quick bite. We can continue after."

We drove a few blocks to my favorite greasy spoon.

"So what's up with you and Shirley? Have you got some kind of old grudge?" Steve asked as we entered the back door to Ray's Coney.

I paused as a flash of anger passed through me.

"It's like you looked daggers at her," he said.

Chapter 4

We took a table and I pushed Steve a menu. "Do you even know who she is?"

"The name's vaguely familiar . . ."

"She writes for *San Francisco Divulged*. Her specialty is building and construction, but it's all dirt. She gets behind the scenes at council and planning meetings, scopes out architects and builders and anything related to the field. She keeps needling her way around until she finds the gossip. A council member whose daughter received a scholarship by one of the development firms with a project up before the board. State funded projects that are over budget. Who's sleeping with who to get what job. Kind of like—"

"Wait, she's not *The Voice from Inside*?"

"Yep."

Steve let out a howl, chortling as his hand slapped the table.

"She freelances for those supermarket tabloids, too, and I've heard her on talk radio dishing her inside poop."

"Some of that sounds like worthwhile public service."

"Yeah, I don't object to keeping people on the up and up. But her tactics leave me livid."

We were interrupted by the waitress, who took our order for coneys and fries. A diet Coke for Steve, a chocolate shake for me.

"So how do you know her...skeleton in your closet?"

I shook my head. "No, no, nothing like that. I went to school with her."

"So she has a background in the field. I bet she was hell on wheels even then."

"We were in the same design class, junior year."

"Lawrence Tech?"

"Yeah. The assignment was to do a building types study. Research, examples, compare and contrast, the whole bit. I did mine on airports. Historical development from the early twentieth century. Saarinen's approach at Dulles, etcetera."

"Broad topic."

"Yeah, I bit off more than I could chew. But catch this, Shirley gets permission to do her study on public spaces—plazas, squares, fountains, malls—anywhere that people congregate."

"Not exactly buildings."

"Right, but close enough for the professor," I said. "So she does the overall study including some piazzas in Italy, the mall in DC and so on. But then she investigates some local examples—Hart Plaza in downtown Detroit and the bear fountain at the Zoo. It was springtime."

"Uh-huh."

"So the project is not just the architecture—form, style, and so on—but the effect it has on people."

"I don't follow," Steve said as the waitress brought our food.

I took a sip of my shake. "Oh, that's good. In her preliminary presentation she notes that she's hanging out in these public places, watching people, taking pictures. What they do. How they interact. And she notices an element of romance. Couples holding hands, arms around each other, sharing ice cream."

"Perfectly natural."

"The professor eats it up. Yes! That's what he wants

to see. How does the space affect life?"

"I still don't—"

"Wait. Here's the punch line. For the final class, we all arrive early to set up our presentations, in the public display hall outside the design studio. When I arrive with my boards—after staying up all night to get them done—there's a crowd around a series of pictures."

Steve looked up from his french fry.

"Hart Plaza, a couple sitting on the concrete benches at the performance bowl. Older man in a suit next to a coed in jeans."

"And—"

"Unmistakably, it's Dean Warner and one of my classmates, Julie Kimball. Side by side. Their hand gestures and facial expressions indicating an argument."

"Ok, so how's that—"

"Wait, there's more. There's a series of photos, looks like the same couple but you can't see their faces—same clothes though—back down one of the concrete hallways, in the shadows. Standing. She's backed against the wall, and they're kissing. I mean passionately. Hands all over the place."

"Whoa, not very academic."

"Yeah."

"So what happened? What did the professor do?"

I shook my head. "Nothing. Shirley didn't show. As soon as the professor saw the photos, he took them down. Of course, the damage was done."

"What? She couldn't face it? What did she say when she came back?"

"She dropped out of school. Never saw her again until today."

Steve's face sagged.

"Steve, it was unconscionable. Posting the photos, outing Dean Warner. In public. No chance to defend himself. Cost him his job, put his marriage in jeopardy. I'm not defending him. But why didn't she do this behind closed doors, handle it privately without causing a school scandal? I didn't know the girl, Julie, but I heard she quit out of embarrassment. In the moment I saw those pictures, Shirley lost my respect forever."

Chapter 5

Back at the site, we stared at the building.

"What now?' Steve asked.

"I'm gonna kill you!" a voice rang out behind me. I turned to see the project roofer shaking his fists at the older man, Matt Lance, who we had seen arguing earlier.

Matt said something back that I didn't make out, and put his hand on the younger man's shoulder. The roofer brushed it off and turned away.

My phone rang. Robert. Crap! I turned it off. I'd deal with him later. I raised my eyes to Steve and sighed. We had tried everything else; only one option remained.

"I'll go find her," I said. *Why wouldn't this night end?*

"Play nice." Steve chuckled.

I spotted Shirley a few dozen yards to my left, talking to a group of men and women in evening wear. As I ambled toward her, she looked in my direction and smiled. Before I arrived, she had released herself from the group and turned my way.

"Change your mind?" Though her eyes were bright and earnest, her smirk irritated me.

I hated to turn a friendly face to her, but I might as well try. "Hey Shirley, your assistance would be helpful, and we'd like to take you up on your offer."

She stood silent, considering me, surveying my grubby clothes, her long lashes deepening the shadows along her eyes. How I hated her judging me. I felt her sizing me up, searching for an angle to use against me. *Forget it!* "Shirley—"

"Wait 'til you see it!" Her eyes grew large. "Of course, the basics are lush—polished wood floors, emerald green leather couch and chair. Mahogany book cases with glass doors. But get this: she hired an artist to embellish the walls and ceilings. His paint replicates the materials and their texture, shadows–everything— dead on. The result is reminiscent of an Italian estate: marble columns lining the corridor, blue sky with cumulus clouds. In the living room, there's a scene of olive trees framing a panoramic view of a vineyard."

Was she being civil?

"I can't wait to see your reaction. Listen, there's something else too. A surprise."

A crane appeared in the background behind her, its trussed shaft rising against the moonlit sky. Steve came up, whistling low. We focused our attention toward the action and huddled into the crowd to watch as men in tan jumpsuits, in the company of uniformed police officers, fastened a cable to the sign framework. Officers spread out a tarp on the adjacent lawn. Slowly, the framework and its mangled sign were lifted from the body, moved to the side, then lowered again and set down on the tarp.

We stared at the tuxedo-clad man sprawled out on the lawn, too much red on the back of his balding head, pieces of broken glass and metal littered on his clothing and the adjacent grass.

I stifled the urge to vomit.

Before turning away, I noticed another item which had been obscured by the sign. A few inches from Jerome's left hand lay a cardboard box, hardcover books in dark colors spilling out on the damp lawn.

"Let's get out of here," I managed to say.

"They'd better hang the rat-bastard," Shirley hissed.

Steve's phone rang. "Hello...What?...Alright...OK, I'll be there in a bit."

He fumbled with the instrument.

"Some of the boys are getting rowdy. I need to go home and settle things down."

To Shirley I said, "Can I catch a ride over with you?"

"It'll cost you."

Hmpf. I pulled the keys out of my pocket. "Steve, take my car. Call it a night. I'll check out the supports with the telescope and snap a few pictures. That's all we can do today."

Steve walked away and Shirley reached into her purse, retracting a set of keys. "Amanda's out of town, so we're on our own, but I cleared it with her earlier."

During the short ride across the street, I considered the box of books. How did it get there? Had it been lying on the grass before the accident? Doubtful. Had Neumann been carrying it? Not likely, in his tuxedo.

We took the elevator to the twelfth floor.

Shirley had not exaggerated her description of the apartment. Curved glass, floor to ceiling, yielding a spectacular view of the civic center and, fading into the inky black, the surrounding golf course. The lack of drapes or any sort of window covering surprised me, but so high up why would you need them?

The interior walls and ten foot ceilings provided ample opportunity for adornment. Murals stretched into the ceiling creating a surreal atmosphere.

"Nice. You were right."

She tilted her head to one side. "More than nice. I'd say it's sublimely perfect."

The telescope held a prominent position along the glass curtainwall. One of those pricey jobs, sleek black aluminum body with an enormous lens.

The lawn across the street glowed under the police

and news-crew lights, the illumination sharply cut off at the roofline. Though I could make out the portion of the roof where the sign had stood, the light was insufficient to review the details and supports.

Dead end. No pun intended.

"Well, that's that. I'll have to pick this up in the morning." I looked at her, a dark curl caressing her forehead. I pulled out my cell phone. "I'll call a cab and be out of your way."

"Hey, would you like a drink? Amanda's not much for booze, but I think there's beer."

"Ok. One."

Blue flame danced in her eyes as she pulled bottles of Miller Lite out of the fridge and popped the tops.

I said, "Those men at the site. That was Matt Lance, he's on the board. What did he tell you about why he wanted Neumann dead?"

"You know the guy?"

"Lance, yeah. I met with the board several times gaining approvals for the project and working out details. He never displayed that type of venom, at least not when I was present."

"During a meeting? *Please.* That type, he'd have two personalities. One stoic, reserved for public occasions. The other passionate, to the point of frenzy. I've seen the ilk: borderline sociopathic."

"Huh. So what was his comment about?"

"Apparently there's—there was—an on-going feud between them. He's quite livid about it."

"What kind of feud?"

"From the way he spoke, this goes way back. Matt Lance was one of the sub-contractors on a housing subdivision under development by Neumann. He started jabbering about Neumann screwing him out of a lot of money. In his rambling on, he used words like beginning, starting off and the like. From what I gather, this occurred before either of them had made a name for themselves. But, sooner than he revealed any more about it, his aggravation reached a fever pitch, shaking his fists and spouting gibberish."

"Hum. Wonder what that's about. Must have been huge, for him to be so keyed up about it years later."

"Well, I've known people to get something caught in their craw and never let go of it."

"Hum." *Yeah, me too.*

"And did you see Nicole Neumann?" Shirley said.

"At the reception hall? She was sitting on one of those hard wooden chairs, surrounded by friends. Pitching back and forth. Those gals were falling over themselves to take care of her. Lucky to have that kind of support. Poor woman, looked pretty messed up. I don't know why she didn't go home."

"I heard she was waiting for the police to confirm what happened. Sitting on pins and needles."

"Knives and scalpels is more like it. Wouldn't get any rest at home anyway. Pitiful. Horrible night for her. I can't even imagine someone I care deeply about being brutally snatched away in such a fashion. The way she was bawling, she must have been deeply in love with him." I finished the last swig of my beer.

"Well, it wasn't mutual."

"Huh?"

"It seems that he mistreated her dreadfully. The other item Matt Lance was all hopped up about."

"What? He always seemed so nice."

"Ken, you trust people too much. Always did. You have to look beyond appearances and what people say. Matt didn't specify, though."

"Humpf. So, Shirley, why did you come here anyway? Back to Michigan I mean."

"Work. Following up on a story."

"Always working, aren't you?" As I studied her,

suddenly her eyes lost their focus, her slender fingers caressed her beer bottle. Even in the lateness of the hour, after the stress of the evening, Shirley's skin glowed softly, the surface layers underlain with a luminescence.

"So what happened back then, Shirley, in class?"

She pushed back her chair. "Are you done?"

"Huh?"

She indicated my bottle, then took it. "I have to get to bed."

She moved away, heading for the back hallway. "You can let yourself out."

"Hey. What about my surprise?" I said.

She stopped, and slowly turned toward me. She wrinkled her nose and tilted her head. "Come here," she said, holding out a hand. I took her hand, soft, warm skin.

She led me across the wood floor, along the faux colonnade in the corridor, to a door painted to resemble distressed wood with iron hinges. She grasped the ornate doorknob and pushed in. She flicked on the light.

The bedroom was appointed in mint green tones with modern, clean lines. The head- and foot-boards were oak planes, with matching dresser and night stand. What attracted my attention, however, were the photographs of entertainment personalities adorning the walls. Old/new pairings of Hollywood actors offset by images from a modern TV series. James Dean looked at me over a cigarette; the adjacent screen shot from *The O.C.* had Ryan Atwood in his leather jacket, smoky gaze holding my attention. Marilyn Monroe in a one piece swimsuit and high heels, next to *The O.C.'s* Marissa and Summer in their bikinis, laying out at the crystal clear pool, their marble-faced mansion in the background; Humphrey Bogart next to Ryan again, both in wife-beaters. Lynda Carter's Wonder Woman, regal head-tilt, next to Summer in her Superhero costume, shiny short pants and long boots.

Shirley tapped the corner of the Summer Hero picture. "This is my favorite."

"Yeah? Remind you of your aspirations to save the world and crush your enemies?"

She twisted her mouth. "Something like that."

"How did you know I liked this kind of stuff?" I said.

She scanned me from the corner of her eye. "I don't know. In school you were always quoting some movie scene or another."

"I was?"

"Let's see. *This was no boat accident.* And then there was: *Roads. Where we're going we don't need roads.* And how about: *If you don't get on that plane right now you'll regret it. Maybe not today. Maybe not tomorrow, but soon and for the rest of your life.*"

I laughed. "Yeah, those were some good ones. I didn't realize you paid attention."

We looked at each other silently, unspoken words filling the space between us.

She smoothed the front of her skirt. "I have to get out of this suit." She disappeared into the bathroom.

I considered the day's events as I shuffled back through the room, examining the photos. We would have to check the roof with the telescope as soon as the sun rose.

Did the audience in the poetry event hear or see anything? There was a parking lot to the North of the building. There was no direct angle to the sign, but perhaps someone parking their car noticed a suspicious act, or a person who seemed out of place.

Exhaustion tore at my arms. I had to go home.

Light shone in as she opened the bathroom door. Bare feet on the porcelain tile, slender legs stood out against a black negligee, bare arms leaning against the door frame. Briefly backlit, the stark outline of her nude torso beneath the sheer cloth caught in my throat.

I was drawn to the narrowness of her waist above the curve of her hips. The light was doused and darkness overtook us. Clothes were pulled, clutched, and torn.

I basked in wanton pleasure and took without remorse. Hot breath enveloped my ear, followed by soft lips. Ensconced for a momentary eternity, we gave in to the basest of our needs. Our breath synchronized and we drifted into oblivion.

When I awoke I felt an ache in my back, a pencil point just below the rib cage. My eyes opened to momentary disorientation. Bed, too firm. Sheets, smelled of musk.

The bed was empty beside me. I swung my legs to the floor, stood. My eyes swept the room. The floor was cleared of everything save for the comforter, which must have slipped from the bed during the night.

Ryan Atwood peered my way over a cigarette. "Hey," he said with remarkable understanding. I nodded in acknowledgment.

Summer, on the other hand, laughed haughtily at me from behind her frame. Hands on hips, head thrown back.

She didn't get it.

An urgency drew me to the bathroom. Water droplets on the shower and sink indicated earlier activity. I took care of business and then explored the apartment.

A breakfast plate had been arranged: fruit bowl of grapes, melon, and an unpeeled banana. Bran muffin. Unsalted butter. Carafe of coffee, which smelled delicious. Silverware precisely arranged. Laptop.

Note: "Had to run. Enjoy. Feel free to use Amanda's

computer if you need to check your mail. She won't mind."

Sun streamed in from the panoramic glazing. I pulled on my boxers and strode to the window. The telescope was easily adjusted and aimed at the auditorium roof.

Though I could make out the pipe supports clearly, I observed nothing notable. I snapped a few pictures through the telescope, for the record. I thought to call Robert, but had nothing to report.

I turned on the laptop, then sat to enjoy the breakfast. I reflected on last night's developments. Perhaps I had been too hard on her. Maybe there was something I failed to understand. Possibly there were reasons for her gossip ways.

There was nothing of interest in my email. I cut up the banana and dropped it on my cereal. After reviewing the Yahoo home page, I keyed in *The San Francisco Divulged* to see what Shirley was up to. Whoa. There was the auditorium sign, laying on the man's back. A smaller photo glared at me. It was of Steve and me, clipboards in hand, cameras around our necks. The article was titled *Sign of a Bad Conscience*, underlain with Shirley's by-line. As first I was startled. Then, I read faster as realization encircled me like a rattlesnake.

In the wake of a man's death, BPW Architects shows little caring...before the body was even removed from the site, they dispatched two of their staff to protect their interests...Ken Knoll led the charge to investigate the fatal accident, not to aid in the resolution to the dead man's family, but to prove the firm's innocence in this tragic event...Not much more than a year ago the firm was shrouded by two deaths as Knoll's secretary was slain, while one of BPW's senior associates was charged with the killing of a prominent businessman. Why is this firm surrounded by murder and mayhem?

I pushed back the chair, threw the napkin on my breakfast dishes, dressed hastily, grabbed my camera and clip board and exited the apartment. I slammed the door behind me.

Bitch.

Chapter 6

As I stomped out onto the street, a speeding Dodge nearly brushed me. The whoosh raised the crusty yellowbrown leaves from the gutter, and they danced like marionettes. Gritty road dust swirled around me and I shielded my eyes.

I was ashamed. My thirst for carnal satisfaction had been fully exploited by her predatory nature, ensnared by her girly wiles and heavenly scent. My guard down, I had fallen prey to the woman I most detested in the world.

Her actions cried out for punishment. How dare she take advantage of my weakness for sex, knowing how I felt about her. Which was what? Disgusted. I made her a ruthless, improper substitute for a reporter.

I crossed Evergreen, skipped over the curb and up the sidewalk and headed for the circular auditorium building. The tented sign structure on the lawn caused my gut to tighten. Separated from the pedestrian walks with heavy yellow police tape, the hulk was like a ghost with no one to spook, except me. Gone was the well-dressed crowd, the police guards, and everyone else.

I'd call Edison to pick me up, as Steve still had my car.

When I pulled the phone out of my pocket, it immediately chirped. "Ken Knoll."

"Cannoli, I've got better things to do on a Sunday morning than answer calls from the police looking for my chief architect. They say you am-scrayed in the middle of their investigation." Robert's words were slightly muffled, as if he was chewing.

"They wouldn't let me—"

"Sergeant Gilmore tells me he was waiting for things to settle down before reviewing the structure with you."

"Well, things got hairy. Then I had to go across the street in order to check out those sign supports."

"I haven't heard your report."

"It was inconclusive." Restless, I headed away from the building, the clip board tucked under my arm. "Give me his number and I will call. I'll apologize profusely." I shoved the camera into my coat and began walking down Evergreen.

He gave me the number. "Oh, and Sue Watts made it down and needs to meet with you before you entangle yourself in any more trouble. Remember, she's on our side. She's a little high strung, but take care of her. I need this liability issue to be a non-issue. *Capisce*?"

"You got it."

"Speaking of trouble, Cannoli, how is it you manage to magnetize every ounce of misery and pull it in your direction?"

The wind gusts picked up, and I found myself walking backwards along the street, the city's 1840 farmhouse—red and white job—to my right. Its low white picket fence reinforced the anachronistic image.

"Cannoli! Are you listening to me? How on earth did Shirley what's-her-name snap a picture of you and Steve on site? And that story! Your antics are getting the firm in hot water. Watch your mouth, and stay away from *The Voice from Inside*!"

Click.

I sighed and kicked a rock into a utility pole. It was Sunday morning and traffic was light. I dialed the police number.

"Hello Sergeant Gilmore, this is Ken Knoll, the architect for the Neumann Auditorium. I'm calling to–"

"Mr. Knoll." Dry. Matter-of-fact. "Where did you disappear to last night? Did I not explain that we needed your consultation? Did we not have an understanding—"

"Well, sir, I was called away. It seemed you were busy maintaining your perimeter, and, well, I didn't want to interfere—"

"Bullshit. Excuse my French, but you knew very well that I was expecting to review the site with you."

"Yessir. I'm sorry, but I'm available anytime today. What works for you?" I was facing straight ahead now, striding along, furthering my distance from the Auditorium building.

"Ten-thirty. On the lawn."

At the sign; he didn't have to say the words. I turned right and headed across the parking lot to Kerby's Coney Island. May as well warm up and have a cup of coffee. I punched my speed dial. "Listen Steve, we have an audience with Sergeant Gilmore."

"Hey, Ken, long time no see. Aughhh. What time is it? Crap. Man, it was a wicked night."

"Can you make it to the site in an hour? We'll walk the project, and take a closer look at those supports. Take my car over, and I'll give you a ride home after."

"Sure, sure. Let me slosh some ice water across my face and I'll be on my way."

I disconnected and the phone chirped.

"Ken, it's Sue Watts. Essential, Incorporated. Robert gave me your number. Of course, you know why I'm calling."

I disengaged my hand from Kerby's door to finish this conversation before entering. "Yeah, right, we should talk about the sign support failure."

"I understand you've started the investigation. Fast thinking for Robert to dispatch you right away."

Robert, trying to save his hide. "Yeah, we were on-site last night, but the police had everything locked down, and there were a few hundred gawkers." I huddled next to the rear of the building, coffee and pancake scents wafting through the building walls.

"Were you able to gather any hard evidence, photos, etcetera?"

"No, the police presence was dominant and prevented any procedural activities." I needed coffee. "But we're meeting on site shortly with the structural engineer."

"Good, good. I want a full report. Let's meet, say lunch at one o'clock at Fish Mack in Royal Oak?"

"Fine."

"Oh, Ken, one more thing."

"Yes?"

"It's very important that you don't talk to the press."

"Oh?"

"They have a habit of twisting things around. We need to keep a low profile. I understand this was on the local news last night, but the sooner this leaves the public arena the better. Understand?"

"Yes." Pray she doesn't see Shirley's article.

I popped a handful of quarters into a red *Detroit News* stand. I wondered how the *News* would handle the story, in comparison to Shirley's yellow rag. I folded the paper under my arm, entered, and slid into a booth. A cheery blonde set down a mug and poured from a pot of steaming coffee. I opened the paper. Nothing. The ceiling mounted TV in the corner of the room caught my attention. *Police are investigating what appears to be a freak accident.* Freak, for sure. *Unclear at this point what caused the structure to give way.* On the hot seat again. I turned to the newspaper comics, when I overheard two elderly women in the next booth.

"I can't believe it, Marlene, did you hear about that

accident last night at the Civic Center? Jerome Neumann was killed!"

"Hear about it? I was there! Ran down the street to take a look after I heard the commotion. I don't understand how that sign could just fall off. We weren't even having a storm or anything."

"You're right. It was even a bit warm. Beautiful evening. Someone is going to get into trouble over that one. Shoddy construction's my guess. No one takes pride in their work anymore. Lordy! Neumann himself! Can you imagine? Donating all that money, having your name put on the building, and then it all falls apart and kills you dead."

"It's a travesty. A plain shame. Now, I'm not saying he deserved it or anything, but did you know he was having an affair?"

My ears perked up.

The first woman said something unintelligible through a mouthful of food.

"Yeah, yeah. She was on the board. All that funny business. Sneaking around. I heard it had been going on for some time."

On the *planning* board? Who? I wondered. Julianne?

"No, really? Must have been some long nights, if you know what I mean. Working late, studying projects. Hey hey."

"I'm sure. Did his wife know? She's an adorable woman. Hear she made a scene at the poetry reading last night. Can't say I blame her, though."

The waitress came by and filled my cup. "Ready to order? We have some tasty blueberry pancakes today."

I shook my head, straining to hear the conversation in the next booth, but the ladies were on to the next topic. Humpf. Neumann having an affair? That nice man?

Chapter 7

Coffee cup drained, I grabbed the clip board and made my exit. The sun had appeared, streaming warming rays across the sky. Sunshine makes me smile. I strode down Evergreen to the auditorium site.

With trepidation, I approached the fallen sign. The stiff green tarp remained in place, draped over the top of the framework, giving the appearance of a dragon on its haunches. I was certain they had removed the body by this time. Sergeant Gilmore and a young, gangly officer stood at attention by its side. As I aimed in from the sidewalk, Steve walked up from the parking lot.

After dispensing with introductions, Sergeant Gilmore led us beyond the police tape.

"Gentlemen," he said. "Here's the deal. I invite you to examine the metal work. Look at it from whatever angle you desire. Don't touch. In exchange for your access, I want your forensic opinion. Agreed?"

Steve and I nodded.

He signaled to the officer, who stripped off the tarp.

Anticipation gave way to puzzlement as I scanned the metal framework. "N-E-U-M-A-N-N" was the shorter of the two signs, its car-length 18 feet was about five feet less than the "A-U-D-I-T-O-R-I-U-M" sign. In plan, the auditorium addition was a 140 foot diameter circle, set into the notch of the existing building where the administrative offices met the library. The signs were mounted to a metal framework set on the roof along the perimeter of the curved building. The base of the framework was comprised of two parallel eight inch high wide-flange I-beams, three feet apart, in two straight segments, with a four degree bend in the middle to follow the curve of the circular building. The parallel beams were joined by five equally spaced beams running cross-wise, and in the same plane. On top of this base were set a series of triangular frames constructed of galvanized steel angles, roughly three feet on center; the three foot short side set on the base, the four foot long side vertical, facing out to the street, with a member on the diagonal side connecting the two. The triangle frames were tied together across their hypotenuses, facing into the center of the roof, and on the street side with steel members curved to match the 68 foot radius. All the components were welded together. We extended three pairs of steel stub columns from the roof framing below the roof's plane up through the roof surface for attachment of the sign frame. The pairs of columns were capped with ten inch square cap plates, drilled with a hole in each corner, to which the wide-flange beams were bolted, four bolts at each column.

What I expected to see was scrapes and cuts. Torn, bent or gouged metal.

None was present.

What lay before me instead represented a metal assembly awaiting installation. The straight lines and ninety-degree bends of the angle frames had been bent askew from the fall, but I was taken aback by its condition. Was this the framework that had been bolted to the roof columns a day ago? Bolts torqued down and tested?

I turned to Steve, who was running his eyes along the framework, inch by inch, absorbed as if he were eyeing the female anatomy.

"Well?" Sergeant Gilmore prodded.

Steve held up a finger. "May we take pictures?"

"Very well," Gilmore said, "but then I damn well better hear a prognosis."

Steve and I circled the metal creature, trudged through the soggy grass and snapped photos. I knelt down where the frame connected to the sign "A," looking for blood. I found a full array of stains and splatters.

Steve and I exchanged glances.

"Is this the structure you designed?" Gilmore asked.

Steve paused in dramatic tension. He consulted the clipboard, to which he had fastened a detail of the frame assembly. "Yes, the components match."

I said, "May we see the roof?"

"Gentlemen, have you no further assessment?"

"Until we see the remaining stub-columns on the roof," I said, "we won't have a complete picture."

Steve was more accommodating than I. "Everything appears in order on this section, Sergeant. I don't see anything unusual."

Through the auditorium lobby, up the grand stairway to the mezzanine, into and down the service corridor to a utility room. From there we climbed the roof ladder, which extended up to a small penthouse, a single room used for storage. It contained the window washing equipment, which was used for both the auditorium building and the adjacent office building. As we passed, I noted the platforms, plywood, ropes, buckets, etc. used by the cleaning crew. We stepped out the door and onto the white TPO roof surface. Thermoplastic polyolefin, a sheet roofing membrane that is unrolled out over sheets of rigid insulation, and the seams heat-welded. It's a product with good UV resistance and puncture resistance. We were standing behind the roof screen, a metal assembly that stuck up above the roof surface. It was constructed of a six-foot high standing seam metal roof, sloped 60 degrees toward the center of the roof, curved to follow the outer perimeter of the auditorium building, set back about eight feet from the edge. The screen was on a triangular framework with base beams and stub columns, like the sign support, and ran continuously along about five-eighths of the building's perimeter. The portion of the circular building facing the public was screened, the remainder faced the roof of the other buildings.

We walked about twenty feet to the end of the roof screen and skirted the end, which placed us in the space in-between the screen and the roof's edge, defined by a twelve-inch high parapet, where the wall below rose above the roof's surface. I advised the others to be careful and hold toward the screen. We didn't need anyone falling off the roof. We were now on the Evergreen Road side, and could hear the Sunday morning traffic below. We walked the thirty feet to the "Auditorium" sign, and behind its framework—still attached—until we approached the six stub columns which a day ago had supported the "Neumann" sign.

Again, Steve and I examined the structure while Sergeant Gilmore and his police officer side-kick stood off to the side.

The stub columns and their cap plates were also in pristine condition. No signs of stress. No scrapes. The cap plates were not bent.

The parapet wall at the roof's perimeter was capped in a formed aluminum coping, which kept the rain and snow out of the wall. It extended across the top of the wall, and down both sides about four inches. The coping was a different story: mangled, dented, crushed, ripped through. Curiously, the heavy damage occurred in a six foot section at the center of the sign's length. Ripped conduit and broken wiring lay on the roof like a snake's shed skin.

Certainly, this was unexpected.

"Sergeant Gilmore," I said. "I don't have an on-the-spot answer for you. The structure appears in order. Obviously the coping was damaged heavily when the sign framework collapsed on it and crashed over the edge. Steve?"

"I'd like, again, to take some photos, and study the conditions before arriving at a conclusion. Sergeant, I don't want to be hasty."

"But what's this plywood doing here?" I said, noting three large pieces of three-quarter inch thick plywood, each more than a half-sheet, lying next to the stub columns.

Steve bent down and shook his head. "Weird."

"You don't have an idea why they are here?"

Steve and I shook our heads.

"Well, then. Time is of the essence, gentlemen. When will you have an opinion?"

"We'll call you the moment we figure this thing out," I said. "What about the forensic evidence on the sign frame?"

"It will be taken to the lab today," Sergeant Gilmore said.

We photographed the conditions from every angle. I looked over the edge of the parapet at the parking lot, and noticed vehicles from Perry Construction and Motor City Sign. Ha! So they were here to protect their turf, investigate on their own behalf. Fine. I would just stay out of their way.

"Alright, Steve, let's boogie."

We shook hands with the policemen, clambered back down the ladder, exited the building and marched in the direction of my car. Two women in a navy blue Grand Am entered the lot, shot in front of us, and pulled to a stop at the sidewalk.

"Was that Shirley?" Steve said.

I took a closer look.

"We just can't get rid of her, can we?" he said.

Nicole Neumann sat in the passenger seat. The moment Nicole opened her door, I heard the screaming.

"No, let me goooo!" Nicole flailed, arms flying in all directions, struggling to get out of the car, her motion restrained by Shirley's arm.

"You don't know what you're doing. I shouldn't have brought you here."

"Lemme go!" Nicole craned her head in my direction. "Ken, Ken! Help me! Please, you have to help me!"

My manhood invoked, I ran over to the car.

"Thank god, Ken. Shirley, you bitch, let me go!"

Nicole tumbled out of the car onto the pavement in a black and white blouse and grey skirt. She looked up at me longingly. She grasped my outstretched hand, and raised herself on wobbly legs. Looking down, she brushed her hands over scraped knees. She then threw herself at me, clutching her arms around me.

"Hey, hey," I said. "It's ok." Wailing noises erupted as her shoulders shook and tears fell on my neck.

"She's all yours, Ken," Shirley hollered from the driver's seat. She gunned it in reverse, then hit her brakes and hit the accelerator in drive. The passenger door slammed shut, and she drove off.

Another car pulled into the lot. "Hey, Ken," Steve said. "That's my son, here to pick me up. Do you want me—"

"No." I motioned him to go. "No, go ahead. Don't forget the meeting with Sue Watts. If I'm a bit late, make my apologies."

"Oh," Nicole sighed and turned her eyes up to mine. "Ken, I'm glad you're here. You are the only one who can help me. You are consistently rational. The police won't do anything. I've told them over and over, but it's like talking to the wall. I explained it last night, and went over it again this morning. Uh-huh, they say. Sure, uh-huh. They don't believe me. They think I'm being hysterical."

Wind whipped at our legs, and Nicole's hair was being blown into knots. "Let's sit in my car." I maneuvered her into the passenger side, ran around the car and slid in, started it up and prayed for the heat to come up quickly.

Nicole turned to me, mascara smudging down her face. Icy blue eyes pleaded with me through the tears. During the months we worked on the auditorium project, she had accompanied her husband to my office many times. For each visit, she had worn a different, new outfit. Stylish. Coordinated. Sleek. Stunning. Beautiful. The mess before me was evidence of the battering she had taken by last night's painful tragedy.

"Ken," she said with a quivering bottom lip, "Will you help me?"

"Of course, Nicole."

"Jerome. You always were kind to him, to us. Treated us fairly and honorably. I always felt like you cared."

"Well, sure, your husband was a nice man. I always thought so," I said.

"Please, please help me. Jerome's been murdered."

Chapter 8

"Murdered?"

"Yes. That Julianne. She's crazy, gone off the deep end. For two weeks she's been stalking us. I spied her at the supermarket behind the Pepsi display, and peeking at me through the Starbucks kiosk."

"Julianne Bodary? From the Board?"

"Yeah. She wears a disguise, this huge stupid blonde wig like Hannah Montana, but it's her. She's not normal. I don't know how she pulled it off, but listen." She cricked her neck and aimed her baby blues up toward mine. "She killed Jerome. And we need to prove it."

"Now, I've met Julianne, and I never noticed anything other than professionalism and sincerity. She seems committed to continuous improvement in the city. I doubt—"

"No, no, no, Ken! She's fooling you with her looks and her smarts. Why won't anyone believe me?" She smacked her hand down on the dashboard. "She's wicked. There's a devil in her. She's been carrying on with my husband. Wednesdays usually. Meeting him in a motel, no less: the Quatrain over on Van Dyke in Warren. Sure Jerome has his faults, but he's mine, damn it, and no one is going to— Damn it!...he *was*." And the wailing returned.

I reached into the back seat and grabbed a box of Kleenex. Nicole snatched one and blew a yard of snot into it. I noticed her peach fingernails were fiercely chipped, bitten to the quick.

"She's been...been sneaking around with him for a year...ah...ah..." She paused to sob. It shook her shoulders. I felt sad, angry, and helpless. I adjusted the heater. Nicole tugged out another tissue, wiped her raccoon eyes and went on. "She didn't make a great secret of it either. I've heard Matt Lance talking about it. He seemed particularly agitated by the idea."

"So they had an affair?"

With sudden alertness, she jerked and began beating me on the chest with both fists. "Don't you...don't you... Don't say that to me!"

I held my breath as she continued to pound me. Suddenly, she shrunk back into her seat and placed her hands over her face.

"Ken, yes, yes...I'm sorry...I'm sorry."

I put my arm gently around her. "It's ok, shhh..."

Several moments later she continued, speaking through her hands. "They were carrying on. She killed him. Murdered him in cold blood. My poor Jerome. What did he ever do to her? Don't you see?"

"No, I don't, Nicole. I'm not following. Can you connect the dots for me? Why would she kill your husband?"

"Because she couldn't...he wouldn't..." Her hands were in her lap now, balled into tight fists. "She reckoned if he wouldn't leave me, then she was going to get rid of him! Vindictive, sorry ass loser."

"Did she tell you this?"

Her shoulders shook in another bout of sobbing. "She...said it."

"When, Nicole? When did she tell you?"

She blew her nose, and threw the tissue into the pile on the floor. "She said...she said...he'd be sorry."

"Did she say that to you, or to Jerome?"

More wailing. "No, no...she said if she couldn't have him, nobody would."

"He wouldn't leave you, so she killed him by having a sign fall on him?"

"There, now you have it! She made the sign fall. His name, don't you see? Kill the sign, kill him. She was on the board. Wipe his name off the building, wipe him out."

I had to admit, it made a certain kind of twisted sense. But murder by signage? How would that even be accomplished? To be certain that Jerome would be walking below at the precise moment the sign was detached and released over the edge. And it would take an army to push the sign, and equipment. Not plausible.

"Help me, Ken. You are the only one who can. Help me prove that she killed my Jerome. Will you do that for me? For Jerome?"

"Well yes, I'll do what I can. Listen, you need some rest. We can talk about this tomorrow, or the next day—"

"No! She can't get away with this! Promise me, promise you'll get the evidence. Find out the proof."

"Ok, yes, let me find out." I paused. "One question, if you don't mind. Why was your husband outside?"

"Huh?"

"What made him get out of his seat and go outside?"

"Oh. He received a phone call. At intermission. He had to go to the office."

"Back home?"

"No, no. The city office. He left to go to the office next door."

"Did he say who he was meeting?"

"No. He just said he would be back for the second...second... half." And she started bawling her eyes out again.

I put my arm around her. "Ok, that's enough. I'll see what I can find out. You have to get some rest. Shall I take you home? Do you have someone to stay with you tonight?"

Nicole nodded. Mission accomplished, she slouched back in her seat. I put the car in gear, and she was asleep before we reached the first stop light.

What did I know about Julianne Bodary? Only her resume. A vice-principal at Troy High School, she rose quickly to that position largely as a result of her work with developmentally challenged kids. The ascent to power was accelerated by the resignation of the principal over a mid-year fiscal scandal and the promotion of the then vice-principal into the top spot. A year later she was appointed to the Planning Board by Mayor Wilkes.

Our interaction was limited to board activities. No red flags. She was proper, thoughtful, a hair more brusquely professional than she was charming, but based on my limited exposure, I found it difficult to imagine her a killer.

I remembered the two elderly women at the coney island talking about the affair. What was notable to me was that both Nicole and Julianne were about half Jerome Neumann's age, with the older of the two, Julianne, in her mid-thirties.

I'd been to the Neumann home, located in the northwest section of Birmingham, on three occasions during the development of the auditorium project. A cozy residence, built in the Cotswold Cottage style and dating back to the 1930s, it reminded me of something out of a fairy tale. It featured a steep slate tile roof, multi-paned casement windows and a large stone chimney. Vines clung to the expansive brick walls and climbed toward the sky. Windows and doors were edged in stone trim, and a patch of half-timber and stucco accented the entrance gable. I had to smile. There's something to be said for warmth as a design element. Give me an earthy domicile like this one over the misanthropic boxes built under the guise of "high design."

Under normal circumstances, my shoulders would relax and a deep sigh would escape as I pulled up the cobblestone drive. But today I worried about leaving Nicole alone. She was upset, confused, freaked out. She needed rest, and someone who could help her achieve it.

I loved the lot. It was deep; a through lot with a gazebo at the other end reachable from Westphalia on the other side, or a long walk from the house. A wild flower garden bridged the property in between.

As we arrived, I noted that the circular stone fountain had already been drained for the season. I turned off the engine and noted a navy blue Grand Am sitting next to the doorway. Shirley Hansen clambered out, slammed the door and charged toward us.

Chapter 9

Uncharacteristically, Shirley didn't speak as I helped Nicole slide out of the car. It was only when we reached the cottage door that Shirley said, "It's ok, Ken, I can take it from here." She pulled out a key and unlocked the door.

"No," Nicole said calmly. She turned to look in my eyes. "Let me get you some tea." She patted me on my back. "Come on inside."

I nodded.

We sat at the kitchen table. Shirley heated water. Nicole picked up a wooden box of assorted teas from a shelf, next to a black and white photograph of her with Jerome. "The elderberry is my favorite."

We sat in silence, played with our tea bags. Shirley looked gently at me; my return glances were of the hostile variety.

"Let me help you to your room, Nicole," Shirley said.

Nicole nodded.

"I think Ken can get back to his day, don't you?"

Nicole looked at me and winked. "Yes, Ken, you have a project to begin don't you?"

I nodded, gave Nicole a hug and said, "I'll be in touch." To Shirley, I gave a curt nod. I walked back through the house. At the entry hall, I noticed a flyer laying on the console table. It was labeled "Full Moon Meter," the poetry organization that sponsored the auditorium event. I picked it up and opened the tri-fold glossy paper. On it was printed the evening's agenda, with a list of the poets and a small blurb about each. Gwendolyn Darmus, Molly Gross, Chuck Carter, Johanna Daltry, Dustin Neihaus. Tacked to the back of the brochure was a yellow sticky-note on which was hand written: 'See you there! - Molly.'

I left the house, got in my car, and eased down the driveway.

The short-lived relief I felt at clearing BPW's responsibility was quickly replaced by the overburdening responsibility of finding Neumann's killer and bringing what peace could be had to the torn heart that resided within the lovely Nicole. Finding the murderer was top priority. For Nicole. To allow the settling of her battered heart toward a new equilibrium.

At the moment, however, I had more pressing matters. Lunch with Sue Watts loomed ahead of me like an iceberg off the port bow. Edison had been given an engraved invitation and I would pick him up on the way, at his tidy 754 square foot home in east Ferndale, a few blocks from our restaurant meeting place on Main Street in Royal Oak.

With his jovial countenance seated in the car beside me, I began sharing my news; the bulletin that was eating its way through my gut. "You'll never guess who I spent the night with, last night."

"Princess Leia? J Lo? Beckinsale?"

I shook my head. "Shirley Hanson."

"Yowww! Get out of here." He cracked up. "Tell me the details."

"Yeah, well, it was a short lived event. She burned me bad in her column this morning."

We turned into the parking lot and I eased into a metered spot. "I'll have to tell you later. Right now, priority number one is prying Sue Watts off our backs. When we finish here, I'll tell you what happened with Nicole."

"Nicole, as in widow Nicole?"

"Right. Let's get in there. Remember, we didn't do anything wrong. We're professionals. Everything went by the book."

"Right . . . so?"

I gave Edison the evil eye.

"Right, shut up. Hey, Fish Mack. I love this place. You know they have a Bloody Mary bar on Sundays that will knock your socks off."

"No Edison, this is a business meeting. There will be no drinking. Not even Bloody Marys."

We entered to a dark, woody atmosphere with high backed booths obscuring patrons and obfuscating the overall view of the interior. Fish-themed mobiles and sculptures hung from the ceiling and walls. Some of the metal sculptures—tidy little events comprised of clean geometric shapes fused into clever caricatures of classic fish—were marked with little white tags. For sale.

A hostess escorted us to a table. Before we picked up the menus, Sue Watts rushed in. A compact five feet, with a very short salt-and-pepper 'do, she wore chunky black bracelets and a flaming red tee dress. She had the figure to pull it off.

"Gentlemen, thank you for meeting me here. Because this is world serious, I rearranged my appointments so I could meet you in person, but unfortunately, I'll have to make it quick." She looked from one to the other of us and back again. "But first, they have a fabulous Bloody Mary bar here, and lord knows I need one. Gentlemen?"

Edison gave me a happy, *told you so* grin. We rose and hustled to the end of the aisle where an arrangement of accouterments delighted us. Tomato juice, Bloody Mary mix, olives, celery stalks, pickles, pepperoni sticks, pickled green beans, cooked shrimp, hot sauce, horseradish, black pepper, lemon juice, celery salt.

A bartender provided glasses pre-filled with a generous amount of vodka, and we custom built our drinks.

The waiter stopped by, moments after we returned to the table, and Sue placed her order—shrimp and eggs. Ready or not, Edison and I ordered as well. When the waiter left, Sue got down to business. "All right, I don't need to tell you why we're here. Ken, why don't you describe what you found at the site."

"First, Sue, let me assure you that we—BPW that is—are not at fault here, and we will find the evidence on site that confirms it, as well as documenting that our work flow for the design was executed in proper order."

"Please," Sue said, "just tell me the facts."

I proceeded to share what Steve and I experienced at the site that morning, beginning with meeting the police and ending with the observation of the clean bolt holes.

"Good, now–"

"Wait, shouldn't Steve be here?" Edison said.

Sue responded. "Steve Dickerson is a consultant to the firm of BPW Architects, not on staff. My concern, the concern of Essential, Incorporated is with you." Her eyes shot from one to the other of us. "There will be no need to take notes, fellas. I'll send you an email later today. First, your documents and files. All need to be put in meticulous order, if you haven't already. Contracts, email, reports, site photos, submittals, inspections, close out documents, the works. I's dotted and T's crossed. Got it?"

"Yes," I said leaving out the *ma'am* I felt like adding.

Our food arrived, and Edison and I dug in hungrily.

"Do you think we'll get sued?" Edison asked.

"A man died yesterday," Sue said. "There most

certainly will be a drive to place blame. The first act for some is to file suit, naming everyone involved. Since a portion of the building failed, causing the death—I'm assuming the man was alive when he was crushed—it would be natural to include the architect in the petition."

"But a portion of the building *didn't* fail," I said.

"And we may have to prove that in court," Sue said. "Now, this is important, so listen carefully."

We looked up from our food.

"No press. No phone calls, no interviews, no discussion, understand?"

We nodded.

"No *yes*; no *maybe*; no *no*. Don't answer questions at all. At most, provide a curt *no comment*. Understood?"

My turn to question, "But isn't saying nothing worse than–"

Sue shook her head. "We don't want to try this thing in the press. We need to be silent. Any comment can be used, spun, twisted. If we need to clarify, provide explanation, we'll have our day in court where we can do so under controlled conditions. We don't need an outsider to mutilate our words or actions."

I nodded.

"Good, now tell me about Shirley Hanson."

I froze.

"Shirley who?" Edison was trying to be helpful.

"Yes," I said.

"You know her, don't you?" Sue said.

Silence.

Sue continued. "Who is this woman? This could sink us, you know. Why the personal attack, Ken? The picture of you and Steve at the site."

"I don't know why she did that."

"Who is she?"

"An investigative reporter. We went to school

together. For a while."

"More gossip than investigation, if you ask me. Why would a friend of yours write that?"

"She's not a friend. Far from it."

"Well. Don't talk to her. She's trouble. Any more like that, we'll be plummeting like a boulder from an airplane."

Edison excused himself and headed for the restrooms.

Sue continued. "I heard about *him* from Robert. Now I see the concern. Edison doesn't have much self-control does he?"

I chuckled. "Well, he's fun when you get to know him."

"Keep him on a short leash, Ken." She folded her napkin and placed it on the table. "Thanks for lunch. I'll trust you'll do the right thing." She got up and walked out.

I wiped perspiration from my forehead. We had to solve this. Nicole claimed it was murder. Could it be? After all, someone messed with those bolts. Finding the responsible party would certainly relieve BPW of any blame. Helping Nicole to uncover a murderer would, in fact, get the firm off the hook too.

Edison returned. "Where's Sue? Gone?"

I looked my friend in the eye. "That was a disaster. I feel like I just got a whoopin'."

"Are you buying? Mind if I get another Bloody Mary?"

"Yeah, yeah. Then let me tell you about Nicole."

"And Shirley."

I finished my breakfast while Edison was creating his drink. I decided to talk to Julianne first. Edison came back clutching his drink, two stalks of celery and a green bean sticking out of the glass.

"You growing a vegetable garden?"

"You never heard of hydro-farming?"

I told him about the morning *San Francisco Divulged* column, indicting Steve and me for "protecting our butts" last night.

He shook his head. "I'll have to read it. She's inflammatory. It's entertaining. What about the widow?"

"She's convinced Neumann was murdered and wants me to find the killer. Claims the police don't believe her."

Edison lifted a dripping stalk of celery out of the glass, tilted his head and took a bite. "About what?"

"She says Julianne Bodary, Neumann's mistress, had been stalking her and must have done the dirty deed."

"You're not going to do this are you? Get involved? You start asking questions and it's going to be bad. You heard what Sue Watts said, not that I would take her directions either, but poking around the same time as the police will capture the eye of one journalist or another and for sure land you in the paper. Not to mention Robert."

"Robert?"

"You're supposed to be investigating the sign plunge for Robert, right? What's he going to say about you investigating for the widow? Conflict of interest."

"No, actually, it's in our interest." I explained.

He shook his head. "Bad idea. But that scene between Julianne and Jerome Neumann was hot."

"What?"

"They'd been nearly shacking up on the side for three years. Scuttlebutt was predicting that Neumann would change horses, and tie the knot with the side dish. Then the wife found out, the couple had their rants and raves, and after it was settled, Nicole was back in the driver's seat, and Julianne was out."

"Right, so Julianne figured if she can't have him..."

"That's lame."

I rolled my shoulders. "It is, what it is." My phone chirped. Sue Watts.

"How much do you trust Steve Dickerson?" she said.

"Steve?"

"You've worked together on other buildings, over what period of time?"

"It's been three years. We must have worked on a dozen projects including The Shops at Silver Pond, Westview Crossing, the McPhail Law Library and a couple others."

"Could he have made an error? Failed to execute an inspection properly? Fudged a report?"

"No, Steve wouldn't do that. He's a good engineer. I doubt—"

"There's no room for doubt here, Ken. And in this instance, good may not be good enough. I see disciplinary action was taken against him eight years ago. A case in Toledo. He was fined, but retained his license. Do you know anything about that?"

I expressed my shock. "No, I don't. There's been no trouble that I'm aware of."

"Keep it that way." The line went dead.

Chapter 10

Julianne, a name that strikes melodies in my heart. Moore. Hough. Nicholson.

I had dropped Edison off, and punched the button for John Boyd, a number I had called numerous times during the planning and construction of the auditorium.

"Ken, how timely! Were your ears ringing? We are talking about the den. It's been a few years since we had a face lift, and in addition to freshening up the decor, we want to look at blowing out this window wall and expanding our horizons."

"Well, John, sounds like an interesting project. I'll leave you to your mulling. I was calling to see if I could trouble you for Julianne Bodary's phone number."

"Sure, sure. Why don't you come on over? We'd love to have your thoughts on our renovation, and I can give you the number then. Shall we say two 'o'clock? I'm sure the missus can set us up with some coffee."

I agreed and hung up. John Boyd's den project was the last thing I wanted to do.

My phone chirped. Paul Larken, Motor City Sign.

"Ken, I'm sure you're looking into the issue with the sign falling from the Neumann Auditorium. We went out there to take a look at it, and the sign is still attached to the framework."

"Yes, Paul. I agree; you're off the hook."

"Yep, so we're on the same page. Good luck with your part of the analysis." Paul rang off.

I zig-zagged through neighborhoods, to Nine Mile and Woodward and pulled into my driveway. A hasty trip inside, past the stripped-off door casings still laying in the hallway and to my bedroom in the back of the house. A quick change, and I rushed back out and jumped into the car. Before long I was cruising up 10 Mile.

I turned on the AM radio and tuned in my sister Ella's program—politics and pop culture—as she hosted a lively conversation with the Republican candidate for governor.

"And with the repeal of the bill we can free up twenty-two million dollars of state funds to shore up our deficit and restore our prospects for the future," he announced.

"Thank you for being with us today Senator Huckleby. Up tomorrow, Wilson K. Mell talks about his book 'Emo - A Lonely Boy's Tears' about the rise of Emo to a national frenzy in the early 2000's. Until then, think quick and turn slow."

"And in traffic, note that Business Loop I-94 along the coast of the big lake south of Port Huron remains closed at this hour due to the movie shoot, which apparently is taking longer than earlier predicted. A Mother's Dilemma *features Kristen Blume and Leonardo DiCaprio."*

I turned down one of the charming streets with ornate iron lampposts and brick pavers, made a left at a three-story colonial revival, and drove deeper into the subdivision. Houses were stately here, with a nice hunk of property attached to each. As I grew nearer my destination I popped a spearmint lozenge.

I was intent on making this meeting with John Boyd quick. In and out.

Boyd met me at the ornate wooden door, dressed in his conventional brown three piece suit—was he ever without it?—bright blue shirt, and plaid bow tie. "Glad you're here, Ken. And how timely this is. Let me show you to the den."

The two story foyer was dark and cold, with green marble walls and a wrought iron stair winding to an upper level.

His wife slid into the space, a wool skirt and hearty brown shoes anchoring her to the wood plank floor. "Oh, John, let's give Ken a moment to catch his breath. Would you like some coffee, dear?" She smiled at me with straight teeth, prim and proper, like an elderly Julia Roberts. Despite her graying hair and yielding skin, her eyes shone brightly and she moved with quick, cat-like movements. John Boyd introduced her as Amira.

We walked through the kitchen, where I accepted coffee in a mug with a Detroit Lions logo. I took mental notes as John described his ideas for a brighter, wider, more playful den. The room before me was worn white plaster walls, imitation rough-hewn beams, and plaid furniture. He vigorously described his vision for demolishing the south wall, expanding into the yard, incorporating a new fire pit, and including an abundance of black hinges and wrought iron.

Amira interjected. "I think we may be holding Ken up from his day. Ken, dear, you wanted something?"

"No, no, I'm happy to advise. But if I could get Julianne's number before I forget why I came..."

"Sure," John said, rattling off the digits. "What's this about, anyway?"

"Yesterday's tragic event, John. I've—"

"Oh, the terrible accident," John said. "Horrible."

Amira raised a hand to her mouth, nodding.

"Not an accident. There's no evidence the sign supports failed or gave way."

"You mean this was deliberate?" John said.

"I'm working to determine that, yes. I want to talk to everyone who was down there yesterday and see if there were any witnesses."

Amira spoke. "And that man, Jerome Neumann. He was killed in such a horrible manner."

I nodded. "I want to get to the bottom of this quickly. Please."

John said, "You know, I never did trust that Molly Gross."

"Molly?"

"As long as she's been on the board, what, maybe two years, she's been mighty difficult to read. She opposed the auditorium project from day one. Couldn't stand Jerome Neumann."

"No, I don't think so, John," Amira said. "She just wanted to preserve the old place; the Fitzgerald Reading Room. Lots of folks wanted to protect it."

"The old rattle trap. Sentimentalists. You can't stop progress. What an eyesore that building was, from the day it opened. I'm glad we got rid of it," John said.

"Now, there was a lot of history there," Amira said. "It was very modern for its time."

"What about Julianne?" John continued.

"I was told she was at the event, and want to ask her a few questions about what she observed, things that may be unusual," I said.

"You'll have a lot of people to talk to. Of course, Amira and I were there as well, but we didn't see anything."

"You attended together, the two of you?"

They nodded.

"Did you see anything at intermission?"

Amira said, "No, we kept to our seats the whole time. No reason to get up. Until, of course, that awful racket before the plunging..." She turned pale and left the room.

John gave me a dirty look.

"I'm so sorry if I upset her," I said. John waved it

off, so I took the opportunity to ask another question. "What about the people around you, sitting in your vicinity. Anything suspicious there?"

"You know," John said, "You should talk to Matt Lance. He was there."

Amira came back into the room. "And he hated Neumann."

"A grudge?"

"Ask Scofield about it," John Boyd said. "He can tell you the messy details. He's over in Lansing visiting his daughter right now, but he should be back home tonight. Now, last night at the poetry reading, come to think of it, Molly Gross's agent Rusty what's-his-name was down in the front row. Sitting next to Scofield. As I recall, everyone in that front row got up at intermission. I remember because Amira and I said we'd move down if one of the couples didn't come back. Afterward, when the show started again there was only one empty seat, next to Scofield. I don't believe Rusty returned."

Amira said, "No he didn't. I kept thinking Scofield should take his hat off, and put it on the seat next to him. Would you like more coffee, Ken?"

"No thank you, I should be going now. I'll put some ideas together for your den, and call you in a couple of days."

I made a hasty exit. Their den renovation would be a thorn in my side.

On the next street, I stopped in front of a lumbering half-timber, and punched in the numbers for Julianne. She was on her way to meet a friend at Donato's Restaurant, and would spare a few minutes if I could get there right away.

What was it that kept Rusty from returning to his seat? I wondered as I drove.

Donato's was an Italian bakery hooked up in front of a charming sit down restaurant. I parked in the back and came in through the glass bakery door. There, at the butter cream frosted birthday cakes, stood Shirley. *Yikes*. Perhaps softly, I could sneak behind her back....

"Ken! Glad I ran into you!"

I shook my head. The confrontation would happen sooner or later. "Shirley. Do you have no sense of propriety? Don't you know you don't slam someone after you...after having a pleasant evening with them?"

"Oh, so you thought it was pleasant?" Smile.

"You know very well what I mean."

Shrug. "Actually, I wrote that before our *pleasant evening*. Just business, Ken. Can't you separate the personal from the work? Has nothing to do with you."

"Nothing? You threw me to the wolves."

"Not you, your actions. Or your firm's actions. By the way, I hear you're investigating the so-called murder."

"Who told you that?"

"Is it true? Obviously, it turned out not to be a BPW problem. Why the interest beyond that?"

"Shirley, don't make this personal."

"That's not personal. But I would be interested in something a little more along those lines...perhaps dinner? And a bit of friendly sparring." Smile.

"I'm not sparring. Last night was a mistake. And after that story I shouldn't be talking to you at all."

"Oh Ken, don't be so—"

Out of the corner of my eye I saw Bryce McClurg coming my way. I couldn't not say hello. "Hey Bryce, popular joint tonight."

"Hi, Ken," he said and turned to Shirley. "Who is this lovely lady?"

I made introductions. "Bryce is the roofing contractor for the auditorium."

Shirley jumped on that morsel. "Oh, then you know something about last night's events."

Bryce said, "Well—"

I jumped in, "Be careful what you say, she's an investigative reporter."

"Oh, how interesting. I love reporters." Bryce showed his pearly whites.

Suddenly the air grew heavy around me. It was time to boogie over to the restaurant side.

As I threaded through the arched doorway, a hostess scowled at me like she expected a toll. Luckily, Julianne came up behind me. The hostess took us to a table.

Julianne wore a loose floral print top and gold dangly earrings. "We have about twenty minutes or so before Michelle arrives." Her dirty blond hair was razor cut and feathered, which had the effect of emphasizing her angular cheekbones. She peered at me through fuzzy grey eyes, bloodshot.

"I appreciate your taking the time to see me. I'm sorry to encroach on your day." I said. I had met Julianne on two occasions previously, both for short board meetings relative to the auditorium project. I found her no-nonsense approach refreshing. Perhaps it was this attitude that helped her make her mark with developmentally challenged youth before she was tagged for the vice principal position at Troy High School.

"It's ok. What did you want to ask me about?"

"I'm sure you have a lot of troubled children to deal with, difficult circumstances, so—"

"Difficult? No, I don't make judgments. There is no right or wrong. Life is a banquet, it's all spread out for you. Everything you could possibly want is right there for the taking. All you have to do is get up off your seat and grab it. Whatever you want. Everyone makes his own way. Being right involves judgment. Who am I to judge others? Who are you? If someone else needs help getting to the banquet table, I'm here."

"That's quite a philosophy."

"It's served me well."

"So, I'll get right to the point. Nicole Neumann has offered the suggestion that you killed her husband."

She slowed her movements and raised her eyes to mine. She picked up her knife and tapped it against the table. Her eyes grew misty and she looked down at her fingers. For a moment I thought she would bring tears. But she didn't. Her expression grew stiff, her eyes small. Her mouth grew hard. "I thought about it."

"Hum?"

"If Nicole told you that, then I assume you know about...our love for each other?"

"Yes, I was made aware of your, uh, relationship with Jerome Neumann."

"Sure, I wanted to kill him. I had three years invested in that relationship. He *promised* he wanted to be with me. He said so. But he couldn't pull the trigger. The wimp."

"You took revenge on him?"

"No, I couldn't. He said what he said, and later his actions denied it. That night—last night—I begged him to reconsider. We—"

"You talked to him last night?"

She nodded. "He was going to stay with his wife. No budging."

"When did you see him?"

"Before the program started, maybe seven o'clock. I arrived early to speak with him. Afterward, I met Michelle in the lobby. I sat through the first half, but developed a stress headache and was forced to leave half way through. I practically bolted out of my seat when they called intermission, and went straight home."

"Did Michelle take you home?"

"No, I went home by myself."

I waited.

She looked at me. Played with her fork. "Did I have an alibi? No. No one saw me once I left the building. No one saw me go home. Yes, I could have done it."

We sat in silence for a moment. I couldn't think of anything else to say.

She spoke first, "Now, if you'll excuse me, my friend will be here any minute."

Chapter 11

Something was off. Julianne had no alibi and plenty of motive. She certainly was forthright in sharing her feelings. I could see her working with special children. From what I understood, she was good at her job.

And Shirley. Did Edison tell her I was investigating? How else would she know?

On the way home I bought a pack of index cards. So much had happened, I needed to reduce it all to writing.

Walter Scofield was just walking in the door when I called him. He agreed to meet for breakfast the next morning at seven at the Original Pancake House. I loved pancakes.

I pulled into my driveway, parked, entered the paneled side door, and hung my coat on a wooden peg next to the basement stairs. I bounded up the three steps into the kitchen and tossed the packet of index card onto the table. The room boasted a built-in booth, with speckled white Formica tabletop and red plastic bench seats. A premium feature in its day, the seating would be ripped out in a few days—perhaps over the weekend—but I had hairier goals to worry about first.

I slid onto the bench and laid out the cards. Each possible suspect got his own card. At this point anyone who knew Neumann and could reasonably be assumed to have been at the event made the list. Cards were inked for each piece of information of any significance. Of course, I had no idea what was important and what wasn't, but the last time dead bodies appeared at a jobsite, I learned to organize the facts, create a timeline, and put the pieces together. If I was going to keep my word to Nicole, I would have to be diligent in my pursuit and painstaking in my note taking.

Chopin's *Minute Waltz* interrupted my thoughts. Shirley. We had exchanged numbers the previous evening, and I had assigned her this spirited tune. But after throwing me to the wolves that morning, I'd have to switch to a more ominous strain, perhaps Chopin's *Death March*. I opened the phone. "If it's not our local hellion."

Sigh. "Listen, Ken, I know you're upset but—"

"No. Livid." I slid out of the booth and began pacing.

"Hey, let's talk, ok? There are things you have to understand. I'm in a difficult position. We could meet—"

"I don't have to understand squat." I opened the fridge. Mustard. Pickles. Pizza box—huh. I opened it. The triangular slices were curling at the edges. I shoved it back on the shelf. "No Shirley, I don't want to see you."

"That's not what you said last night. The way you touched me, a fervent glow of sun on my bleakest perimeter."

"Listen, I felt it too, but I was wrong. I'm not going to play games with you. If you can't be straightforward, just leave me—"

"No games, Ken. I want to talk, that's all. If we could wrap our minds around each other like we did—" She cleared her throat. "Let's make it casual...somewhere neutral. We could meet at George's Coney on—"

"You haven't heard me, Shirley. Listen carefully." My jaw was tight. She was pissing me off. I raised my voice and it echoed in the sparsely furnished house. "Last night was a mistake. I don't want to see you.

Don't want to talk to you. I'm not available. I'm going to be alone tonight. Just me. By myself. I'm going to the crash site, alone. Then I'm going to dinner, alone. Got it?"

"But—"

"Don't say it. Don't say anything. Don't call me. And leave me out of your blog." I closed my phone. Hard.

I collected the cards, careful to keep them organized by suspect. As I stretched a rubber band around them, they blew up and scattered over the floor. Down on my knees, I pushed them into a heap, tapped them into a ragged pile, and wrapped the rubber band around. I grabbed my windbreaker and slammed the door on the way out. Once in the Taurus, I started the engine and shoved it into gear. If I didn't calm down, this would be an ugly night.

I focused on taking even breaths.

A few minutes past seven, the sun was setting and my eyes locked on the blank space where the "Neumann" sign should have been. The "Auditorium" sign appeared forlorn against the darkening sky. I turned into the empty parking lot, cast in a pinkish glow, and pulled up next to the west sidewalk, nearest to where the sign had plunged onto an unsuspecting Jerome Neumann. The wind picked up as I exited the car and a chill went through me. I sighed.

I started on the north side of the building, the opposite side to where the sign had fallen, for a cursory look. The Auditorium was designed as a circle in plan, the east portion a tangent to the existing civic center offices. On the north side in the "v" where the old and new were attached was a small loading area where supplies or sets could be delivered to the stage, and a trash enclosure with two dumpsters. The loading area was devoid of vehicles. I went to the dumpsters, lifting each lid in turn. Nearly full of trash bags and boxes. They must not separate things here. Tisk, tisk. I wondered if yesterday's trash would yield any clues. It stunk. I was not about to find out.

The sidewalk around the end of the building led me to the narrow concrete pathway which paralleled Evergreen Road. This side was used by staff only. I wanted to take another look, sans crowd. The area was still cordoned off with yellow police tape, the metallic hunk gone—carted off to the police lab. Deep ruts in the grass near the road indicated where they stationed the crane to lift the fallen sign earlier in the day, after Steve and I had met with Sergeant Gilmore. In the muddy patches I could make out footprints left by police who had investigated, as well as hundreds of foot marks from the previous night's crowd, which had edged in on the yellow tape. My eyes followed the sidewalk off to my left, to the door to the administrative offices where supposedly Neumann had been summoned during intermission, a half hour prior to the sign's dive. He must have been killed as he was walking back along this stretch. Perhaps after meeting with his killer?

My eyes were drawn skyward to where an enormous moon peered at me. I smiled at its corpulence, glowing bright against the inanimate building. I swore it smiled back.

I caught a whiff of something sweet, and heard the hollow tap of footsteps approaching. A striking blonde rounded the corner at the end of the building, her head turned toward the police tape. She continued in my direction.

She moved like a Latin dancer sashaying to her own internal rhythm.

"Oh!" she said. "I didn't know anyone would be here." She came within an arm's length of me and stopped.

Seriously, was that—? Clear blue eyes set the perfect distance apart? Check. Crisp cheekbones? Check. Welcoming mouth? Check. The famous birthmark on her cheek clinched it. How was I so lucky?

"It's ok, I wasn't expecting anyone to be here either."

"I couldn't believe that horrible accident last night. I was driving along here and, I don't know, I had to take another look at this."

"You were here?" I said.

"Yeah, I was late, arrived just before intermission."

"Just before the sign fell from up there," I pointed above the roof's edge.

"Umm, down to here...marked by the police tape." She pointed her high heel at the spot. Black, lots of straps. If they were any taller she'd be on ballerina toes. *Painted* ballerina toes.

"Right."

Her glance lingered on the grassy area, the otherwise manicured lawn broken with muddy sores and gouges where the ground had been punctured and scraped. Then she backed up to the brick wall, chewed on her lip and said, "So, are you driven by morbid curiosity, as I am, or are you here for the view?"

"Doing a little investigation."

"For who?" She raised an eyebrow.

"BPW, the design firm."

"Ah..." she said. Then as recognition flashed across her face, she added, "The architect."

I nodded.

"So, you must be in the hot seat right now, with the sign falling off and...everything."

Internally, I grimaced. "Yeah, I'm working to get to the bottom of it."

"Hello," she said offering her hand, and when I took

it she placed her other on top, a pair of thin metal bracelets clanging in the dull silence. "Hello, I'm Kristen—"

"Kristen Blume. Yes, a pleasure to meet you." *Screw you Shirley.* "Ken Knoll. At the risk of sounding like a silly fan, I admire your work on *Richmond Place*, and I was quite taken with that girl you played in *Dancing for the Defense*...what was her name..."

"April Dancing. I loved her too. So quirky." She smiled. Wide. "It's not silly at all, Ken, I always appreciate a kind comment about my work." She tossed her head back. "I thought about being an architect." She raised her leg, placing her foot against the wall behind her. What great legs! I always relished those thighs, shown off to good advantage in the courtroom scene of her movie. "When I was just a girl, I read a biography of Frank Lloyd Wright and was taken with his intensity and imagination. Later on, I looked into architectural schools, like U of M."

I smiled.

"Why the big grin? You don't think I could be an architect?"

"I'm sure you'd be amazing. But we're fortunate to have you on the screen."

She shrugged it off with a shoulder roll, which I found oddly alluring, and said, "Were you here, too, when it happened?"

"No, I was called in after the sign fell. You're in the movie they're filming in Port Huron, right?"

"*A Mother's Dilemma,* yeah. We'll be there all week...You know, I grew up right next door."

I angled my head toward the subdivision behind her.

"Not *literally*," she slapped her palm jokingly against my arm. "Huntington Woods."

My heart raced. Here she was, famous actress, and she had walked right onto my project site. "I don't believe I've met an actress before." *Come on Cannoli! That's inane, can't you be more creative?*

"Ditto...about architects, I mean. All those thoughts about becoming one, and I can't remember the last time I met one in person." The wind picked up and Kristen crossed her arms. "It's getting chilly. How about we get a drink? I'd like to hear more about your architectural vein, as well as your tendencies toward the morbid." Her lips curled slightly.

"Actually, I had my heart set on having a bit of Pad Thai at Emerald's around the corner. Would you like to join me? The place is unassuming, but the food is fabulous. You can tell me all about your curiosities, and I'll share mine."

She tilted her head and pursed her lips. "Are they still around? Yum! I didn't realize how hungry I was until just this moment."

Chapter 12

Thankfully I had cleaned out the car over the weekend so I offered to drive.

Kristen glanced at the only other vehicle in the lot, a fire-engine red muscle car. "But my Mustang! I love that car! I rent it every time I'm in town."

"I've always had a passion for Mustangs," I said.

She dangled the keys. "Ok, you drive!"

"Ahh, the magic words." Once we climbed in and were on the way, my internal ruckus began.

She said yes. This is not the way things had been going for me the last few years, or well, ever. *Edison was not going to believe this.* To share dinner with *Kristen Blume*! But the cards called to me, and the thought crossed my mind that this would have been better another night, when I was not so distracted. I had to get those cards back in order, prepare for tomorrow's interviews. Review today's discussions.

What was I thinking? I was catching a break here: Kristen Blume. *Couldn't I enjoy this unique moment; one that may never be repeated?*

"Geez, it must be five years since I've been to Emerald's."

Inwardly, I sighed. *She was sooo cute!* Now I was thinking like a teenager. I had to get a grip. *Seriously, when was the last time I had a date with an actress? Ok, I realized it was not a date, but what was it? Dinner, the two of us, together at one table. Talking. Kristen Blume.*

"Mind if I turn on the radio?" she said.

"Go ahead." Wow, she was beautiful.

Come on, Cannoli, she used to live here, she has friends in town. Could have asked anyone from the set. But she's with you. Wait. I need to relax and enjoy the moment. Before I wake up. Wow, one of the most gorgeous women in the world wants to have dinner with me.

I told myself to shut up.

"Oh, I love this song!" Kristen began snapping her fingers. "*I had a barbecue stain on a white t-shirt, she was killin' me in that mini-skirt...* Oh, yeah." She was dancing in the seat.

And she liked Tim McGraw. I did deserve this, didn't I? And after that long dry spell after the divorce. After the broken relationships...After waiting for Gwen, only to lose out when she was snatched up by Robert. After Mary—and what she did to me. And poor Isabelle. What a mess that was, for me, for the company. Yes, I did deserve this.

Now I was getting ahead of myself. Deserve what? It was dinner. But after all my woman trouble; after the crap with Shirley.

Shirley! Now, why did I have to think of her? I needed to put her out of my head, or I would spoil this. Get back here, in the moment, with Kristen.

Nothing fancy, Emerald's was located in an office building on Ten Mile, the parking lot bordering on Northwestern Highway. We got out of the car and headed in.

The building's office lobby was closed, but the restaurant had a separate canopied entrance off the rear. Once elegant, the faux-leather booth material was now cracked, the simulated wood laminate worn, and the huge aquarium dingy looking. The food, however, was excellent.

The dark-haired waitress brought shrimp chips and

hot tea with our menus. Kristen opened hers right away with "I'm starving!"

I already knew what I wanted.

"I haven't had drunken noodles in so long!" Kristen said.

She put her menu aside and turned her chin up at me. "So, in your architectural work what kind of buildings do you do? No, better question, what's been your favorite project?"

"Ten, twelve years ago I worked for a developer named Sawyer Green. This guy was making money hand over fist—"

"You know there's a movie called *Soylent Green*, about an overcrowded future, everyone is starving and there's this new food ration–"

"Yeah, I know. The guy used to get kidded about it."

"Don't you love it? Go on."

"He built shopping centers all over the country. Anyway, he hired us to design his home, a twenty-five thousand square foot *palace*. Didn't care about the budget, just wanted to have the look. We went crazy. Clean lines, floating ceilings, mitered corner glass. My favorite indulgence was the bar top that popped up from a recess in the floor. I loved the huge two-sided fire place, with limestone from a quarry in Rogers City and a black walnut mantel. We designed a rooftop garden, a walk-out from the master bedroom. Flat planes of manicured green, edged in cast stone. My kind of client."

The server came to take our order, and Kristen commenced an explanation of what she wanted. "Do you use holy basil or sweet?"

"We use holy basil."

"Perfect. What kind of soy sauce?"

"In that dish, I believe it's black."

"Humm, is there any possibility you can prepare it

with mushroom soy sauce instead of black? Also, may I have some fish sauce on the side?"

The server nodded, writing intensely.

"Also," Kristen continued, "I'd like a side of corn fritters, but I don't want the chili sauce. May I have some peanut sauce instead?"

The waitress nodded, I ordered the Pad Thai. After she left, Kristen turned to me and said, "My grandfather always told me to get my money's worth, and get exactly what I deserve. And it's a habit I continue to employ."

"And what do you deserve?"

Kristen wagged a finger at me, "That would be telling...How's the investigation? You couldn't have done much since last night."

"You'd be surprised. Let's see...I was on the roof this morning with our structural engineer and the police detectives, reviewing the supports and condition of the roof. Interviewed two people who knew Neumann. Had a long discussion with the widow. She swears her husband was murdered."

"Murdered? How would you murder someone with a sign? Or even coordinate the passing of someone below as the sign fell?"

I shook my head.

"I like it though," she said. "The whole murder by fallen sign thing," she said, nibbling around the edge of a shrimp wafer. "Not *like it* like it...you know what I mean. It would make a spirited movie."

My God she is beautiful. Seriously, how is this supposed to work? She lives in LA, travels the world. And me, just a stiff in a regular job. But it's just dinner.

"Speaking of movie," I said, "tell me about *A Mother's Dilemma*."

"It's about a girl who surrogates for her mother. Her mom's only forty-five. Had the girl and her twin sister as a teen. The father disappeared before they were born. After years of broken relationships the mom finally has a nice man in her life, marries, and they try to have children. After a miscarriage, her doctor tells her she can't have a child. So the daughter, Aly—who wants to see her mom happy, offers to surrogate."

"Sweet kid, big sacrifice. You play the Aly?"

"Right, but wait. She carries the child to term and the parents, her mom and her new husband, are racing to the hospital from across town and are broadsided by an SUV as the girl is delivering. Killed instantly."

I set down my fork and took in that turn of events.

"Compelling. There are legal issues, but the girl basically is left with caring for her half-brother as her son. She's on her own, right, didn't plan on having a baby! Now her mom's gone and she's left with this remembrance of her, and dealing with caring for a newborn. To top it all off, she's a special needs teacher and was committed to a year-long fellowship in Italy. The plan was to have the kid, turn it over to her mom and scoot off to Europe. Well, it's her career, right? So she takes the kid with her to Turin and gets to know her son...brother while she works her passion. It's mixed up."

"A lot of questions. So why are you filming here, in Michigan?"

"Story is, she grew up in Port Huron. Has the baby here. She doesn't get along at all with her sister, Melody, but now there's this tension because, of course, the baby is her sister's brother too. I filmed a few scenes along Lake Huron with the sister, arguments mostly, before she leaves for Italy. And I'm still to shoot scenes which take place later, when she returns."

I pushed my plate away.

"The look on your face," Kristen said quietly. "I hope the audience gets it like that."

"It's so serious. My goodness, how would you...How could anyone?"

"Right."

And suddenly, Kristen actress became a girl sitting across from me. A flesh and blood person with flaws and dreams and heart and tears.

And I liked her.

We sat quietly for a moment, then were interrupted by the waitress. "Everything ok?"

We mumbled noncommittally.

I changed the subject. "Where are you staying? You have relatives in town?"

"Yeah, my parents are here, but I'm at a hotel. I can't sleep at my parents' while I'm working, with the late hours covering rewrites and meetings."

"When you're not chowing down with the local architect."

"Exactly."

"So, you said you aspired to become an architect? What happened?"

Kristen took a sip of her drink. "Dave Fuller."

I cocked my head in question.

"We had a project, junior year of high school, for art appreciation. Visit an art gallery, take in a movie at the DFT, something cultural. Then write a report. Dave and I sat beside each other in homeroom and he was a Yamasaki fan, and, of course, I'm mad for Frank Lloyd Wright. So we decided to team up and do a compare and contrast on Wayne State's McGregor Memorial— one of Yamasaki's finest—with Wright's Turkel House."

"Palmer Park, isn't it?"

"Exactly. I was geeked about it. I'm still hungry for architecture. Every time I go anywhere, I find the local treasure and check it out."

"Must have been fun, with the architectural passion

the two of you shared."

"You would think, but Dave had a different kind of passion in mind, as we took a snack break in his car at A&W. My shake ended up in his lap."

"Ouch, did that dampen his spirits?"

"Be-dump-ump. Yeah, well, we both felt kind of rotten about it after. Things were awkward at school...I threw myself into drama, with winter and spring plays. That summer I played Annie Oakley at the Baldwin in Royal Oak. "

"So, I have Dave Fuller to thank."

She made a noise in her throat. "What about you, always wanted to be an architect?"

"Since I was fourteen and read Wright's biography."

"I wonder if he ever realized how many young people he inspired."

"Yeah."

"Who do you think did it? I mean you're convinced it wasn't an accident, aren't you?"

"Oh, I'm certain it wasn't."

"Want to tell me about it?"

I looked in those piercing blue eyes, points of light dancing, dark brown edge rimming her irises. "Ok. The first half of the program went off without a hitch. Intermission, Neumann got a call to meet someone in the office—this I got from his wife—she didn't know from who. There's a path, the one we were on earlier tonight, connecting a side auditorium door to a back door into the offices. After the program started up again, Neumann never returned to his seat. The sign fell twenty minutes later and Neumann was crushed by it."

"So he was on his way back from the offices."

"That's the working theory."

"Who was this call from?"

"I'm working to find that out. I talked with a couple of people, his mistress Julianne for one." I gave her the run down.

"But of course she claims not to have done it."

"Right; she admits to being furious with him, but didn't kill him."

"Do you believe her?"

"Umm. Yes. I mean she showed sincerity, but what do I know?

"You said two people."

"Yes, I talked to John Boyd this afternoon, director of the planning board." I gave her the short version of my visit to see him.

She grew a sly smile, "Wait, you don't have to get up early do you?"

"Actually...I'm meeting Scofield for breakfast." *Oh, now why did I do that?*

Kristen moved her food around on her plate. "You should talk to Matt Lance."

I looked up. "Why do you say that?"

"Look, Boyd's wife told you Matt had a grudge against Neumann. Grudges matter."

"Sounds like a bumper sticker."

She jabbed me in the arm. "Ok, ok." I said. "No, really, I'm meeting him tomorrow afternoon. I have a meeting at work right after lunch, and then should be able to sneak out. I've arranged to meet him at three."

She smiled at me. "You're a good man, Ken Knoll."

A balding guy in a blue suit two tables over whispered to the woman next to him and pointed in our direction, then wandered over. "Excuse me, you're Kristen Blume, aren't you? I love you! I can't tell you how much..." he gushed on, Kristen smiling. She autographed his napkin and he swaggered back to his table.

Meanwhile, I felt my own fireworks beginning. *Slow down Cannoli, wait this out.*

She shook her head. "Nice man." She pouted. "Well,

would you like to see me in the afternoon? I have a scene in the morning, but my portion is short and I should be done early for once. How long do you think you'll be tied up?"

"No more than an hour, depending on his information. And, yes, I'd like to see you."

"Well, why don't we meet somewhere at fourish? Which part of town you gonna be in?"

"We're meeting next door to the auditorium, at the city offices, so how about The Golden Pear on Twelve Mile?"

"Perfect."

"Excuse me, Kristen Blume, right? I love you!" Another guy, skinny jeans and kinky hair. "Can I get your picture?"

She agreed, and I took a photo of the two of them with his camera. Lucky guy.

When he was gone, she folded her napkin and stood up, placing the cloth on her seat. "I'll be right back." And she headed for the ladies' room.

Ken, you are so lucky! Don't breathe, don't move, let it be real. I pulled out my phone and wrote a text to Edison. "Hey pal. Guess who I'm dining with? Kristen Blume. Yep. More later."

I looked around the restaurant. Fish. Paintings. Drummed my fingers on the table. Strange not to have heard from Shirley. *What? Shirley again?* I warned myself not to ruin this. *Think of Kristen.* There. *Could I possibly ask her for her phone number?* She had mentioned seeing me the next day. I could ask for her number. No, she wouldn't give that out. *This evening was almost done, maybe I could end it with a kiss? No way, too forward. Not gonna happen. Forget it.*

She returned to the table and sat down. "What time is it?"

"Nine-twenty."

"Oh God! I need to get my beauty sleep. Four am call. Are you ready?"

I nodded and moved to slide out of the booth.

"Wait. Hand me your phone."

I did as instructed.

She took the device and started punching buttons. "Oh, you have a text message. Who's Edison? You don't mind if I peek, do you? '*You dog.*' Now what's that about?" She gave me the evil eye, giggled, and punched more buttons. "There, my private number. Call me tomorrow? No excuses now."

I felt myself grin. We walked out.

She slid into the driver's seat and we drove back to the lot where my car was parked. She cut the engine and got out as I did.

"Well, Mr. Architect, you gonna kiss me? Don't make me wait 'til tomorrow."

I leaned in and planted one on her. Her lips were soft, smooth, delicate.

"*Ciao* for now!" and she was off.

Chapter 13

I drove home happier than I'd been for a long time, the memory of Kristen's lips on mine engendering a smile the whole trip. It didn't seem real. I thought about phoning Edison, but I wanted the moment to linger. Like a soap bubble floating in air, I knew it would pop any second.

After I entered my house, I placed the still messed-up cards on the kitchen table, strode into the living room and plunked myself into an easy chair. I was too keyed-up to go to bed, though my lack of sleep the night before would come calling soon. I didn't even pull down the shades. I sat, closed my eyes and thought about Kristen. I pulled out my phone and looked at her number. I slumped back. Kristen Blume. Oh my. Kristen Blume. I liked the way she smiled, one side of her upper lip curling just a bit—yes, like Elvis.

Kristen.

The phone chirping woke me with a start. Kristen! Perhaps she was calling me. No, it wasn't. I glanced at the clock. Eleven pm.

"Nicole, hi, what's wrong?"

"Ken, please, it's terrible. The police are here and—" Her voice cracked.

"Are you at home?" I jumped out of my chair.

"Yes. There was a break-in. Oh, Ken."

"I'll be right there." I grabbed my jacket and flew out the door.

What fresh hell was this?

* * *

"Hello, Ken; thank you for coming so quickly." Nicole stepped back from the door, then grabbed my arm. I gave her a hug, looking beyond her to see Officer Tallman sitting comfortably in an easy chair, footrest up.

To her, I said, "Well, I see you've been well taken care of."

Officer Tallman spoke, "Cannoli, you gettin' around to all the crime scenes today? I should just turn my radio off and follow you around."

"You two know each other?" Nicole said.

"When you renovate the police station you meet all the cops. Every time somebody throws on a pot of coffee and lays out donuts, they come running."

Officer Tallman moved toward the door. "Funny guy. Well, this is my cue to leave. Now that you've got Cannoli here, ma'am, you should be fine."

"Hold on a second, Tallman; don't rush out so fast."

"Ken," Nicole said, "It's ok." She placed a delicate hand on my arm.

"If you don't mind, I'd like Officer Tallman to tell his side of the story while he's here and the information is fresh. It might be harder to secure his attention later."

"I ain't got no story, Cannoli. Just plain facts."

"Well, then, we should all have some wine." Nicole said. "Ken, would you mind? There's a bottle in the kitchen."

I went for the supplies while Nicole fidgeted on the sofa. I returned to the living room and poured two glasses. I was about to pour a third when Officer Tallman spoke up.

"Nothing for me."

I handed a glass to Nicole, then took one myself and joined her on the sofa. "So tell us what happened at your end."

"Ok, but I gotta make it quick. I was like this. We

were on widow watch—sorry, ma'am—doing a drive-by of the house with every loop around the neighborhood. Mackey had the new car, the Charger, lucky S.O.B. By nine-thirty, the house was solid dark, so we knew the missus had gone to bed."

"Uh-huh."

"Around ten-forty, Mackey picks up movement on the south side. Lady has French doors facing the flower garden. Guy comes out of the house, no lights on. That points to trouble. There's a bit of moonlight, but that's it. Mackey watches as best he can and sees the guy half jog into the back yard, but then his line of sight is obscured by the shrubs."

"What did he do next?"

"He calls it in, and follows the guy into the yard. I pick up the call and start heading over, from about a mile north. The guy runs through the yard clear through to the other street. It's a deep lot. Mackey gives chase and intercepts him before he can get into his vehicle."

"And this was Bryce McClurg, the roofing contractor?"

Nicole caught my eye. "That man, from Jerome's project." She sniffled.

"Yeah, funny ain't it? On the roof this morning, breaks into the widow's house tonight."

"Was anything taken?" I said.

"The lady says not."

"I checked my jewelry, the computers, laptops, everything seems to be here." She crossed her arms and rubbed her shoulders as if experiencing a shiver. "That man. Here. In our house."

"Are you sure, ma'am, you don't want to press charges? After all, he was on the premises, even if he didn't take nothin'."

Nicole shook her head slowly. "Any other time, maybe, but with everything that's happened. I...I can't."

Officer Tallman turned in my direction. "Maybe when the wine wears off, she'll reconsider."

"Well!" Nicole said.

"Tallman—!"

"Sorry, ma'am, I take it back. Thieves like McClurg shouldn't get away with it, that's all. Listen, I gotta get back to the station. If you change your mind, give us a call." He handed Nicole a business card and walked out the door.

Sensing that Nicole needed a comforting touch, I took her hand and led her to the sofa where we sat next to each other.

"I'm sorry this had to happen to you."

"I was asleep. I didn't hear anything until the banging at the door. I went to see what was so damn important, and there were the cops. Oh...Ken." She raised her brown peepers to me as they began to fill with tears.

"Nicole, it's ok; breathe." I snatched a box of tissues from the end table. "Here."

She took one and blew her nose. "It's so hard. I never thought I'd—"

"You want to tell me about it? Why would Bryce break into your house? What about the alarm system?"

"I don't even know if I set it. Thank God, the boys are at my mother's. Imagine if they had been here."

"I'm surprised he did this, with you home..."

She shrugged.

"And nothing was taken?"

"That just it, I can't stand the thought of the police prying, and the newspapers! TV. I'm surprised they're not here already...after last night. Scavengers. No more cops! I'm not pressing charges, I'm not! Even though he...he...OH GOD!"

Her head tilted forward, hands coming to her face. Her shoulders shook as she cried. I gently put my hand on her back.

After a few moments, she nodded and said, "I don't know how to get through this, but the cops can't know about it, that's for sure."

"Wait, what? Did Bryce take something after all?"

She nodded. "A frame with that woman. I found it last week. Cleaning his room. You know, men are so messy. I straighten up every day. Jerome, he has this safe behind the picture of the '68 Tigers. I was curious to see what new thing he had there. Usually it's contracts and recordings, once in a while he buys old coins. But this! That horrible woman, the one that's on the news. I could have smashed his favorite liquor bottle I was so angry. I could have...I don't understand, we had gotten through the argument about that hussy from the board. Jul..Julu...What's-a-hoosit...Shit."

"Now, Nicole, just relax."

"Well, Ken, why would he do this? He told me he loved me, and wanted to stay with me, never mind Julu..So why this anchorwoman? What's the deal?"

"So this was a photo, of the two of them?"

"Oh, much more. It was like some sick souvenir of their tryst smartly framed, and she wrote on it such a horrible perversion! Slut!"

"Did you confront him about it?"

Nicole squirmed. "It made me furious! How could he do that to me?"

"How furious were you exactly? So furious that..."

"Oh, I was livid... OH NO!!!" She recoiled away from me on the couch, a dark scowl crossing her face. She leaked all over like a busted hose. "Not, no, no...no, Ken, get away from me. How could you even think that I could, that I could..."

I struggled to get my arms around her and held her tight. Gradually her sobbing died down.

Gently, my words found air. "I remember our

meetings. The two of you stood out to me. The way he pulled out your chair for you, the way he looked to you first for an opinion before rendering his own, the way he brought you a coffee, mixing in the Sweet-N-Low and creamer. Seemed to me he cared about you deeply."

A little smile. "Thank you for saying that. I appreciate you."

I nodded. "I'm sorry to keep on, but I have to ask you a question. I don't know the piece you're talking about, but you've seen it. Who was it?"

"That one who anchors the news, well used to, on 4."

"Bailey Justine?"

"Yes, her."

"You know Bailey Justine recently became a network news anchor. With her rise to national status, she's pretty vulnerable to, well, innuendo. That framed souvenir, is it the kind of thing a network up-and-comer would pay money to keep from surfacing?"

"Well, yes, maybe. I don't know. Ken, I can't think about this anymore. But, Ken, don't tell the police. Ken, whatever you do. I can't stand this coming out."

We remained quiet for several moments, leaning against each other on the sofa, and I became aware of the floral scent of her hair.

"Ken...Ken, I'm so grateful. For everything you're doing. I always liked you. You know, when you were dating Dani..."

"That was a long time ago."

"In college."

"Dani and I were in college—you were sixteen."

"Yeah, well, I'm not sixteen anymore. Ken, do me one more favor? I can't stand to be alone. Not tonight. After this. Would you stay with me?"

"Sure, sure," I said. "I'll stay as long as you need."

Chapter 14

I awoke on the couch. Silence. No one was up. We had sat for a while, embracing each other, listening to each other breathe. Finally, wordlessly, Nicole got up and walked into the other room. Presumably, she had gone to bed. I made myself as comfortable on the couch as my height would allow, set my phone alarm, and closed my eyes.

Five am. The poor girl. She was a bundle of nerves. Trauma left its mark. She needed someone with her now, and my day was booked.

I needed to move, stop by home to shower and dress for my breakfast meeting with Walter Scofield. An idea popped up, and my fingers found the speed dial.

"Hi, so now you want to talk? Or yell at me?" Shirley answered.

"I deserve that, but listen. Nicole needs your help."

"I know, she's so distraught."

"More. There was a break-in here last night, and she's—"

"Whoa, what? Break in at her house?"

"Yes, she can explain. She called me about eleven last night and the police were here. I stayed over because she was so frightened."

"And now you need someone to relieve you, to baby sit Nicole?"

"Well, I wouldn't put it like that, but yes. I need to get on with my day and—"

"And I don't?"

"Forget it." I hung up. Stupid.

Chopin's *Minute Waltz* erupted. I opened the phone, but didn't say anything.

"Look, I'll be there in a little while," Shirley said. "What about the boys?"

"They are at their grandmother's. It's just Nicole, and she's still sleeping."

"All right, get out of there if you must, I'll be there in half an hour. I have a key, lock up."

* * *

It was supposed to be a quick stop home to shower and dress, but I couldn't resist firing up my laptop to check out Shirley's column. She wrote:

After months of sit-ins, demonstrations, etc. the sign is finally gone....But which of the wackos took it down?

1. The Mothers for Historic Preservation, who argued that the unique character of the Fitzgerald Reading Room was worthy of retaining for its historic contribution to the City of Southfield

2. Board member Molly Gross, whose startling poetry raised more than a few eyebrows with her line in Overturned: *"the Benefactor and his beauty become a screaming wreck"*

3. Talbot X, the mysterious underground organization that plagued the project in secret and whose exploits varied from graffiti on the contractor's job trailer to sabotage of their equipment

4. A crazed fan of architect Arne T. Fehn, the Fitzgerald Reading Room's original architect, noted for his also controversial five story cylindrical aluminum Student Union building on Wayne State's downtown Detroit campus—commonly referred to by students as "the beer can"—who protested the new addition wildly. Based in Ann Arbor, the fans boast a national membership. Did they have a nasty member amongst them?

Did a participant of one of these groups fell the sign in retaliation for the building renovation that took down the Fitzgerald Reading Room?

Here's another stumper: What was it that took Neumann out of his seat to wander over to the city offices just a few feet from where he met his death?

High-tailing it out of there, I zoomed to the Original Pancake House on Woodward. Home of the Big Dutch Baby—a gigantic apple dumpling pancake I always ordered and then forced myself to finish. Delicious.

Walter Scofield's dark bushy eyebrows and black-rimmed glasses reminded me of Dick Purtan, local icon radio personality. Purtan had graced the airwaves for more than 40 years, charming listeners with his quick wit and homespun charm, and had only recently retired.

"When can we get the sign back up?" Walter Scofield wasted no time on pleasantries. He hijacked the conversation as if he had called the meeting.

The waitress came and we placed our orders.

"This was not an accident, Walter. The perpetrator needs to be caught before we re-install the sign. Or they will do it again."

"Don't you see, that's what they want! We can't give in to terrorism. We have to put it up right away, tall and bright and shiny in the night sky. Let them see we can't be intimidated."

"What about the widow? Out of respect for her."

"Humf." Scofield continued. "Well, can we salvage what fell?"

"No. The roof is undamaged, but the frame is toast. It will need to be remade."

"Well, let's get on that right away."

Here was this sixty year old man, who wanted nothing if it wasn't for the good of the city. Of course that was admirable, even if occasionally he was stubborn as a mule. One time, he held up a board meeting because his petitioner's packet was incomplete. Sharing was not good enough; he insisted on having a copy made before continuing.

"Let me ask you another question, Walter. Let's talk about Matt Lance."

"Matt's a good man. He's been on the board for more than seven years, taking time away from his business. Why, he sometimes works late studying up on proposals."

Our steaming food arrived.

I dug in and continued. "I wonder if you could tell me about his past. I have some information that perhaps Jerome Neumann wasn't his favorite person."

He stared at me, demur eyes calculating, weighing, playing out some scenario in the depths of his mind. "Yes, there was bad blood between them. It's not a secret, though the information is probably guarded more than others. What is your interest?"

"Well, one man is dead, the other carried a grudge. Was the issue enough to make Lance want Neumann dead?"

Scofield licked his lips. I had aroused some primeval instinct in the man, could almost see his canine teeth lengthening before my eyes. He was intrigued. "It was 1982. Matt Lance was an upstart, a hustler. Always trying to get ahead. He had recently married and had a young family. The Novi/Wixom corridor was drawing an enormous amount of activity. The town was growing, and every developer worth his beans had a project going. In comes Jerome Neumann, only a few years older than Matt Lance, but a mover and shaker. He had irons in fires all over the Midwest. Matt went to work for Neumann's development company. Quickly, Matt learned the ropes and was on his way to earning his own fortune.

"During this time, Neumann engineered a plot to develop a piece of land along the northern edge of Eight Mile that was said to be undevelopable. It had previously played the role of dumping ground, and soil borings showed no bearing capacity whatsoever. In addition, the property was emitting methane gas. Trouble is—or rather the opportunity was—that this piece of land was prime real estate. Surrounded by sixty thousand residents within a two mile drive. Forty-five thousand vehicles per day on Eight Mile Road. Retailers longed for the location. Neumann did some performas and confirmed the gold mine. Well, Neumann could see the young Matt's mouth watering at the proposition.

"And here's where the going got sticky. Along came a land reclaim company out of Texas that sold Neumann a bill of goods. Guaranteed they could drill into the ground, pressure fill with some proprietary lightweight slurry that would not only create a load bearing matt on top of the trash, but the material would coalesce together and form a seal against the methane erupting through the surface.

"Neumann was hooked, as was the green Matt Lance."

"What happened?"

"Neumann put together a REIT—a Real Estate Investment Trust—to raise the capital. He had buyers— Kmart, notably—and there were others. Each would only go through with the purchase if the land was proven buildable."

"And in order to prove it, they would have to hire this company to do their magic."

"It was a slam dunk, right? Pay the money, reclaim the land, make the deal. Any investor would pay big to obtain a return like that."

"And Matt Lance was in on the ground floor."

Scofield nodded. "Neumann talked him into mortgaging his house, taking out credit cards and throw that money on the pile as well. Matt Lance bet everything. It was no-lose scenario."

"But he lost."

"The company took the money and left town. They never had a real system. Tampered data. A good story, that's all. Of course, Neumann promised he would make good, eventually. But it wasn't enough. Matt Lance could only juggle his creditors for so long before he was in deep trouble himself. And then his wife left him. That turned out to be his biggest heartbreak. They were only married five years.

"Lance of course blamed Neumann. Never forgave him for the financial trouble, but what meant more to him was the loss of his true love."

"What happened?"

"It took Matt Lance a long while to get back on his feet. He changed jobs, paid all that money back. Slowly, from his earnings."

"All that time, the anger must have grown to a rage. After thirty years, he must be fairly venomous."

The waitress arrived with more coffee. I had slowed down eating my breakfast, listening to the story.

"Let me ask you about Saturday," I said.

Scofield nodded as he dug into his plate.

"You were there. I understand you were sitting in the front row. Did you notice who was sitting next to you?"

"Well, Rose and I—you remember my wife—we were lucky enough to catch the middle two seats on the left side. That agent, Rusty Wagner, sat on my right. He was alone, and God, that wore on my nerves. Wouldn't leave me alone. Guy could talk the leg off a dead man. Kept jabbering on with his war stories. The first half of the program up on stage was terrific. I don't do much poetry, but the lineup was mesmerizing. And to my good fortune, the moment the lights went up for intermission, he was off like a lightning bolt."

"You don't know where he went?"

"No, Rose and I went out into the lobby to grab a coffee, decaf of course—thank God they had a decent brew. People were lined up across the lobby. We stood, talking about the highlights of the night—Rose and I. I don't remember seeing Rusty anywhere near there, but of course I wasn't particularly looking for him. We returned to our seats just in time."

"What about when the program returned, after intermission. When did he get back, do you remember?"

"He never came back. I was glad. I could think for a change, and then—"

He let the sentence hang, looked down.

"What about you," I prodded. "Did you see anyone else out in the lobby?"

Scofield stared at me. "You'll have to be a bit more specific than that, Ken, there were a lot of people..."

"Of course. Jerome Neumann, and his wife Nicole."

"I saw Nicole in that bright yellow dress, with some girlfriends on the other side of the lobby by the stairs. Neumann wasn't with her. We got our coffee and didn't hang around. Went right back down. Didn't see Rusty again. Or Neumann. Sat and looked up at the stage. Half the poets were still up there. Molly Gross sat quiet as a mouse. Looking off into space."

"Neumann received a call at the end of the first half of the program. Would you happen to know who called him? Did you?"

"No, I didn't call him. Don't know anything about that."

Chapter 15

The Scofield breakfast left me with more questions. And fatter, definitely fatter. I had a burning desire to talk to Bryce and get to the bottom of what had happened at Nicole's the prior evening. He was a subcontractor on the auditorium project, and I had his number in my phone. To my surprise, he was amenable to meeting an hour later.

When I checked with Shirley she said Nicole was "moody as a caged tiger."

I phoned the office. "Rita, it's Ken."

"I know."

"Would you let Robert know that I'm going to miss the project manager's meeting this morning?"

"Uh, huh. He's not going to like that."

"Would you please tell him?"

"He arrived in a foul mood. What did you do to him this weekend?"

"I didn't do anything, but the Neumann thing is on his mind."

"Humf. Anything else?"

Rita was always a spot of sunshine.

I needed to see Molly Gross. Boyd had given me her number, but I wasn't quite sure how to approach her. I wondered what, if anything, she had seen from the stage.

A man answered when I dialed her number.

"She's unavailable. May I take a message?" He didn't sound like he meant it.

"This is Ken Knoll. I'm sure she has a busy

schedule, but it's important that I speak with her today."

"I'll leave word. She likely won't be returning calls today. She's feeling a bit under the weather."

That I believed. We all did.

* * *

I'd been to Bryce's shop a couple of times. It was a big box/little box arrangement, with the metal-walled shop–slash–warehouse in the back and the brick-faced office in the front. The building was in an industrial cul-de-sac near the intersection of I-75 and 14 Mile Road—easy freeway access north and south, and a handful of miles from east-west thoroughfares I-696 and M-59.

Bryce, dressed in blue jeans and grey logo t-shirt greeted me easily and walked me through the reception area and conference room, back into a small kitchenette, complete with full size refrigerator, two microwave ovens and dishwasher. I noticed counter appliances—toaster, toaster oven, blender, electric can opener, coffee maker.

"Would you like some coffee? I made it a few minutes ago."

"Great."

He opened a cabinet door and pulled out a china mug with his firm's logo on it. We'd previously met in the conference room, which had its own coffee maker. "I had no idea this was back here. All the comforts of home."

Bryce chuckled. He had a relaxed way about him, ruggedly handsome—think Marlboro man—and was adept at creating rapport. "This *is* home, during the week. I live in Dayton. Annabelle, my wife, stays down there with the kids when I have a job going up here. I'm usually on site four or five days, then back home. It will go on for a couple of months that way. I have another shop in Dayton, and split my time depending on the work. Between the two I can cover Michigan north to Saginaw, west to Lansing, and south into Toledo. From Dayton I can cover the southwest corner of Ohio."

"That's a large area. You must be doing well."

"Can't complain. Let me show you the apartment. I share the kitchen with the staff." He strode across the room. "It's arranged like an onion, layers of personal space."

We entered an office with file cabinets, a large desk and matching credenza. "This is mine. I keep the sensitive files in here—accounting and personnel records. Gloria handles project-related paperwork in the main office—you've met Gloria."

"Yes, efficient gal."

"Very."

I noted with interest the framed photographs and memorabilia that adorned the wall opposite the desk. Mickey Mantle autographed baseball; photo of Barbara Eden as Jeannie with a string of beads from her costume, under glass; Green Hornet's mask from the TV series with photo of Van Williams dressed as Britt Reid. "Impressive."

"Thanks. I have a new one here." He opened a drawer. "I haven't had a chance to properly frame it yet." He extracted a slender plastic box, an inch high. Inside was a long piece of grey paper, with printing on it, the first quarter reading "Friday" with a red painted slash, the second quarter read "Saturday" with a star, the third quarter "Sunday" with a moon. Across the top was printed "Woodstock Music and Art Fair." The last quarter of the ticket said "THREE DAY TICKET $24."

My eyes widened. "Woodstock? Impressive."

"Thanks." He pointed through the open door behind him. "I've got a full bath back here, and a bedroom. Not home, but not bad."

"Makes it easier to bear the commute."

"Yeah, that can be good and bad. But I work like a dog when I'm here, then relax when I'm home. But enough of that." He indicated the direction back the way we had come, and said, "Why don't we get to business. Let's head over to the conference room. You probably want to talk about the roof damage, get things cleaned up. I could have met you on site—"

"Well, this isn't about the project, Bryce. I have a few, more personal, questions."

"Oh," he said as it dawned on him. To his credit his expression didn't change perceptibly. He closed the door to the kitchenette and stepped back into his office. "Give us some privacy." He motioned to a chair opposite his desk, and his eyes settled on mine.

"It's about Sunday night."

Bryce nodded, but didn't offer the first words.

"I'm getting all this through hearsay. Nicole Neumann is sort of a friend and I offered to make some inquiries for her."

Bryce fished a cigarette pack and lighter out of his shirt pocket, then apparently thought the better of it, and laid the lighter on his desk. I hesitated, eyed the lighter, admiring its sleek black look, with a Jack Daniels logo affixed in brass. He fidgeted, picked up a pencil and started tapping it, "You know me, Ken, I'm a no-nonsense guy. Just come out and ask me. I'll tell you the truth."

I sat forward. "Ok, well, the police picked you up. After you, apparently, had been inside the Neumann residence while Nicole was sleeping. What were you doing there?"

He sighed. "Neumann had something of mine; I went there to retrieve it. I'd been in the house before. I knew right where it should have been. I didn't want to bother Nicole for it, at this difficult time, so I waited until she went to bed."

"What were you looking for?"

He shook his head. "Sorry. Sensitive documents. The kind nobody needs to know about."

"Did you find them?"

"No, turns out they were in my office all along. It was a mistake. Should have looked here first."

"Nicole claims you *did* take something."

"I already told you, I didn't take anything. Nicole is distraught, so out of it with the death of her husband, in that terrible manner, how would she know? She told the police nothing was taken."

"She says it was a picture in a frame. It was in Neumann's office earlier in the day. After you left, it was gone."

"Picture? Why would I take a picture? I already told you I didn't take anything."

"Hmm," I said, and decided to drop it. "Do you know Molly Gross, by the way?"

"The poet? Yeah, I saw her at the poetry reading Saturday night."

"I mean, personally."

He picked up his lighter and played with the cap. "No, never met the woman."

"But you were at the event?"

"Yeah. Scofield gave me a ticket. Poetry's not my thing but I'd read Molly's book."

"Book?"

"Yeah, about relationships and honesty."

"Oh, didn't realize." I paused. "What did you do during intermission?"

"Intermission? Took a leak, got a beer."

"Did you meet Neumann? During intermission?"

"Neumann, no. I tried to get hold of him earlier in the day, but he never returned my call." Bryce straightened papers on his desk. "Anything else, I really have to—"

"One more question, Bryce. This is important. I understand you were friends with Matt Lance."

"Matt, oh yeah, we go way back. Why?"

I shook my head. "Just something I'm checking on. How long have you known him?"

"My dad was a bookkeeper for Matt at his business, Auto Engineered Parts. Matt, I guess, was good to work for. At least Dad never complained."

I nodded.

"Then, last year, I joined Toastmasters. Thought I'd learn public speaking skills for the job. You know, it helps to attend these facilities association gatherings, give a lecture about caring for the roofing materials, maintenance things like that. Matt Lance was in the Birmingham group. They meet monthly, and I participated whenever I was up here and my schedule would allow. But I still don't see—"

"I'm sure it's nothing. Well, thank you for your time. Hopefully we can work together again soon."

"Perhaps so."

Chapter 16

What happened at Nicole's break-in remained unclear. Nicole claimed something was missing; Bryce asserted he took nothing. I believed Nicole. But I've been wrong in the past.

Something was off. From the moment I hinted at the break in, there was a note of—not hostility, Bryce was *seemingly* just as forthcoming as before—insincerity perhaps? Bryce exuded confidence in every circumstance, but I felt the undercurrent of a feeling being covered over. Like software chugging away in the background while your computer worked at a muted pace.

I headed back to the office, an easy ride south on I-75, then I-696 west to the Telegraph Road exit. It was still morning, barely.

Robert Westin stood at the receptionist counter talking to Sally. Grey suit, perfectly creased. Black hair, dusted with grey. Business short, perfectly in place. A "healthy" tan, ice blue eyes, chiseled features. Richard Gere handsome in *Pretty Woman*. What grated me was his stupid tie tack, a white whale chomping a wooden row boat in half: Moby Dick.

"Cannoli, a word."

He stepped into the small conference room by the lobby. I followed and set down my briefcase, a soft leather job.

"Cannoli, I don't like repeating myself. We went over the program for tomorrow's presentation earlier and—"

"At the PM meeting? Why did you do that?"

Icy blue stare. "You can catch up from Wally. I don't appreciate you blowing off the meeting at the last minute. We need all cylinders functioning together. Teamwork, right?"

"Yes, sir. But I had—"

"I don't care, Cannoli. Don't let it happen again. Got it?"

"Yep."

"Good. Now, are we ok for tomorrow? You're responsible for the fly-through and the stacked model. We don't need any bumps."

"It's dynamite. Edison is on it; you know he's a wiz."

"Yes, but I also know he's a bit off center. This is on *you*. And another thing. Sue Watts is all over my ass. Are we clear on this sign catastrophe?"

"Yes, sir. The sign supports were clearly tampered with. We checked the bolts, did everything by the book. There's nothing to snake back on us."

"Good." First smile of the day. "Keep it that way. Get Watts everything she needs, so she'll stop calling me."

"You got it." Robert strode out.

I slung my briefcase over my shoulder and went to my desk. Turned on my computer, grabbed my coffee cup and headed to the kitchen for some joe.

Wally was at the coffee. "Cannoli, looks like that trouble's been following you around again. I won't ask what kind of weekend you had, but why would you skip the PM meeting when you knew you'd be on the hot seat?"

"Nice to see you too, Wally. I'm jumping into this investigation. That's more important than procedure right now. Robert told me you'd fill me in on tomorrow's presentation."

He gave me time, players, script. "We'll have a dry run here tomorrow morning before we hit the road. Maggie is finalizing the take away."

"Has Robert seen it yet? You know he's going to bleed all over it."

"Yeah, he never knows what he wants until we give him something first. Don't worry. Maggie is used to it."

"Right on that. Good, good. SOP. Last minute as always. I'll check on how Edison is coming."

Val's Market, the third largest supermarket chain in Metro Detroit with 62 stores, had optioned the purchase of the six Dizzy's Supermarket locations, a small independent chain that had been losing share in recent years. Two of the units were in Detroit proper, the others edged the city. Val's was soliciting proposals to explore renovation options. Five architectural-engineering firms were to propose schemes to update and expand Dizzy's typical plan into a layout that incorporated Val's much larger prototype. Competition. The successful firm would obtain the commission to expand and renovate the six stores. To make matters more exciting, each Dizzy's store was located in a strip center owned by developer Walter Gruen. By Val's contract, Gruen would be required to update those six centers. The architect hired to do the supermarket renovation would have an edge on the design contract for the strip center.

We had done work for Gruen in the past—six years past—but when the patriarch retired, his son John went a different direction, preferring quickly produced projects for low cash to quality architecture. Now, the old man would be involved, at his own request, as these new footprints would radically alter the shopping center's appearances. My trip to Gaylord the prior week was an effort to "grease the skids" with the old man.

I reviewed Edison's work. Impeccable, as usual. He

knew how to make that software sing and dance, beginning with a stacked model, a 3-D image of Dizzy's showing demolition of the walls required for the expansion, new steel framing, walls and roof; interior rearrangement. In the 3-D "exploded" view, with old pieces flying off and new pieces flying back on, it was a thing of beauty.

As a surprise bonus offering to Val's, we had studied the six site plans, determined an approach to the store expansion layout, and laid out the additional parking that would be needed. We liked to stay one step ahead of the competition.

"Edison, this is smashing as always," I said. "On the Greenfield site, let's show another fifty spaces along the side here, instead of at the road. Put some landscaping in there."

"Sure."

I noticed the physical Neumann Auditorium model on the reference table behind him. "What's going on here, Edison? What are you doing with that?"

"I was just playing. Trying to visualize what happened with the sign." He turned to the model to illustrate. The auditorium addition was three-quarters of a full circle, attached to the existing rectangle of offices. The model showed clearly the circular building, parapet wall along the perimeter of the roof and the three foot high "NEUMANN AUDITORIUM" sign letters following the edge of the perimeter. Eight feet further back stood the sloped standing seam metal roof that followed along the curve as well. As I watched, Edison took the sign and demonstrated the fall over the roof's edge.

Seeing the action in three dimensions, something occurred to me which was not obvious before.

"I don't know, Ken, how can this sign fall? It's about eighteen feet long, and attached to these wide-flange beams at the base, right?"

I nodded.

"So the sign is relatively light, but those beams weigh a ton. Not like someone can push that construction over the roof's edge."

"No," I said. "And what doesn't make sense is that the parapet was only damaged in the middle third of the sign."

Edison looked puzzled.

"Look here, Edison. The sign is curved and base beams are in two rows, bent at a small angle in the center. The sign is on a concentric circle with the building's parapet. The moment the sign and base start to tip forward—toward the building's edge—the extreme ends of the curved base reach up into the sky and could easily fall without touching."

"Ahhh, but the middle, the tangent. Has to make contact. Even if a giant was on the roof pushing the sign over, it must have touched the parapet. Probably mangled it pretty good."

"In the middle."

"Right. There were no signs of explosives, were there?" Edison said. "No gun powder, scratches from shrapnel."

"No, nothing like that."

"Someone couldn't have pushed the sign over, it would have been way too heavy for that."

"Right."

"So," Edison smiled. "As far as I can see, there are two explanations. A windstorm, twister, tornado, or—"

"Edison, there were no tornadoes the other night. It was a clear night, remember? A bit on the warm side, definitely no *weather*."

"Earthquake. An earthquake could have done it. Lateral accelerated motion. Rocked the sign back and forth, in sync with its period. Then boom, the building dips down below grade line just as the sign topples, eliminating the possibility of impact."

What was he smoking? "Edison, there was no earthquake. We would have felt it or heard it on the news. Besides, what about the missing bolts? No, something else. But you did give me an idea."

I pulled out my cell and hit Steve's number. "Steve, could you tell by examining it if the sign frame had any unusual stresses placed on it?"

"Unusual stresses?"

"Yes, like if an earthquake had shook the sign back and forth? Or if there had been some explosives placed underneath that blew the sign up off the roof and over the parapet?"

"Well, yeah, sure. Either of those would have created some stress fractures. Maybe not to be seen with the naked eye, but if you're looking for it..."

"And we are. So if you find some of these stress fractures, you could then postulate what happened to force the sign from the roof?"

"Well, we can get an idea of what types of loads were placed on the sign. Force of impact, in an ideal world anyway. This sign support frame is all hacked up; it took a beating from the force of the fall itself.

"Oh, by the way, I got a call from Sargent Gilmore earlier. They are releasing the framework and it's heading over to the testing lab, MEC, for evaluation. I'll give them a heads up about the additional information we're looking for. Originally they were tasked to determine how the sign landed, what hit first, force of the blow on the ground, and, ur, body."

"Perfect; thanks, Steve. Keep me in the loop on that will you?" I said.

"Me too," Edison mouthed.

I hung up and asked, "Want to get some food?" Then, glancing at Edison's computer, I added "Do you have time?"

"Heck yeah," he said. "But let's make it quick. Robert wants to see the final product before he goes home."

"Sounds like Ray's Coney is calling us."

We walked in behind a group of high-schoolers. Ever since the school had rescinded their strict "eat in" policy, all the lunch places, especially Taco Bell, Papa Romano's and Ray's Coney were swamped with teens. Ray's was a dive, the ultimate greasy spoon. But what it lacked in atmosphere, it made up for in the largest pounds-per-dollar lunch around, except of course, for Taco Bell.

"So...you and Kristen Blume?" Edison said while we waited for a table.

I smiled at the mention of her name. "Yeah."

"How did this happen?"

I explained meeting her at the site, asking her to dinner, and having a great night. In the middle of the explanation we were walked to a table, and a waitress took our order right away.

"So you just ran into her? She just showed up?"

"Isn't it amazing?"

"Pffdt."

"What's wrong?"

"She was running around during the madness Saturday night. I didn't even get a hello. You get dinner."

"Edison, she doesn't even know you."

"You either, but apparently that didn't matter."

I didn't get Edison. He had so many girls, lined up one after the other. He was dating a *Sports Illustrated* model for crying out loud. Not to mention he used to live with QDivine. And now he's jealous of *me*?

My phone chirped as the waitress brought our coneys, fries and Cokes. *Sue Watts*. Great.

"Where are you on that report?" she hollered.

"It's practically done."

"And perhaps you can explain how Shirley Hanson got the information about Neumann leaving his seat to go to the office, which she published in this morning's column?"

"I don't know. She finds things out. She's an investigative reporter, that's what she does."

She hung up.

I sighed. "She's like a pit bull."

"Who, Kristen?"

"No, come on, Sue Watts. I used to think she was cute, when she was selling the insurance. Now that she's backing it, it's another matter. The sooner I get to the bottom of what happened, the better off we'll all be."

"What about Nicole?" Edison said.

"Nicole? She's stunned, taken aback. She's—"

"Not how *is* she, but what *about* her? Do you trust her? Could she have done it?"

"No, Edison."

"Well, she asked you to find the killer, right? She put you up to this hunt."

"Exactly. She suspects Julianne, though I don't know if there's anything to it."

Edison picked up a fry and dipped it into a puddle of coney sauce that had slopped onto the plate. "Maybe she just said that to keep you from suspecting her. Maybe Neumann's phone call from the office was a diversion; a red herring."

"You've been reading too much crime fiction. You should have seen her. She's beside herself."

"Are you sure your feelings aren't coloring your opinion?"

"Huh?"

"You *did* date her sister. Maybe you had an eye for

the younger sibling."

"Edison, what has gotten into you?"

"I'm just saying, maybe you should look at all the possibilities. Not to mention she's an actress. She could be using you."

"Nicole? She's not an actress. Lately, she's been a trophy wife. Yeah, she studied film at Grand Valley, but that hardly makes her—"

"You're forgetting that sexy shaving commercial. The one with the football player. Brett whatshisname."

"Favre. Yeah, I forgot about that. Well, that doesn't make her an actress."

He looked down at his empty plate, surprised—apparently—that it was empty.

"What about Bryce McClurg?" I said. "What do you know about him?"

"The roofing contractor? Not much."

"Hmm."

"Maybe try Wally. I bet he has stories," Edison said.

"Yeah, Wally. Good idea. What about Molly Gross?"

"*Extreme Honesty* Molly Gross? I know that she's a fake."

"I'm talking about the poet from Saturday, on the planning board. Don't know anything about *honesty*."

"Yeah, yeah. Then you don't know Molly. She professes this theory about living a principled life based on honesty. She says when you are gut honest, blatantly sharing inner feelings, it helps you develop good relationships; relationships built on honest truth, no game playing. This builds a series of bridges: first respect, then trust, ultimately love."

"Other than the blatant honesty part, it sounds like a good theory."

"The theory's fine, but it's hard to swallow from someone that doesn't believe it herself."

"Explain?" I took a sip of my Coke.

"Well, a couple of years ago I went to a book signing in Southfield. I was all excited about meeting her and everything. She gave a little talk, it was great. Afterward there was a book-signing line and so I stood around waiting for her and when she finished, I went over and told her how much I enjoyed the theory and always try to be honest and not hold back."

"Uh-huh."

"I asked her how she liked doing the book signings, and touring around. She told me everything that was great about it: meeting people, listening to people's stories about how their lives where changed. We had this deep conversation. She confessed to considering assembling people's stories into a book called *The Amazing Results of Extreme Honesty.*"

"Still not sure where you're going with this."

"Two days later, I happened to be in Cleveland— went to see my Aunt Gladys, who has a condo on the river, an atmospheric place, leaded windows and a big fireplace. Old phonograph too, and a collection of Eric Clapton vinyl that will make your eyes water. Enjoying the tunes and catching that spectacular view of Lake Erie, sunset pink bleeding across the waves."

"Edison?"

"Oh, yeah, well we went to this humongous book store in town and sure enough, there she was again! She was just finishing signing books and Aunt Gladys was still exploring the cookbooks, so I hung around to talk to Molly. I told her I had an idea for the results book and asked her if she's thought any more about it. And you know what she said to me?"

"Uh-uh."

"*What results book?* That's what she said. *What results book?* So I explained about meeting her, and how she told me about it. I had this idea for a website to promote the project. So she goes *I'll have to think about it.*"

"She had no idea what you were talking about."

"Disavowed our conversation entirely. Pretended she didn't know me, didn't remember our conversation, nothing."

"Well, I'm sure she's busy and—"

"And nothing. She's a fraud. Bet she'll use all those ideas we talked and not give me credit."

"Not remembering you doesn't make her a fraud, Edison."

"Yeah, well." He paused. "On those sign supports, is Steve going to check on them?"

"Yeah, he's having the police lab send the framework to MTE."

"It's like March all over again."

"What's like March?" I said.

"Remember when the auditorium project was just starting, all those demonstrators? That sit-in by the tree huggers? Not to mention the vandalism when the construction started up—the job sign, the construction trailer got spray painted."

"Right, exactly."

The waitress came and took our plates away. "Gentlemen, any dessert here?"

"Does Willie Wonka like chocolate?" Edison said. He ordered a chocolate sundae.

"Nothing for me." I had to get this paunch off my mid-section.

Officer Tallman entered the back door of the restaurant. He looked around, spotted me and walked over.

"Hey Ken, what's happening?"

"That's what I'd like to know," I said. "Edison and I are just finishing lunch, wanna join us?"

He pulled out a chair. "Sure, thanks."

"Hey Jim, how are those Dobermans?" Edison said. His sundae arrived and he dug in.

"Great. Booker loves the rec room and is real protective of Emily, especially when one of her uncles gets too close. Crash loves to play catch. He's going to enter the Frisbee championships when he's a bit older."

"Anything new on the Neumann case?" I said.

"You know I can't talk about that."

"Come on, Jim, I gave you some good stuff on the roof, didn't I?"

"Well, let's see, I remember you said something like you'd have to think about it."

"Uh, well, I talked to Steve Dickerson earlier, and I understand the sign framework is on its way to MTE. They will do a good job. And if anyone can figure out how the sign was made to lurch from the rooftop, Steve can."

Jim coughed. "Oh, I do have something for you. You had asked me about the call Jerome Neumann received on the night he died, during the night's presentation."

"Yes?"

"Here, let me locate it." Jim pulled out a small black notebook and began flipping through pages. "Right, a call was made at 8:42 pm from Conference Room 102 phone at the city offices to Jerome Neumann's cell phone."

"How long was the call?"

"Forty-seven seconds."

"Anything else?"

"Nope, that's it. Oh, and Cannoli? You didn't hear it from me."

The good officer ordered his lunch and Edison and I made our way back to work.

My thoughts returned to the spring time protesters and mischievous acts that Edison and Shirley had mentioned. They stemmed from historical groups and sentimentalists looking to block change. The majority of the building area that was cut up for the Neumann Auditorium addition came from the Fitzgerald Reading Room, which had been an addition to the library in 1966. Donated by real estate developer Ralph 'Jazz' Fitzgerald, the structure was a shocking architectural statement which rocked the art world and started tongues wagging, some unkindly. The reading room itself provided useful services and opened the library to community involvement. Forty-five years later, it was tired, it was old, and it was still ugly. Community leaders were in agreement that the replacement with a new structure was an exciting addition to the neighborhood.

Opponents provided that it was destroying a landmark that should, instead, be restored to its preeminence. Outrage varied from polite disagreement to sit-ins and destruction of property. At the sit-ins, you could meet your opposition and talk to him. Of course, the physical damage was done under cover of darkness. What galled me was the attack on private property. What grounds did these people have for destroying the contractor's trailer? He was simply doing the job he was hired to do.

When we arrived back at the office, I shooed Edison out of the car. I preferred to stay and make a few calls from the privacy of my automobile.

"But will you be coming back in?" Edison asked.

"Yeah, yeah. I have to write that report for Sue Watts."

Edison slammed the car door and I dialed Molly Gross. She answered personally and agreed to speak with me the following morning.

I closed my phone. As I started toward the office, the phone ringing startled me. The display said "Kristy."

"Hello," I answered.

"Are you sure?" she said. It was *her*.

"Kristen! What a nice surprise. Good to hear from you. Why does my phone say 'Kristy'?"

"That's what my friends call me. You wanna be my friend, don't you?"

"You know I do."

"Ha! Would you like to see me?"

I smiled. "Yes, I have one more meeting, and then I'll be free. I'll call you when I get out, probably around four-thirty."

"Perfect. *Ciao!*"

Yes, this day would be something special.

I pushed Nicole's speed dial number. "How are you?"

"That's a fine how-do-you-do for someone who walked out on me this morning."

"Sorry, Nicole, I had to get to work. Wasn't Shirley there when you woke up?"

"Yeah, she was here. It was a surprise, though, to not have you here."

I heard talking in the background, high pitched and fast, like children. "Your kids are home?"

"Yeah, they came by for a visit. They're on their way out the door now, back to Mother's. I understand about your work, but I needed you this morning."

"Why, what was wrong? Couldn't Shirley—"

"Forget it. Sometimes it's just nice to talk to a man, you know?...Oh, I guess you wouldn't. A-hem. Well, how about an update?"

I had let her down. Some special kid-glove treatment was in order now. "Why don't I stop by and give it to you in person? Say about ninety minutes from now?"

"Oh, Ken, that would be wonderful. I'll make tea."

I called Kristy to delay our time by an hour. She was understanding. I climbed out of the car and strode into our office. Wally was at the water cooler.

"Hey, Wally," I said, "You know Bryce McClurg, the roofing contractor at Prime Roofing?"

"Sure, Cannoli. Any other questions for me? The wife called a minute ago asking me to take her and the kids to the mall tonight. Anything I can do to delay my departure would have my endorsement."

Wally had six kids and a full size van to cart them around in.

"What do you know about Bryce McClurg?"

"Single ply EPDM, TPO, I believe he does a bit of built-up, but I could be wrong. Nail him early, because—"

"No, not his business. What do you know about *him*?"

"The man?"

Wally didn't have anything solid to share, but he would make some inquiries.

At my office I started banging out the report for Sue Watts. It was slow going. Facts, time, conditions. Dry, dry, dry, even with the murder. I got to the end of it. I checked it over, decided it was ok, and sent it to Watts via email.

Done.

I jumped online for a little background research on Rusty Wagner, Molly Gross's agent. Where would we be without search engines and Google?

Then it was off to the Matt interview, a quick stop at Nicole's, then Kristen. Blume!

Kristy.

No way.

Chapter 17

I strive to capture the enviable spirit my high school forensics teacher once attributed to me. A spirit of hope and optimism infused into the Matt Lance interview would, ideally, disarm him into spilling everything he knew.

Mighty Mouse blared from my pocket. "Edison, miss me already?"

"Hey, are you still here?"

"No, I'm on the way to see Matt Lance. What's up?"

"Uh-oh. I have to show you something. It's important. You are going to want to see this."

"I won't be back at the office today. Can it wait until morning? I have a couple more stops to make after Matt."

"Um...hmm. Well...you need your eyeballs on this. Trust me."

"Can you tell me over the phone?"

"Not really. It's a lookie."

Sometimes, in dealing with Edison I felt like a parent trying to get something out of his kid.

"Well, I'm meeting Matt Lance at the Southfield city offices, can you meet me there? We could talk for a few minutes before I shove off for my next stop. Meet me at four-thirty."

"Sure, City of Southfield. See you there."

Whether through his charm or because he had information on somebody, Matt Lance always seemed to have office space available to him at the city offices. He appeared gruff to me, and at seventy, I wasn't sure how far his charm would get him with the office staff. That situation would change soon enough, as Matt was one of the first who had rented space in the new office building under construction immediately south of city hall. We were currently completing the inspections for a Temporary Certificate of Occupancy on the three upper floors of the eight story building. Matt had secured an office on the top floor and would be able to move in before the end of the week.

Why he needed an office on this side of town, I didn't know. Matt Lance was in the automobile parts business, having perfected—in the late '70s—a method of producing parts to spec out of plastic materials that cost pennies less to produce than their metal counterparts. The business grew and his fortune was made. He maintained an engineering office about ten miles east, in Clinton Township.

The glass door was framed in aluminum which had lost its sheen, and into the corners of which dirt had made its way. Matt stood in the cluttered hallway, arms open like a Walmart greeter.

"Ken Knoll, never thought I'd see you again so soon."

"Hello Matt, thank you for meeting me so quickly."

"Follow me. Forgive the stink and stain; they don't know how to clean around here. If it was my place, I'd make 'em scrub with vinegar and baking soda and get that dank smell out of here."

"Oh, come on, Matt; it's not all that bad."

"That rose scent is merely a red herring. A discriminating nose could tell."

We strode down a side corridor, past a secretary who sat behind a putty-colored steel desk piled high with manila folders.

His tiny office was enclosed by ceiling height demountable partitions finished in faded grass cloth, with a roughly textured 2x2 ceiling darkened by dirt from the heating vent. Matt offered me a molded plastic Eames chair.

I sat and he tilted his head in question.

I jumped right in. "I have a few areas of inquiry. First—if you don't mind my being blunt—I heard there was a topic on the board's agenda, business where you and Jerome Neumann didn't see eye to eye."

"About that landscape ordinance? Hell yes! I told that joker this was a city matter, and we needed to get our ducks in a row. If Southfield is to remain viable in the 21st century, we need to maintain order and make it pretty. Ken, this isn't new to you. You gotta have corridors of light. Buffer zones on axis creating breathtaking vistas." He slapped the table with his open palm. "Heh, heh, heh. The future is ours if we take it."

I shrugged.

"He didn't see it that way. Thought appropriating land—that's what he called it, though we weren't *taking* it—appropriating the land for landscaping was a violation of private property. Those developers are ego-centric. Why look at what he did to his wife! Cheating on her—and I don't excuse that hussy we have on the board neither. I'm not surprised he was killed by the sign. It was destiny. The hand of Karma. Every act of evil is repaid by the passing of dark shadows across your life."

"No, Matt, it was not so much Karma that did him in. The sign was deliberately plunged."

Matt peered at me from behind thick grey eyebrows. I waited for him to verbalize his thoughts, but nothing came my way.

"Let me ask you about something I overheard at the site Saturday night, after the sign fell," I said. "You were talking to Bryce McClurg. He made a remark that he was going to kill you. Do you remember that?"

"Not specifically. Bryce and I go way back. We're always joking around. Bryce is a good kid. Whatever it was, didn't mean nothin'."

"Did you enjoy the event? I mean before..."

"Oh, me, not so much. I'm not a poetry kind of guy. It was for my date; it was all she could talk about for a couple of weeks beforehand."

"Your date?"

"Amelia Day. You met Amelia; she's right out front here." He motioned out the door. He yelled, "Amelia, come on in here for a minute."

And then I understood how Matt had acquired the office. Amelia was forty-something with a dark brown page-boy and wore a loose-fitting red print top that did nothing for her round figure.

I asked Amelia, "And did Matt treat you to something special at intermission?"

"Well, not exactly. I stayed in my seat the whole time. He kept getting up, but he had other things on his mind which distracted him from bringing me anything back."

I looked quizzically at the pair, she with her hand on his shoulder.

"Matt, what made you so antsy? Bored with the program?" I said.

His eyes turned downward, "Nothing like that. The poetry was all right, for what it was."

Amelia spoke up, "He wasn't feeling well, he—"

Matt said sharply, "Amelia!"

"It's no crime, sweetheart," Amelia said. "He had diarrhea. He was up and down all night."

"Pish," said Matt.

Follow-up questions were niggling at my brain, but I didn't want to embarrass the man.

"Oh, by the way, Ken, when will those new offices be ready?"

"Just a couple of days, it should be all set." I looked at Amelia, who was still stroking Matt's shoulder with her stubby fingers. "I know you're anxious to get out of Amelia's hair."

Amelia said, "No, that's not it. Matt likes to work late at night when no one is around. We *always* kick him out at dinner time. Nobody here works late enough to please him."

"You want to take a peek?" I said.

Matt's tired eyes grew bright. "Now? I've only seen a model. If we could see the real thing, that would be something."

"What would be something?" a husky female voice chimed in from behind me. Shirley. My heart rate spiked. "Hi, Ken; annoying the hard working people of the city?"

"Hey," Matt said, "You're that investigative reporter, aren't you? Shirley..."

Shirley reached out her hand and introduced herself to Matt and Amelia. "I've seen your name in the city notices, Matt. I'm sure you were as devastated as I was, two nights ago when the building's sign—designed by this man right here (she put her hand on my shoulder)—plunged into the heart of the man who donated three million dollars to the project."

"A travesty." He glanced at me, as if acknowledging that our conversation would remain between the two of us.

"Ah-hum," I said. "Nice to see you, Shirley, but we were about to scoot."

"Next door?" Shirley said. "I'd love to see it, too. Are you playing tour guide?"

I couldn't figure a quick trick to make her disappear, so we all trouped next door, including Amelia. I ran interference with the contractor, who provided hard hats. We signed the log and piled into the elevator, its interior lined in protective cardboard, and rode up to the ninth floor. The elevator doors opened to a collection of boxes stacked high and tall shelving piled with all manner of construction tools and supplies—a contractor's staging area.

Matt's office was in the high rent wing, a single-loaded corridor with office windows to the exterior, the walkway overlooking the triangular atrium space from which two office wings sprang like butterfly wings. The stainless steel railing was comprised of solid posts supporting braided stainless steel mesh panels, overlooking the full height space. Eight story tall glass on the far side looked out toward the city's golf course.

"Fancy shmancy," Shirley said.

Amelia's wide eyes echoed the sentiment.

While the rest of us hustled into Matt's office, Shirley stayed behind, leaning against the corridor railing.

"We'll be returning downstairs in a minute," I said. "Don't go too far."

"Do I ever?" Shirley smiled.

Matt's new office suite was comprised of a small lobby and two generous offices, the larger of which included a restroom.

A clattering, followed by a shrill scream, erupted from beyond the office. I raced to the door. I saw Shirley at the far end of the corridor, sprawled out on the floor by the elevators. As I jogged to her, I took in the sight of a stack of storage shelves tipped over beside her.

I offered my hand and helped Shirley to her feet. "What were you doing?"

"It's all right, Ken. Nothing broken."

Boxes, screws, and acoustical ceiling grid track and hanger wire were strewn about. "Were you climbing the shelves? Why?"

"Nothing that matters now." The camera poking out of her pocket gave her away.

"To take a picture?" I said.

Shirley looked at her feet, and brushed dust from her black slacks.

Matt and Amelia slowly approached us, shared their concern for Shirley's well-being, and were reassured as well. "You're thoughtful, really, but a minor tumble wouldn't begin to retard my momentum. I'm fine."

Amelia leaned in and whispered to Shirley, "Good thing you weren't wearing a skirt and hose, dear."

"Everyone ready to head back?" I asked.

We signed out and returned our hard hats. Matt and Amelia gave their thanks for the tour. Shirley raced off toward the near parking lot, while I circled around to the other side of the building to where I had left my car. As I approached the parking area, a Camaro screeched into the lot and bounced to a halt in a handicap parking spot. Edison jumped out.

"Ken, glad I caught you."

I looked at where he parked the car and frowned at him.

"I'll just be a minute." He held a manila envelope. "Wait until you see this. Look."

He pulled out a stack of 8x10s and I began to review them one by one. They were taken after dark, outside under the night sky. I recognized the subject as Edison's model girlfriend Jeanelle, with her enormous eyes, mile-long legs and black dress. What was she leaning against? A metal framework of some kind, wide flange beams, tube steel, metal angles slightly bent.

"You took pictures of your girlfriend the other night, against the murder scene?" I said.

"Isn't it cool?"

The pictures were printed in black and white. Taken from various viewpoints, the accent was on Jeanelle, the steel members a backdrop.

"I'm surprised the cops let you take pictures. They had a no-camera rule."

"I know. It was hard with them watching, but my little palm camera worked well. But look, here." Edison pointed to the bottom of the photo where I could make out the victim's legs beneath the wreckage. He slid out the next photo. "Here, I blew it up."

I saw black satin pants on thin legs, pinned beneath the triangular steel shapes. Shiny black shoes stuck out. The edges of the heels were not crisp. There were clumps of something sticking to the edges, with spiky strands poking up, backlit by the headlights of a passing motorist.

"Grass?"

Edison nodded his head. "And dirt, scraped onto the sides of his heels."

I looked at Edison. "Good work." My phone chirped. Kristy.

"Hey, where are you?" she said. "I can't wait to see you!"

"I'm at the Civic Center, but I still have a couple of—"

"Me too! Can I see you now? Oh, there you are!"

Her red Mustang pulled into the handicap space next to Edison's. She bounced out of the car, all legs and heels, tan and beautiful.

I shoved the photos back in the envelope, mumbled "Good work, Edison," and thrust them back into Edison's palms. "Here comes your introduction."

"Kristy!" I said opening my arms for a hug.

She stepped into them warmly, then, glancing at Edison, pushed back and said, "Oh, hi!" To me she said, "I'm sorry to interrupt, but I couldn't wait to see you, Ken."

"It's wonderful. This is my friend and associate

Edison Edwards. Kristen Blume."

Edison giggled. "It's a pleasure. Wow, I can't believe I'm meeting you right now."

Kristy tipped her head sideways and posed, as if waiting for Edison to take her picture. Her eyes flashed on me. "Ok, I gotta have a quick shot at those lips." She grabbed my face between her soft hands and planted her lips on mine. Briefly.

She backed up, gave a little wave, then said "Ciao for now!" She skedaddled to her car and pulled out.

Edison shook his head. "What was that?"

"What do you think?" I smiled. "Kristen Blume."

"That was *not* an introduction, she barely looked at me. And that kiss in front of me? What kind of standards is that? I thought she was cool. I'm sorry, but that's not how you treat people. I redecided. I hate her."

Chapter 18

Gone was the person I had left, sleeping fitfully, a few hours before. Nicole wore a skin-tight mandarin-red dress, patterned with white lightning bolts. The square neckline accented her collarbone, against which lay a cornicello suspended from a thin gold chain. Tall and lanky, the dress came to three fingers above her knees, and she moved like a panther, her body both firm and curvy. Lipstick matching the dress complemented her coffee-with-cream skin tone.

She met me at the door with a brief hug, and I caught a wisp of *Opium*. "Hello, Ken; thank you for coming by. I really appreciate everything you're doing for me right now."

"No problem, Nicole. You are the one with the burden." Was her hair different? It was swept back into a French twist.

She led me to the sofa. I sat in the wing chair. She offered coffee; I turned her down. Thoughts of the scene between Kristy and Edison niggled at me. I relayed to Nicole what had transpired during my poking around since her last update. I left a few choice things out.

She leaned back on the sofa. "Thank you for sharing the details with me. I feel so much better with you looking out for me, and putting the screws to Julianne."

"That's fine, Nicole. We have to get to the bottom of this. It must be hard right now, emotions and all. But I have a question. Yesterday, in my car, you told me Julianne said she wanted to kill your husband."

Nicole studied her hands for several moments. When her attention returned to me, her mouth was set in an ugly line and her eyes had turned to stone. "That bitch. Jerome told her it was over, and her reaction was violent. She told him he would be sorry, if she couldn't have him, no one would."

"You heard this?"

"Jerome and I had our problems, what married couple doesn't? Financial, of course. His sister always sticking her nose into our business—at times I think she's worse than a mother-in-law; my penchant for order perpetually disrupted. At least that's what he called it. Especially our dresser. That man drove me crazy with his pocket stuff. Every damn night. He would undress and put handfuls of crap from his pants on the bureau. Change, paper clips, scraps of paper he wrote numbers on. That's how I found out: a sticky note, mixed in with the change. The woman's hand writing caught my attention—you can always tell—and those seven words said it all. 'Call me at six. Hogs and quiches.' After I survived the initial shock, I let a long interval pass before I did anything. Took note of things—changes in his mannerisms, work hours, what he wore—and thought about our life together, about myself and what I wanted, before I broached him on it.

"Eventually he was forthcoming, slowly at first, but then he let me in to the whole of it. We stayed up three nights in a row, the first one spent throwing things at each other. Well, I did most of the chucking, but then I'd have to clean it up anyways. I thought I was prepared, but emotions have a mind of their own. After that conversation with her, he told me about it. 'No uncertain terms,' he said. I was scared to death she would come in here some night, and slash his neck with a butcher knife or something."

"That's a little melodramatic, don't you think?"

She threw me a glance. "What?"

"Julianne strikes me as someone a bit more rational."

"Do rational people do the mattress mambo with married men? Come on, Ken, you're supposed to be on my side."

"I'm just saying, if she said no one would have him, she must—"

"*If?* No, Ken, she said it. Jerome told me."

"Seems to me there's room for doubt here. You only have your husband's word, for what she said."

"Get out." She stood up and pointed at the door.

"What?"

"You heard me. Get out. I don't need you disputing me. I need someone on my side."

She tore across the room and marched down the bedroom hallway. A door slammed. Probably nerves. She was distraught. I could have been kinder. I drummed on the arms of the chair, deciding, pulled out my phone. No messages. I sighed, checked my email. A few things from work needed tending to. Information Wally needed for a client; a question from Edison. I hated those little keyboards. I checked my calendar for the next day, sighed, and decided I may as well call it a night. As I stood up to go, I heard a door crack open. Nicole appeared in the hallway, squinted my way, smoothed the silky front of her dress, walked over to the sofa and sat down.

"What do we do now?" she said so quietly I had to strain to hear.

"Red looks good on you," I said.

She turned a cold stare in my direction. Bit her lip. Burst out laughing. "Ken, you are a charmer. I'll give you that."

"I should have been more sensitive."

She tilted her head sideways. "Yes, you should have. But let's forget about it."

I had to change the subject to something unpleasant, an item which might upend those tender emotions, step on her fragile mind, the condition of which had been made worse by what just happened. I moved to the sofa and sat next to her. "Nicole, I'm sorry but I have to ask you about something. Your husband must have had a will."

She looked at me quizzically.

"Have you thought about it at all, I mean..?" I wondered if she knew how she fared. Who stood to gain financially from Neumann's murder? Who had that kind of motive? I couldn't say those words.

After a moment her nose flared and her eyes brightened. She nodded. "Yes, Ben Proctor wanted to get that done right away, reading the will. Do you know Ben?"

I shook my head.

"He's a friend of Jerome's family. He's the attorney who handled all his affairs. The legal establishment of Jerome's charities, the trust funds for the kids, his stocks. He wants to read the will Saturday, when everyone is here."

"Everyone?"

"Yes. Jerome's brother Neal lives here, in Warren, and has promised to help me with the arrangements, once the remains are released." Her lids closed and her bottom lip began to tremble.

I reached my hand over and patted hers.

"Jerome's older brother Vincent in Utah. I talked to him earlier today, and he's waiting to make travel provisions until we know for certain when the ceremony's going to be. Thank God, my mother is taking care of the kids, so I can handle all this."

In this moment, Nicole was the picture of strength, the charged emotion of a few minutes ago, dissipated.

"When do you think that will be?" she said.

"Oh, the body release. I can't say for certain. I've gotten to know one of the cops—"

"Officer Tallman, the one who was here Sunday?"

"Yes, right. I'll check with him. He'll know. I can't imagine it would be more than a few days."

"And I talked to Dani too, she's coming in on Wednesday."

"Is she still in New York? I haven't talked to her in, well, in quite some time."

I had fond memories of dinners with Dani and her family. Her parents owned a large home—a mansion—in the Palmer Park district in Detroit, on an amazing residential street, rich with architectural detailing, west of Woodward near Seven Mile Road. Dani was twenty at the time, an art student at Wayne State. Her younger sister, Nicole, was just sixteen and in high school.

Dani and I met, quite accidentally, in the heart of Detroit one sunny fall day. I had been surveying the nine block neighborhood north of Grand Circus Park for my thesis on reviving urban play spaces. My study site consisted of twenty-story high-rises, old theater buildings, and ramshackle storefronts. I counted stories, sketched elevations and took notes of details; stone, brick, rusted metal. After completing my notes about the theater faces on the southernmost block, I crossed the street to take a break in Grand Circus Park, the semi-circle center of the wagon wheel street layout that spoked into downtown. I noticed Dani, settled onto a bench, feet up, sketchbook in her lap, glancing back and forth at the 200 foot tall spire on Central United Methodist Church, which butts up to Grand Circus Park from the east side of Woodward. The church was built in 1866 and made a striking landmark at the corner of Adams.

As her slender fingers worked pencil on paper, the sun's rays ricocheted off Dani's cheekbones as if deflected by heat, and glanced from her burnt umber hair as if rushing from fire. Unaware that I had stopped to stare at her, I was startled when she said, "Majestic spires rise to meet the sky, yet our planted feet implore us not to fly." She smiled. "But we have to remember to, anyhow."

We shared the afternoon, talking about art and architecture. Later we walked to Greektown and dined on saganaki and grape leaves. And that was how it began. Our interracial relationship caused a ruckus with our friends, even in 1992 Detroit. For two years, we explored, tested, tasted each other. Eventually our relationship gave out. I don't remember why.

"She's still in New York, still married. I told her you were helping me out. Told her you were single."

"Oh, Nicole."

"Well, she still cares for you, you know. Of course she wouldn't let Chad know about it."

Chad was the med student she married.

I couldn't have asked for a better segue. "I remember you were a few years behind Dani and me. You ended up studying at Grand Valley, didn't you?"

"Oh, yes. I loved the downtown campus, more earthy than that spread out field of green with structures on it at the main campus."

I laughed. "Didn't you study film?"

"Cinema. A lot of classes watching movies, dissecting films, analyzing directors. *Casablanca. The Crucible. Five Easy Pieces.* Junior year I made a PSA about going green with laundry detergent. Highlight of my scholastic years."

"Did a little acting too, right?"

"I did some black box theater; I remember a vignette about babies in cribs with humongous toys. Oh, and I appeared in my friend Tanya's short skit on football half-time shows. Funny piece. Whatever happened to

her? Oh, I know. She married that football player—
Woody Nichols—the one she was trying to impress
with that play. Why?"

"Just curious. You snagged some work later, too,
right? A shaving commercial?"

"Oh god! Have you seen that thing? I hammed it up
pretty good. Never got much play in the States,
although I understand it was dubbed and broadcast in
Asia. Can you imagine?"

As I pondered her acting wiles, and thought about
whether any of this currently was acting, we were
interrupted by a knock at her front door.

The door opened and Shirley stuck her head in.
"Forgive me for barging in like this, Nicole. I wanted to
check on how you are doing."

"Come on in. Ken and I were just talking."

Shirley wore a silky ivory blouse and tight black
skirt. "Ken, you're back again."

"I was just going to say that to you." I stood up from
my seated position on the sofa. I became aware of a
sudden chill in the air. Goose bumps spread down my
arms like a wave of wind across a wheat field. My eyes
darted from Shirley to Nicole, whose bright veneer
warmed the space between us. The gap felt charged
with static electricity, but I sensed she was putting up a
chilly slap hand to Shirley, who, on the other hand, held
her entire being open to me, a refreshing warm embrace
to my neck, shoulders. I could sense the prickly current
she shoved toward Nicole.

Shirley smiled. "Nicole, how are you fixed for
dinner? We could order something."

Nicole looked to me. "I was going to ask Ken if he
had any plans."

"Actually..." I said.

Shirley said, "Ken, would you like to join us?" She
seemed to overlook the fact that Nicole was looking to

have dinner with me, not her. But the point was moot, since I had a hot date.

"Sorry, ladies. I have to be going. Nicole, I believe we've concluded our talk for now?"

She gave me a slow nod. "Thank you for coming by. Talk to you tomorrow?"

I moved toward her. "Yes, of course." We had an awkward moment, tipping back and forth. I ended it by taking a step backward. "You ladies take care." With a nod to Shirley, I said, "Thanks for coming by this morning."

Chapter 19

I arranged to meet Kristy at Chuck and Maria's house in Grosse Pointe. These clients had the unpronounceable last name of Kwiatkowski. A record producer at West Canfield Records, Chuck had engaged BPW Architects two years prior to execute the design of his home. His wife, Maria, enjoyed modest success painting still life and her whimsical pewter sculptures were a hit in local galleries.

Driving down Jefferson Avenue toward the heart of the city, I enjoyed the scenic vistas of the lake dividing Detroit from Windsor. I passed the yacht club, churches, and stretches of sand along the road. Suddenly a flock of pesky Canadian geese filled the sky. An older couple sat on a bench along the water, facing the lake view as a freighter crawled along the horizon. I smiled at a young couple, jogging and pushing a baby carriage on the asphalt path next to the road. A teenage girl walked a pair of frisky spaniels.

Five communities make up the area, from Grosse Pointe Park, closest to Detroit, to Grosse Pointe, Grosse Pointe Farms, Grosse Pointe Shores, and finally Grosse Pointe Woods. It is one of the most affluent areas in Metro Detroit, boasting a plethora of historic homes, and a host of prominent residents such as Anita Baker and William Clay Ford, Jr.

Red brick, slate-roofed educational facilities and ornate churches are integral to the landscape. The K's street lay just a few blocks east of Grosse Pointe's posh downtown area.

I drove up two blocks from Lake St. Clair to a short, tidy street comprised of several-million-dollar homes. Streets were arranged in straight blocks in a grid pattern, with telephone poles and electric wires overhead. I watched as a bald man carried packages in from his Lexus. A gangly red-headed girl in jeans and a hoodie rode a bicycle in the street. On the next block, teens played Frisbee with a sandy-colored retriever. A surprise to me were the political signs: school board, commissioner, vote yes!

I braked suddenly when a ball bounced across the road, followed by a shaggy-haired boy in a knees-long Pistons jersey. A moveable basketball pole with Plexiglas backboard showed that you can't take the fun of street play out of a kid, no matter how wealthy his parents might be.

Brightly colored leaves littered the lawns and filled the gutters on each side of the street. Halloween decorations were showing, pumpkins on porches and white sheets of ghosts hung from second floor balconies. I loved the oak trees, measuring up to a staggering five feet in diameter. Houses in brick, stone, stucco and half-timber construction prevailed. Occasionally, an out-of-place home constructed of shiplap siding stood in humble relief. The occasional French copper mansard roof offered a European flavor. Hedges towered above pedestrians, brick walls and an occasional wood fence obscured views into back yards. Front yards were well tended. It's such a simple thing, but I'm amazed at the variety of driveways: asphalt, brick pavers, an occasional concrete driveway. My favorite was constructed of bricks laid in asphalt in a tractor-tire pattern.

Three story homes were mixed in with two story homes with plenty of turrets, towers and stone balconies. Sculptures were not common but sculptural details such a decorative lamp post abounded. Front yards were expansive and sculptured, both in shrubbery as well as stonework.

Looking back from the middle of Chuck and Maria's street, I could catch a glimpse of Lake St. Clair—merely a patch of blue—as the grade dropped off in the direction of the water.

We designed the K's home in a traditional exterior, three stories tall with two stories of living space capped by a steep mansard rising another story-and-a-half. The clients were in Europe until Christmas, touring Belgium and Luxemburg. They had requested that I stay there when I could, in order to explore options for a renovation. We had surveyed books and magazines together, the couple pointing out photos of homes and details they admired, to give me a feeling for what moved and interested them. Remarkably, their tastes were very much in line with each other. Maria kept me up to date on her artwork. A varied and prolific artist, her work graced walls and recesses throughout the home.

I had ordered dinner from Marcelli's, a four star Italian restaurant in Grosse Pointe Shores. They did not do take-out, but three years earlier I had remodeled the chef's home, and when I called him, Voni promised to arrange a meal I could put together off-site. When I stopped there on my way to Chuck and Maria's, I was pleased to find chicken Marsala, corn salsa, truffles with chocolate sauce, and a bottle of California White Zinfandel. Voni had organized the dinner in remarkable china tureens that I promised to return.

I pulled up to the house ahead of Kristy, parked my Taurus on the brick pavers in the circle drive in front of the manse, a blemish on a perfect face. Windows throughout the home were steel, black, with smaller panes arranged to suit whatever room they graced.

Generally, they were in a horizontal orientation, giving the feeling of playful art. The arched doorway at the main front entrance was cut up into panes that mimicked the arch of the doorway. The steel mullions dividing panes of glass were small in cross section, offering a dainty appearance.

A carload waited for me to carry it inside: the dinner, which Voni's staff had arranged in sturdy cardboard boxes; my pocket of index cards; a large leather portfolio; and my overnight bag, which I always stashed fully packed in the car in case of a spontaneous business trip.

A flood of memories, of the material selections, the design meeting, and the construction, came to me as I unlocked the sturdy wood door and pushed in. I stood in the great foyer for a moment, indulging in the atmosphere. The space rose two stories, with a second floor bridge cutting through the air above. We had designed the interior of this home in zones, connected by four themes: art, both the owner's and purchased; white walls in a variety of shades and textures to create a backdrop, a stage, for the action to occur; nature, in the form of plant materials, large leaved live plants in the kitchen and breakfast nook, to silvery dead branches in the dining room; and crisp rectilinear lines and patterns. To the left of the main entrance foyer the kitchen lay toward the front of the house, with the hearth room beyond. Between the kitchen and the entry hall stood the dining room. Straight ahead of the entrance, the living room took a wide berth, with the grand staircase to the left. Immediately to the right of the foyer was a small library and beyond, along the right side of the residence, the game room and extra bedroom. I understood from Chuck that these spaces delighted the grandkids.

I returned to the car and began unloading. I hustled

my portfolio into the kitchen, with its textured white plaster walls that continued into breakfast nook. In-between, the walls were formed into planes and cubes which pulled out and pushed in various depths at heights varying from four feet to seven, which created visual interest. Kentia palm trees and ferns with sweeps of delicate fingers provided a leafy backdrop. Earth-tone countertops in travertine complemented the wood flooring, as well as the terra cotta floor tile on the stairs which led to the breakfast nook and beyond to the hearth room. Situated at the garage level, the kitchen offered an extraordinary high ceiling. Tall windows welcomed streaming sun to sail into the space. An open cube shelf over the recipe counter held pewter figurine sculptures made by the owner, Maria K.

I set up my index card review on the wooden table in the breakfast nook, a hexagonal pod, jutting out from the side of the house. It rose four steps up from the kitchen, while the ceiling was dropped at the same time. This brought the ceiling down to below eight feet. Continuous windows along the three projecting sides provided a beautiful view into a vined garden landscape and birdfeeder. Maria had crafted a floor cloth, painted with a serigraph mimicking the work of Leroy Neiman.

The formal dining room, just around the corner from the kitchen, welcomed my dinner as I set the table, keeping the lids on the tourines as Voni had instructed. He had also packed circular microwaveable hot packs. As directed, I nuked them for sixty seconds and then slid then under the chinaware.

The room evoked a formality by its crisp features, set off by the wood columns which staked its territory at the main entrance hall and the kitchen. Matching wood comprised the plank flooring, the wide trim around the windows, the china cabinet, and the fireplace mantle. Sculptural relationships were made through the use of German pyramids, incense smokers, and carved figurines. Traditionally intended for Christmas holiday, the K's displayed these year-round.

My watch said I had half an hour. I shuffled upstairs and inspected the bedroom Chuck had assigned to me. The last time I had stayed here, he called me a week after he left town to confirm that I was following his instructions. He had told me which room to take, and advised me with regard to his staff, which came in on Tuesdays and Fridays to freshen up the bedrooms, and keep the house in order generally.

The room was like a hotel room made up by your favorite aunt. Ivory sheets lapped over hunter green comforter, roll top desk and padded rolling wing chair, silver antique framed mirror over the desk, two oil paintings, both nautical: one a close-up of a sail and boom with heavy stitching; the other a close-up of the bow with waves chopping and spray coming over the deck.

I stripped, took a shower, and changed into a fresh set of clothes: grey suit and a blue pinstripe shirt. I went back down to the breakfast nook and studied my index cards.

There were too many things that didn't make sense. Were Nicole's instincts correct? Did Julianne mean it when she said she would kill Neumann if he wouldn't have her? She was one of the last people to see him, having met him before the program. And she walked out at intermission with a headache.

What about Matt's old grudge; was it enough to cause him to take action? Did some new occurrence trigger the old feelings?

And then there was Nicole. I longed to trust her, but what if on the night in question Neumann had changed his mind? What if he decided to leave his wife to be with Julianne?

What about the people who were against the project? Mothers for Historic Preservation, Talbot X, and fans of architect Arne T. Fehn? The site experienced vandalism and destruction before and during the auditorium's construction. Did board member Molly Gross, who had vocally objected, play a part in this?

What questions did I need to ask, and of whom?

Maybe instead of poking around in all directions I needed a trick to get the murderer to show himself, to make a move. But how?

Suddenly, I realized there were a few things I needed to follow up with Bryce. I made the call and arranged to meet him for breakfast the next morning.

I sighed. It had been a long time since I had had a real date. It would be nice to have a relaxing night with Kristy; forget everything else—work stress, projects, and yes even the case. Oh crap—*and* the presentation to Val's Market.

There was a knock. I could hardly wait to see Kristy's reaction to this place. I opened the heavy wooden door. Kristy was a vision: startling blue eyes, bejeweled neckline, "v" cut black dress with a black matador jacket. She held out a bouquet of lavender and white orchids. "Here, Ken, these are for you."

"Beautiful. And so are the flowers. No one ever gave me blossoms," I said.

I led her into the dining room.

"How lovely," she said.

The small hallway between the kitchen and the dining room was fixed with a china cabinet. There I found a crystal vase for the flowers. Kristy helped me arrange them in the vessel, as we looked at each other over the rim, through the pods of blooms. The work clothes I'd donned hardly seemed appropriate, given her lovely evening frock.

"Hungry?" I said.

"Famished. It smells marvelous in here." I saw her move her eyes from the dining table, to the crystal chandelier, to the windows with the crisp oak trim and the ornamental divided windows. "But I want a tour of the house first."

We started back at the formal entry hall. A half-size equestrian statue stood as a regal sentry in the two story portion, immediately upon entering. The geometric squares of wrought iron that formed the bridge railing above us matched the motif of the steel windows. At the end of the hall, beneath the second floor balcony, a large painting of a dramatic sunset at Stoney Creek Lake provided a focal point on the wall above a console table. Two black metal sconces flanked the artwork. Kristen marveled and I beamed at her excitement.

We entered the living room, grounded in terra cotta floor tile with chocolate grout, inset book cases in white shelving with metal halide downlights framing a cut-out fireplace opening—no mantle. An oil landscape of Central Park lit up the space above the fireplace. Blockish leather couches in copper penny with suede pillows and white leather slab chairs sat on a rust-and-black oriental rug. Tall windows cut into the two story space, framed in steel with rectangular panes in horizontal orientation. The three pairs of French doors were fit with steel framed window lites to match, and opened onto a Loggia—stone columns framing the view onto the built-in pool.

We turned into the game room to the right, with its glass block walls to the exterior Loggia, letting the light in, and out, but creating a self-contained environment. I put my arm around Kristen's waist, pulling her ever so slightly closer, our hips touching. She pointed out the stainless steel trim on the out-looking windows.

She placed her arm around me as well, and we walked to the library study, which stood on the other side of the grand foyer from the dining room. In unison, we looked up at its two-story space lined with books along two sides, a spiral stair accessing a catwalk to the upper level of books. The catwalk opened onto the second floor hallway, overlooking the living room.

"Marvelous," she said.

We returned to dining room. Her eyes were bright, lips slightly parted. As I leaned in for a kiss, she dropped her hands and moved slowly away. She said, "Let's eat. Then you can show me the second floor."

She walked to the table. "It looks great."

"Wait." I pulled a packet of matches from my suit pocket and lit the two long white candlesticks and dimmed down the lights. I served. I opened the lid, and aroma from the chicken dish filled the room.

Kristy appeared amused as I attempted a waiter's flourish, dishing the dinner onto our blue and white china plates.

"Marcie, my best friend on the set, told me we are going to extend our stay in Port Huron. Milo—the director—has ordered a couple of extra scenes to be written between my character, Aly, and townsfolk. How she gets the low-down on this stuff before it comes down the chain I don't know."

"And who is Marcie?"

"Oh, didn't I tell you about her? She does hair, and she's the best! Mine and Amanda's; Amanda plays my sister. I swear whenever we're in trouble, she kicks it for us. Love her to pieces."

"Sounds like you have fun working."

"Oh, we do. Like today, Ron—that's Ron Johnston, he plays Amanda's boyfriend, took it upon himself to play this little trick on Amanda. It's her birthday, and she knows he's a trickster, so last night he put a creature in her dressing room toilet."

I raised my eyebrows.

"It's this green monster head with great big teeth. It barely fits through the hole in the seat. He has these two green arms he's holding over his head, with suction cups that stick to the bottom of the seat cover. When you lift the lid, the monster is like coming out of the toilet."

"I bet that went over well."

"Right, so this morning we're getting ready and all of a sudden we hear this huge scream."

I shake my head. "He got her good."

"Yeah, I think she's still mad."

"Hilarious."

"I know, right? But she'll get him back. Look out for that one!" She cut up her chicken in little bites, nibbling each one with petite teeth. "How was your day? Making headway—Oh, how was your talk with Matt Lance? Did you find out about the grudge?"

I gave her the five minute run down on our conversation.

"Well, I can see how he would have this grudge, deep animosity back then. But it was years ago, right? Doesn't hold water for me. What else? Did Scofield tell you anything important? Oh, and why did Bryce break into Nicole's?"

I caught her up on those events, too. "I feel like I'm chasing my tail. I guess this is how detective work goes, one piece of the puzzle at a time, but I wish I could have a big splash all at once. Force the killer's hand."

"Like in the movies, plant a story and make the bad guys jump and do something stupid."

"Well, now you're just making fun of me."

"It could work. Maybe you could talk to the papers."

"No, did I tell you about Sue Watts? I've been ordered to stay away from the press." She settled into silence. I got a flash. "But you don't."

"I smell something cooking! Sizzling in your eyes."

She tapped my arm. "Give it up, Cannoli."

"My sister, Ella, has a local radio talk program on Entertainment and Politics."

Kristy's eyes flashed. "Ella Polaris is your sister?"

"You know the program?"

"Hell yes, I know the program. Ella is a little firecracker. She's so sweet and accommodating at times and then other interviews she tears into someone and shreds him a new one."

"That's my sister."

"So, I go on the show, under the pretense of talking about my movie. And during the talk I mention something about the murder investigation. A little nugget that will jolt the murderer into making a stupid move."

I nodded. "Yes, yes, it could work. And Sue Watts doesn't have to know it came from me."

Kristy said, "I have to clear the appearance with my agent, but should be ok."

She set down her fork. "Yum, that was delicious. You sure know how to make a girl feel special." I smiled. "Just tell me one thing, Ken Knoll. What happened with Bryce? Did he actually take something from Neumann's office? Or did Nicole make it up?"

"I don't know. He wouldn't admit to a thing, but more is going on that he's acknowledged. I talked to him a few minutes ago and set up a meeting for breakfast tomorrow." I paused. "No wonder I look like this," I said, pointing at my stomach, "with all these work breakfasts and things."

Kristy looked sideways at her truffles, as if deciding whether or not to indulge. "Come on," she said. "You look fine. Are you going somewhere fattening?"

"Just a coney. Kerby's by the auditorium."

"All the way on the other side of town." Her eyes fell upon me. "You're going to have to get up early again."

I took Kristy's hand and led her into the kitchen nook. "Come, let me show you what I have in mind for this place."

We climbed the grand staircase, between the living room and the kitchen. The second floor was barbell-shaped in plan, with two bedrooms at one end—the one over the kitchen/hearth room to which I had been assigned, another over the dining room—and the master bedroom suite filling out the other end. In the middle "handle" portion of the barbell, a wide hallway overlooked the two story living room in the back, and the entry foyer with its equestrian statue in the front. Tucked into the corner between the foyer and the master bedroom space was the upper portion of the library.

"Come, let me show you the attic." I opened a door to a stairway. We climbed up and found a cavernous space overtaken with darkness, open trusses, and raw subfloor. With two rows of fluorescent lights and no exterior windows, the space had an eerie, artificial feeling. As we studied our surroundings, we could "read" the roof shape, tall perimeter walls, pitched in at a sixty degree angle, rising up to a shallow peak.

"It's like a tall cave," Kristen said.

I nodded. "Plenty of opportunity to create something." I led her to the middle of the floor. Toward the front of the house over a small width of space, the roof projected ten feet out. "We're standing over the foyer, and this projection is the covered entry. My thought is to make this a loft room, open up a window here, over the entry below, to bring in natural light." I walked toward the center of the space, under the main ridge. I pointed to the floor. "Open up a stair here going down to the hallway bridge below our feet, between the two bedroom wings."

"Even with the window, won't this be kind of a dingy space?"

I smiled. "Wait there's more." I tilted my head, looked up toward the roof, pointed. "Open up a large opening in the roof here, eighteen feet square, and build a skylook."

Her eyebrows were now raised. "I'll show you the sketches." We returned to the kitchen breakfast nook, and I pulled the portfolio from behind a small china cabinet, and placed it on the table. Unzipped, we discovered a pile of sketches. Perspective vignettes of the loft room, a spiral stair to the skylook: an octagonal sitting space, benches all around, with arched windows 360 degrees around the perimeter. Exterior views of the addition from the street and yard.

"Ken, I love this idea! The intimate loft is a great workspace, raw character, lots of sunlight. And that cupola will make a great party space. Can you imagine have a few couples over, and retiring up there, under the stars? What great conversations would break out." She smiled.

I said, "Do you think the copula will work from the street elevation? I'm concerned it may overpower the facade"

"Don't worry, it's sublimely perfect."

We moved into the hearth room and made ourselves comfortable. We leaned back on the green leather sofa. I placed my hand across Kristy's, and she responded by flipping her hand over and interlacing our fingers. I wrapped my arm around her shoulder and pulled her closer. She turned her head, her cheek soft against mine. Soft, supple lips. I leaned in and we kissed, firm but not too firm. I leaned her back on the sofa and we kissed for a while, my hands exploring her silky back and narrow waist.

"Oh Ken, I can't believe you seduced me with your

sketches."

We retired to the upstairs bedroom. The ceiling boasted a skylight big as a pool table. We doused the lights, stripped down to our underwear and slid under the sheets. The stars nearly rained down on us, and a jovial moon, not quite full, laughed.

"So, Mr. Architect Sleuth, who did it?" She snuggled closer to me, her thigh smooth against my leg. Her crystal blue eyes twinkled in the starlight.

"Not yet. I'll see Bryce in the morning. Then, finally, an audience with Molly. Earlier today I was told she wasn't feeling well. But I tried again this afternoon and was able to secure an appointment for tomorrow morning. I'll sneak into the office before the presentation."

She caressed little circles in the small of my back. "My, you have a whole road rally of running before you even get to work."

"Uh-huh."

She looked down at my chest. I evaluated her dusty rose lids and long dark lashes. I *love* girls.

"Ken," she said softly. "I have to leave early."

"Oh, good. So we can get up together and help each other get dressed."

Her eyes returned to mine. "No, I have to leave at three for an early call."

"Umm," I said kissing the soft spot where her neck met her shoulder. "Then we'd better—" I slid my hand along her bra band to unfasten the clasp. She leaned into my ear. "Ken, wait. Not tonight. It's late, I have to get some sleep."

"It will help you sleep."

She grinned at that. "Yes, I want to, but...please...I like you, I've just got this pressure, making the film, I want to be my best."

"Oh, I'm sure you'll be wonderful." I said, halfheartedly. I sighed. I struggled with the abrupt halt to my passion, and wrestled with the frustration for several minutes. Yet, I was determined not to let the evening be spoiled. I held on to her words and smiled. *Kristy Blume likes me.*

Three a.m. came early. I roused to the sound of Tiki bar music. Kristy turned to the side of the bed and the high pitched, tinny strings—her alarm—ended abruptly. It was dark. I felt the cool rush of air as she receded, then snuggled deeper into the covers to assuage the loss. Dimly, I was aware of the shower running and woke a few minutes later when she kissed me goodbye, a deep *wow* kiss full of meaning and unsaid words. And she was gone.

In the moment I fell back into the mattress, I became wide awake. Like the sudden clearing on a steamed-up mirror, my thoughts turned to the women in my recent love life.

The slide show began with Gwen, hot redhead principal of the firm. Gwen, the little spitfire who was so tender and affectionate to me, whose Achilles heel was trusting others too much, or not trusting herself enough. Or both. It was a cruel reality that brought her to her knees. I felt for her, and her hasty departure. Sadness erupted into compassion, leeching out from me to comfort her, wherever she now laid her head. A twinge of sorrow made me catch my breath. We would have made a sturdy couple, complicated by our work relationship, sure, but with so much in common, I felt a real rapport that would sustain us for the long haul.

Mary came next in my picture show, the relationship that almost was. Our Christmas brawl—over my leaving the holiday meal with her family, to help out a childhood friend—was the straw that led to our break up. Of course, her devious spirit wouldn't have served us long term. Not at all.

I thought of Shirley, hot-blooded beast from my past who in a matter of hours incited me with passion that raged from my pores until—Crap.

Come on, Cannoli, shake off those Shirley thoughts now.

Chapter 20

I padded to the bathroom and ran cold water over my face. Damn, these old memories. I needed to forget those women and focus on the one who just left my bed. This girl was seriously serious. I mean, a Hollywood woman who protects herself, that's unexpected, a cause to relish. I felt a welcoming nudge from a future time line, one in which, for once, I got the girl. The right girl.

Still in bare feet and boxers, I hustled down the carpeted stairs and cut through the short hallway into the grand kitchen. If I could find the coffee, and work the fancy coffee maker, I'd have a cup of joe. Corn flakes, sugar, coffee. Ha! Starbucks, the good stuff.

Once I had the coffee going, I cranked up the laptop. What was Shirley up to today?

No Signs for a Family Tree.

Southfield, Michigan. As the police investigate the death of Jerome Neumann, the prominent business man whose $3 million donation made the new library auditorium a reality, and who was killed last Saturday when the sign bearing his name plummeted from the building, an odd morsel finds its way to this reporter's ear.

First, a history refresher. Forty years before Neumann, there was another donor to the Southfield Public Library. Ralph 'Jazz' Fitzgerald, well-known to the community, commissioned the last significant project in the library's history, a project which fell to serious criticism, in fact notoriety, at its completion in 1966. Said, by Detroit Free Press *art critic Noel Graham, to be 'a bombastic framework' with 'puke-colored tile,' the Fitzgerald Reading Room proved to be a boon to the library: an ultra-modern asset to the public at large.*

Now the quiz question: which member of the city's Planning Board, which had governing authority in making decisions for the contemporary project, is the granddaughter of the library's previous donor?

Answer: Molly Gross, nee Fitzgerald.

One questions the motivation of Fitzgerald's granddaughter, who joined the Board only a few months before this project was slated, and expressed vocal opposition during the review period. Were there ulterior motives in obstinately challenging the project? Particularly considering the Fitzgerald Reading Room, her grandfather's pet project, was destroyed in the making?

Why didn't she recuse herself?

This reporter has seen a sign of a family tree.

Huh, Molly Gross?

I poured myself a cup of coffee, spread out the index cards and added an entry for this latest development. Was it true? Shirley was usually right; I'd give her that. I made a note to discuss it with Molly at our meeting that afternoon.

Meanwhile, my thoughts turned to the meeting with Bryce and my number one goal: getting to the bottom of the sleep trophy issue. Did he take it or not? Bryce's memorabilia collection featured an assortment of public figures. From Nicole's description, this piece would appeal to Bryce's taste. How could he resist a trinket symbolizing Jerome Neumann's tryst? Plus, its value probably skyrocketed the moment Neumann died.

Or, was Bryce simply trying to remove it before Nicole discovered it? To protect Neumann, somehow?

I drove to Bryce's office. The clock had yet to strike six, traffic was on my side, and I arrived ten minutes early.

When we were settled into his private office, Bryce said, "I know you're going to ask me about that night at Nicole's again. Your time is as valuable as mine, so rather than waste it on trivial matters, let's move on—"

"Breaking and entering isn't so trivial." From my position in his guest chair, I took a pencil from the leather cup next to his blotter and began drumming it on his desk

"Yeah, well, I told you I was looking for some documents Neumann had, and—"

I shifted forward and gave him my best Sam Spade. "Drop it, Bryce. I know you took it. Nicole discovered it earlier in the day and—"

He sank back in his swivel chair.

"Yeah, she found it. Then later, she couldn't find it. Right after your little escapade."

He put his hand to his chin. "I was hoping to avoid that." His eyes rolled. "What did she say?"

I shrugged. "What do you think? Finding some artifact of her husband's affair."

"She thought it was Neumann's?"

"Well, yeah. The poor girl was beside herself, having discovered her husband's tryst. The police at the house. What do you know about it?"

Bryce opened his desk drawer, picked up a framed object and handed it to me. A shadow box, an inch or so deep. The moment I laid eyes on it, I understood its significance. Bailey Justine was a local icon, the Channel 4 news anchor who had achieved celebrity status through appearances at media events and charity fund-raisers like the DIA black tie gala and

Cranbrook's Serious Moonlight. Always stylish. Sexy and seductive, but with an air of charm and dignity; think Grace Kelly, Ingrid Bergman.

Justine always wore the same bracelet: a wide black leather band sporting two rows of matching pearls. She'd wear it with a pearl necklace or a leather choker. The bracelet became synonymous with Bailey Justine. Now her bangle was in front of me, beneath it affixed an open note card, graced with a crimson kiss print and a handwritten note: *Sweetums, love the rose boffing! Bailey.*

Bryce interrupted my thoughts. "It wasn't Neumann's. It was mine. I lost it to Matt Lance in a poker game."

I settled back in my chair. "Steep prize."

"Yeah. I figured I'd win it back the next time that we played. Never thought Matt would give it away, to Neumann no less. Matt told me 'I owed him money. I was going to get it back. He wouldn't take 'no' for an answer. Then, after what happened to Neumann on Saturday..." He paused. "I knew where Neumann would have kept it. Plus, I really didn't want Nicole to discover it, especially now. What she must have thought."

The man before me was contrite.

"What about the 'I'm gonna kill you' comment I heard you make, to Matt, at the poetry event?"

"Yes, I shouted at him, because he gave my memento away. I told him I had to get it back."

The corners of his mouth were tense. Bryce's head snapped in the direction of the door. "Excuse me, I'll be right back."

Bryce walked out, then I heard animated talking in the front office. I peeked through the crack at the door. Was that Shirley?

Hastily, I returned the sleep trophy to the drawer. I

strode across the room, tugged the door open and walked through the kitchenette into the office. Shirley stood in the receptionist area, pale pink blouse under a black blazer. Black skirt with dark hose, one knee bent to good effect as she rested the toe of her platform heels on the vinyl tile and her eyes on Bryce.

"Ken Knoll, happy Tuesday! I didn't interrupt, did I?"

"Shirley—" I exhaled.

Shirley tilted her head. I glared. Bryce looked from one of us to the other and said, "Look, is there something...?"

"I think we're done here, Bryce," I said. "Thank you for the information. I'll be in touch."

Shirley grinned at me. ""Bye Ken."

I stormed out. What's with that girl? And what was she doing with Bryce McClurg? I stomped across the parking lot to my car, climbed in and sat, staring at the weeds along the road. I pulled out my cell and punched the speed dial for my sister Ella. She was an early riser, and I knew I could catch her. "How'd you like to have Kristen Blume on your show today?"

"Ken, I was just noodling how to fill my last three segments. I had an author drop over the weekend and the producers aren't able to fill the slot. How do you know Kristen Blume?"

"I have my connections. She's on location this morning, but afternoon rush hour should be perfect."

"Have her people call Tad."

"Great, thanks." I left a message for Kristy.

Bryce's sleep trophy, should I believe him? Did he give it to Matt, who passed it to Neumann? Roundabout, but plausible. I would check with Matt. It looked like Bryce was a dead end.

No pun intended.

Chapter 21

I had one more call to make before I pulled out of the lot. Most everyone would be at work by seven, even the boss. I dialed. "Robert, it's Ken. I've been thinking about this afternoon's meeting with Val's Market. How about if Wally take the lead? He's up on Walter Gruen's shopping centers as much as anyone, and he talks a mean game."

"No, Ken, he doesn't know Dizzy's," Robert said. I could hear the clicking of his mouse in the background. "More to the point, we have our team identified in the proposal, you know that. You are familiar to all the players on this project. They're expecting you."

"Wally knows them too. A couple of months ago he took Wilson Swentworth to a Tigers game and the two of them hit it off." Swentworth was the real estate representative for Val's and an important go-between for the market and the shopping center owners.

"Hmm, maybe we should include Wally. Good suggestion. We can always use an additional team player. But you've got to lead the show."

"Listen, I have a pile of work to get through here and—"

"No buts, Cannoli. I've scheduled a dry run for later, I think eleven, Rita can confirm that for you."

And he hung up.

The phone chirped in my hand, and I thought it was Robert calling back, but it was Officer Tallman. As I answered, a pick-up truck sporting the *Prime Roofing* logo pulled into the lot.

"Cannoli, I have some news for you."

"Hey, Jim, how's it going?"

"Everything's copasetic. Sunday, Monday, Tuesday progress is being made. 'Course this turns out to be murder it will have doubled our statistics for the year. Hey listen, you might be interested in this little tidbit from the lab. But first you gotta share something with me."

Horse trading; what did I have to offer? "There was grass and dirt wedged into Neumann's heels."

"Tell me something I don't know."

I watched as another vehicle entered the lot. Employees were arriving for the day.

"How about this. Did you know Molly Gross is Jazz Fitzgerald's granddaughter?"

"Cannoli, I can read. That Shirley's on top of things, isn't she? Call me when you can do better." He disconnected.

I banged my fist against the dashboard, then dialed back. "Jim, don't be so hasty."

A grunt.

"Here's something, but it must remain off the record. The other night, when Bryce McClurg broke into the Neumann home, he *did* walk out of there with something. But it's not related to the case."

"Why don't you let us decide that? What was it?"

"Can't tell you, Jim. But it has no bearing, honest."

"Pish. You heard of obstructing justice?"

My stomach tightened. "I know you guys are shorthanded. It's not pertinent, no need to waste time on it."

"All right, I'm gonna let that go for now. What else you got? This is a real juicy morsel here."

I scoffed. "That's it right now."

"Cannoli, you owe me another piece, a little one." He paused. "Ok, here goes; there was dog hair on

Neumann."

"What kind of dog?" If I remembered right, Neumann once wanted a schnauzer but they never got a dog because Nicole has allergies. The Neumann's didn't own any pets.

"Golden retriever."

"Huh. Anybody on your suspect list have a dog?"

"We're checking that right now."

Code words meaning: I'm not telling you. At least he gave me the tip. "Thanks, Jim."

"Yeah, remember you owe me."

I looked back to the building. Shirley was still in there. What was she doing? It was awfully early for a visit. I started the car and pulled out of the lot.

* * *

Back at the office, I dumped my briefcase, punched on my CPU and headed back to see Edison.

"Hey, buddy, how goes the battle?"

He looked up from his work and scowled. "Fine, fine."

"It doesn't sound fine."

He raised his head. "The boards are over there." He pointed to a reference table under the window. I flipped through the illustrations. Leave it to Edison. A perfectly coordinated, smashing presentation.

"This looks good. Why the gloomy face?"

"Oh, it's this damn MicroStation. I hate this program." He shook his head like a dog caught in the rain. "What's up? Anything new?"

"I talked to Nicole last night. The will won't be read until Saturday and I need to know who will benefit."

"Who's the attorney?"

I shuffled through my index cards. "Ben Proctor."

"Oh. I know Sylvia, one of his paralegals. We used to party downtown. You know, she's a hellova rapper. Last month at the slam she kicked the shit out of Wes

Kite. I'll give her a holler. She's good people."

"Cool."

Edison turned back to his computer and scowled. "Grrrrr."

"When you're done barking at your computer, let's talk about Molly Gross."

Edison looked up, "Yep."

"I found out this morning—in Shirley's column no less—that Molly Gross is Jazz Fitzgerald's grand-daughter. How did we miss this?"

"As in Fitzgerald Reading Room?"

"Yes, the very same."

"Whoa. That means..."

"Yeah. We need to find out if this is true."

"Can't you just ask her next time you see her?"

"That, I will. We'll see what she has to say for herself. Maybe the old Ken charm could work his magic."

"Huh?"

"You know, Kristy just showed up in my life out of nowhere. Maybe my luck changed with the full moon; no more back seat to Edison Edwards."

Edison said, "You're nuts and I'm skeptical. Kristy? So now you're getting familiar?" He paused while I considered him. "Kristen, or whatever, is trouble with a capital 'T'. No offense."

What is his deal? Edison has the babes, why couldn't I? Was he jealous?

My phone chirped. Steve.

"Qué pasa, Ken? What's the good word?"

"Hey, Steve. Preparing for a presentation this afternoon." I leaned over to Edison and said, "Oh that reminds me—Edison, Robert set up a meeting room to go over all this. Can you find out where we're supposed to be?—Sorry Steve. What's up?"

"I just wanted to pass this on. I got a call from the

MEC lab. The sign frame was released from the police lab today. MEC's truck is on the way over there to pick it up."

"Great; thanks, Steve."

Wally came into the back room. "Why does it always look like a disaster back here?"

"Hey Wally," I said, scanning the piles of foam core and illustration board, the countertop littered with cans of paint and fixative, the cutting board on the big table with shavings from where renderings had been mounted and trimmed. Maybe he was referring to the samples—rainscreen system cut in half, miniature skylight, cast stone slabs. I shrugged. It looked ok to me. "If you're looking for Edison, he just went to check on something for me."

"Cannoli, I was looking for your ugly mug. You asked me about Bryce earlier."

"Yeah, yeah. What did you find out?" I sat down on a stool next to the cutting board.

Wally remained standing. "Well, there's never a shortage of interesting things to find out. I had to talk to a handful of people for this little nugget, but—I don't know why I didn't think of this to begin with—this morning I casually checked with my buddy Max Klein over at Provost Tanner. You know, they're the construction manager for the south addition to Universal Mall. That project has hit more snags than panty hose on a porcupine. Me and Max go way back, you know that right?"

I shook my head.

"Yeah, we ran track at Troy Athens High. Max was always a long man, liked 1600 meters. Me, I was quick and short. One hundred, two hundred, you know. Well, back in '88, Coach Tanner put us together on a relay team for the 4x400. I thought he was crazy, not doing either of us any good, but he had confidence. Max ran the third leg and I anchored. We took it all the way to the state finals. But, in the end Pioneer bumped us off.

"Anyways, Max tells me he had a run-in with Bryce McClurg back in 2000. He was the General Contractor on a substantial addition to a third party auto supplier by the name of JIN Engineered Products out in Clinton Township. The owner had a facility doing pretty well in a metal building—not much improved from a pole barn if you ask me, but there are a lot of them out there—made plastic parts for the cars that once-upon-a-time used to be metal. Saved the Big Three a ton of money in pieces, and made a goodly sum on orders. Eventually, they needed to expand, blah blah blah. So the architect designs an addition to the eave end of the building, sets the new roof just a few inches below the existing—"

I knew what was coming.

"And of course the thing leaked like a sieve."

"And Bryce McClurg was the sub-contractor."

Wally nodded his chicken-faced head. "Right. He was sub to Provost Tanner. Neumann had a fit. Don't blame him none, water dripping into his research lab."

"That's what it was?"

Wally nodded. "With the expansion. Eighteen thousand square feet of lab where those guys took things apart, measured, tested, what have you. Built like a clean room."

"So the moisture was more than an inconvenience."

Wally drew a finger at me. "Bingo. It lost him time, it lost him dollars."

"And he blamed the roofer? With a design like that..."

"Yeah, from what I understand, Bryce had warned them when he submitted his bid. No one listened. Even after, he was a gentleman about it, patched the leaks ump-teen times. Hired MTE out of his own pocket to find where things were going wrong. In the final analysis, the only answer was that the addition was designed wrong."

"Well, of course, you know in snow country you have to have eight inches minimum at the roof offset. And with all that water sheeting off the building, I'd leave better than a foot."

Wally nodded. "McClurg tried to steer the discussion in that direction. Neumann wouldn't have it, and the architect—Wesley Kiles out of Dearborn—their lawyer claimed that the contractor didn't build to the intent of the plans and therefore assumed the risk of failure."

"Uh-huh, that's not going to play."

"Right, bullshit, the architect screwed up. Shame it was one of our boys, but the truth is the truth."

"So what happened?"

"Neumann had the building torn up, built a parapet along that stretch, re-sloped a gable into the metal roof."

"Wow, must have had it torn up for a while."

"Max told me they had it down and back up in nine days. They had crews run long hours. Of course, it cost. And Neumann back-charged McClurg."

"This was 2000 you say?"

"Yeah. Fast forward to last spring. Municipal auditorium project. The project is awarded to Perry Construction and they sub out the roofing work to Prime Roofing."

"Whoa. Bryce McClurg. He didn't know Neumann was involved?"

"Didn't know or didn't care. Neumann put up the money, but it's a city project. Who would question the funding? Anyways, Bryce gets the job, signs contracts, orders materials. Somehow Neumann finds out and tries to have Bryce McClurg removed from the project."

"Removed? How could he do that?"

"Believe me, three million bucks carries a loud voice. From what I hear, the city thought about it. But all the contracts had been signed and there was no logistical way to have him detached."

"Hmm. I never knew about this. Why didn't I hear about it?"

Wally studied at me with eyes cold as marble. "You don't have to know everything Cannoli. You only think you do. That's why you asked *me*, isn't it?"

Chapter 22

My intention was to find out about Molly's relationship to Fitzgerald, get a bead on her insincerity in the "extreme honesty" theory, and to check Rusty's whereabouts when the sign fell.

Molly's condo stood at the northwest end of Southfield. Manicured lawns, heavy on perennials and climbing vines. The flagstone walk leading to her door was trimmed in roses and Shasta daisies.

My phone rang. Edison informed me the dry run for Val's Market had been changed to a lunch meeting. Good news: I didn't have to rush the interview.

I buzzed and the door opened a moment later. A slender woman with a pale oval face and stringy long, straight black hair blinked at me.

"Good morning, Molly."

With a flourish of her bare arm, she gestured inside. The sleeves were cut off her tie-dyed T-shirt and hung down to her butt. I took two steps into the foyer, laid in Pewabic tile, trimmed in walnut. A familiar voice cackled in the next room.

Shirley stepped out of the shadows. "Hi, Ken. These are the coolest people."

I tried to hide my surprise, "Oh, hi, Shirley." I stuffed my hands in my pockets.

Molly spoke, "You two know each other?"

Shirley said, "We go way back, but we recently became reacquainted."

"Well, show the man in, Molly," said the gruff looking, older man on the couch. I followed Molly in.

He got up and offered me a meaty hand. Barrel-chested and ruddy-complexioned, he stood only as tall as my nose. "Rusty Wagner."

I introduced myself.

"Molly told me you'd be coming. Let's get to it," he said.

Molly stood still, her eyes and lips twitching, reminding me of a stringy haired mouse. "So many interruptions. I must get back to planning our reciting season. Perhaps the two of you will understand that time doesn't stand still."

Shirley spoke first, "Well, you've given me enough. I really do appreciate the time."

I leaned over in Shirley's direction, "What enough? What did she give you?"

Shirley shushed me and I said, "Molly—I have a few questions, if you don't mind."

She shrugged. No one invited me to sit down, so I remained standing. Shirley, despite her announcement, made no move toward the door.

"I'm investigating the events of two nights ago, when you were on the stage reading your poetry and—"

"I wasn't reading."

"I'm sorry, I understood that you were on stage at the time."

"Yes, but I wasn't reading. I was reciting."

"Right. Can you tell me what happened?"

"I already told her," she pumped her head in Shirley's direction. She exhaled. "And I went through this with the police yesterday. Why ask me? What's the value to it?"

"I have to run," Shirley said. "Nice to have met you both."

"You don't have to say that," Molly said.

Thankfully, Shirley left the room. I felt myself relax when the door closed behind her.

"Molly, please. Just a few questions. What did you think when the sign fell?" I said.

"Think? I don't understand."

"You heard the noises, you stopped reciting. What was going through your mind?"

"It sounded like the building fell apart. It would have been ok with me if it had."

"Oh?"

"You know I was opposed to the project from the beginning."

"Yes, I'm aware of your disposition. But why?"

"Reasons? The Fitzgerald Reading Room was of pure design, an iconic symbol of bravery and justice. For it to be replaced with a parody of modern architecture is an insult to—"

"Molly!" Rusty shouted. "Remember who you are addressing. And would you two please sit, let's be civilized here."

I put my hands out in a *hold on* motion. "It's ok, Rusty, I'm not taking offense. But a seat would be nice, if you don't mind, Molly. This won't take long."

She sighed, walked to the couch with Rusty, and sat on the edge at the opposite end. I took a wing chair opposite them.

Molly looked at the carpet as she spoke. "The Fitzgerald Reading Room should have been kept intact, with technology improvements, sure. That would have suited me fine."

"Is that true, Molly? Let me ask you a question. With your philosophy on extreme honesty, does it make it impossible for you to lie? Do you ever do anything wrong, or are you always right?"

"Life is a continuum of experiences. It's not so much about right and wrong but finding the higher quality of moments within ourselves. What we need to hold, is the truth within us. Only then can we share honestly with others."

I couldn't let that one get away, "So are you willing to break the law, if the higher quality of moments requires it?"

Rusty spoke, "Now, now, don't get all word smithy on us."

I had researched Rusty the day before and I had been looking forward to meeting him. His history read like that of a mythical warrior. He enlisted in the Army, became a member of the elite Underwater Demolitions Team, and completed two tours of duty in Vietnam, in '66 and '67, concluding with the first battle of Saigon where he lost his right leg. He attended college on the GI bill, studying the writing business and earning a degree in journalism at Oakland University, which opened the door to a job covering sports for *The Detroit News*. The bottle got the best of him and he was fired after a short stint. A bout of freelance travel writing followed. He then secured an editorial position with Macmillan Publishers in New York, where he worked for twenty some odd years before hanging out a shingle on his own. Now he worked as an agent, representing sports writers, mystery authors, and poets.

But there were a few blanks to fill in.

"Rusty, how did the two of you meet?"

"If you have some questions for me, let's do it now," Molly rubbed her hands together.

"All right, then," I said. "What did you do when the sign fell?"

"As you said, I was reciting at the time. Surrounded by others. That screeching sound. I froze, unsure of the protocol."

"Did you get off the stage, go back to the city offices, and meet Neumann?"

"No, I didn't meet Neumann. That would not be part of my reality."

"So you stood?"

"For a few moments. Then I took my seat on stage."

I nodded. "It came to my attention today that you are Ralph 'Jazz' Fitzgerald's granddaughter."

She looked at me, blank-faced. "My greatest honor was serving a tribute to his memory." The edges of her mouth turned up. "In my mind, I dedicated the night to my grandfather."

"Then it's true?"

"Yes, Ken."

"About that, Molly. I have a friend, Edison Edwards, who attended one of your talks in Southfield and according to his memory, the two of you spent considerable time talking about your book idea for a collection of stories about the results of *Extreme Honesty*. A couple of days later, he made it a point to visit your lecture in Cleveland. I understand you reacted to him as if the two of you never spoke."

"I see a lot of people. If your friend was offended or angry or frustrated, I encourage him to express those emotions."

"But surely an extended discussion on so definite a topic, kicking around ideas for your next project would stay in your memory. So you don't believe him? You think he's lying?"

"Sometimes it's the juxtaposition and both are true...most times it's better to find the common ground than be right about who is telling the truth."

I decided to try another tack. "Rusty, where were you after intermission?"

"You know in the business, you have to keep on top of things. I was checking with booking agents, scheduling conferences in June."

"Uh-huh."

"But, I ran right over to Molly when the sign fell."

Of course, Molly couldn't have met Neumann—she

was on stage. But honesty was in question. How is it to be determined who is being truthful, when all parties claim to be, even those who make a career out of it?

Chapter 23

I left Molly's house feeling uneasy. I felt like I knew less about them than when I arrived. Sometimes you can't get under the skin of people you meet in life, no matter how much time is spent together. Regardless how hard you try, you have no idea how to 'read' them, don't know if they're serious or cracking jokes. This was the situation with Molly and Rusty.

Rusty and Molly were an unlikely pair. Far be it for me to know what an agent looks like, or what an agent-client relationship should be, but something was off. I circled around the ideas for several minutes, then shrugged. With all their attendant quirkiness, they were probably harmless.

This lunch with Robert and the gang was a thorn in my side. I had plenty to do and sharing lunchtime with the office crowd could only add to my commitments. I was sure of it. Robert liked to orchestrate the assembly of people, pull them together in one place and direct their interaction, like that team building workshop he shipped us to the year before. Four days of playing follow the leader, catching each other blindfolded, and knocking beach balls around. Funny thing is, it worked. But with his authoritarian rule, why bother? The complexity of his psychological issues was nearly as abstruse as mine.

Of course, the Val's Market opportunity was top priority. Potentially six shopping centers to renovate. I heard the manager of Gruen Properties, John—son of the founder—was considering making BPW the "architect in charge" for the next five years. This would give us a ton of work to add to our backlog.

I pulled into the Deli4 parking lot and squeezed my Taurus into a space behind the building, between a Hummer and one of those monster Ram trucks. The rear glass door took me into a space with dim light and I took a moment to adjust my eyes. Our group was already seated at a picnic table near the front. Wally and Robert on one side, Edison on the other. The red-and-white gingham table cloth and wrought iron candlesticks did not do much for me.

"Glad you could make it, Cannoli," Robert said. "Now let's get down to brass tacks."

Robert was interrupted by a skinny youth with closely cropped hair and an apple cheeks smile. We had not yet reviewed the menus, so he would come back. Conversation halted briefly as we studied the offerings, printed on white copy paper, folded in half. Each sandwich was named after a celebrity. I smiled at The Britney, a baloney sandwich. After we placed our orders, Robert continued.

"We've had a minor reprieve. The presentation's been delayed. You can be assured that the competition will not rest on their laurels. Let's take this time and add some knock-your-socks-off material to our presentation. I'm throwing it out to you. What's the best use of this wrinkle in time? I'm looking for options."

Edison spoke first. "How much time do we have?"

"I don't know," Robert said. He adjusted his tie tack, the Addams Family's "thing" hand reaching out from a black box. The fist held a pen which had scrawled on the side of the box: *Help Me.* "At least a couple of days. Once they get the word out to everyone, it could be more."

"We could add another fly-through. It would take a

few hours to set up, but it could be rendered in two nights."

Robert nodded.

"We could assemble additional Project Experience references," I said. "Photos, descriptions. We only have—"

"Boring. Next?" Robert said with a wave of his hand.

"Out of the box thinking is what we need," I said. "Who's our competition for this commission? Retail architects with a decade or more experience. Same as us. Retail architects who have worked on projects with these developers. Same as us. But what's the differentiator? Why pick BPW? What do we bring to the table?"

"I'm listening," Robert said.

The sandwiches arrived and everyone dug in. A pitcher of Coke was placed on the table.

"We should team up with a general contractor. Retail is fast paced. Once they make up their minds to move forward, the countdown begins to open doors and ringing cash registers. Instead of traditional project delivery, we go design-build."

Robert shook his head. "The old guy won't go for it. He's been doing this for fifty years. He believes in designing the right thing, then bidding it out to the most qualified contractors. I doubt we can sell him on a non-conventional delivery system."

"Then we have to make it appealing," I said.

Wally spoke up, "What if we do the construction management ourselves? That way the control remains in the designer's ball field, but we bring the advantages of reduced schedule."

"No, we're not entering that side of the business." Robert said.

Wally said, "Some of these projects we practically

do it anyway. It would just be more formally assigned to it."

I said, "Maybe we should go the design-build route, with an established contractor. It may be more convincing."

"Look," Wally said, "We can plot the phasing ourselves and not rely on a contractor to come up with it. Through creative phasing and innovative construction techniques like building components in the shop we can cut costs and time. We can design common elements to the six-pack of renovations, which can be shop-built before plans are even completed. And we can design some areas of selective demolition around that pneumatic destruction equipment I've seen around. It can work wonders for improving the schedule."

"I like it," Robert said. "Wally, put together something we can look at tomorrow morning. We can offer those services. Ken, help him out with this. Put your heads together for an exciting option."

Wally and I gave each other the *crap what have we gotten ourselves into?* look.

"Now," Robert said, "Who's got a new hot actress girlfriend?"

Gawd. How did he find out?

"Ken's been seeing Kristen Blume," Edison offered. Innocently, I'm sure. Certainly Robert was jesting.

"She's not another one like your last girlfriend, is she?" Wally said.

"Oh yeah, she was a piece of work, wasn't she, Cannoli?" Robert said. "Extra wicked."

I wanted to sink under the table.

"Maybe you should do a background check on her," Wally said. "As famous as she is, there should be a lot of dirt to find out, not like last time."

They all laughed.

"Come on, guys, that's not very funny. We lost a good person in that episode."

It got quiet at the table.

"Just don't tell Kristen about Mary," I said. "I mean if the opportunity should present itself. I don't know if you all will be meeting her, but if I do..."

"I already told her," Edison turned his eyes down at the table.

"What?"

"She called the office looking for you and we had a little conversation."

"Oh, Edison, tell me you didn't?"

"She already knew, Ken; she was just looking for confirmation. It's not like I blurted it out or anything."

"How did she know?"

"I wondered about that part too," Edison shrugged. "But she wouldn't tell me."

"Not too tough," Wally said. "You date someone like that, word gets around."

As I walked to my car, I heard heavy footsteps behind me. Edison's customary hiking boots were slamming on the ground as he caught up to me. "I found out some information. I tried to get your attention in there, but—"

"What is it?"

"You're mad at me I can tell."

"Edison, I really care about this girl. She's—"

"Kristen Blume, I know."

"No," I said. "It's not that. I mean, she's funny, spontaneous. Her view of the world makes me glad there are people like her walking the planet. Of course, it's silly. We live in different circles. Stratospheres. I don't know what kind of future we could have. And she's only going to be here for another week or two."

Edison's face grew serious, his chubby cheeks dropping their sheen, eyes sunken. "Now I've ruined it for you. I didn't mean to, it just came out."

I considered Edison for a moment. There weren't many innocents like him around either. "It's ok. I'll talk to her about it."

Edison's eyes livened. "I hope she understands. Let me know, ok?"

I nodded. "Now, what was it you had for me?"

"Sylvia, my friend at Ben Proctor's office, called me before lunch."

Edison pulled out a piece of paper from the pocket of his Dockers. Anticipation kicked up my heart rate.

"The will is long, and goes on about people and circumstances of daily life. Things that meant something to Neumann. The bartender at Tom's Oyster Bar, the owner of the 7-Eleven, stuff like that."

"What?"

"To each he left a little something. Barbers, secretaries, the minister at his church. Oh, and this is funny. To his mail carrier he left five hundred dollars in chips at Dave and Buster's."

"The video game restaurant?"

"Yup"

I failed to see the humor. "What about the main players? His wife and Julianne?"

"I'm getting to that. Ok, his fortune was about 29 million. Of which he divided two million among charities, and left five million to Julianne."

"Whoa. Heavy payment to the other woman."

"Yeah, but she coaches a summer hockey league for the Boys and Girls Club. When I go hang out, I've seen her there. She is kinda cool."

My watch said time to go. "What else? Any more surprises?"

"There's only three more beneficiaries. He left each of his kids three million, and the bulk of his estate, Sylvia figures it totaled up to about 17 million, to his wife Nicole."

Chapter 24

I stopped by home, took in the mail, dumped my dirty clothes and replaced my bag. It always stayed in the car, just in case business took me on a prolonged trip.

Twenty minutes later, I reached Southfield's city offices and strode into the cubicle zone searching for Amelia or Matt. The space was disorganized, with putty- colored metal desks arranged willy-nilly, the occasional faux wood-grain side table piled with paperwork. Matt was right. The place stunk. Boyd or Scofield would know if there were any remodel plans.

The short hallway by the office Matt had occupied the day before appeared abandoned. Since he was squatting, I had no idea if he would have claimed the same office again. Amelia appeared from one of the offices and closed the door.

Startled, she shook when she caught sight of me, then regained her composure. "Oh, Ken. Ha. How nice to see you again."

"Hello, Amelia. Sorry if I spooked you. I'm looking for Matt Lance."

"Quite all right. I have a low shock threshold. Matt's down there, third office on your left."

I nodded my thanks. Matt was sitting at the office desk, fingers flying across a computer keyboard. I knocked on the open door.

He turned his head up. "Oh, hi, Ken. Let me finish this sentence."

I waited.

"There. Working on memoirs. This is going to be a hoot. Have a seat."

He pointed to a metal rimmed chair.

"Now, what can I do for you? You said you had some follow up? Hold on a minute; where are my manners? Would you like some coffee? The stuff they have around here tastes like iron, but sometimes I crave heavy metal. Hehehe. There's a vending machine, too. Coke?"

"I'm fine, thanks. I understand you know Bryce McClurg, the roofing contractor?"

"Sure I know him. Why?"

"Well, I heard recently there was some bad blood between him and Jerome Neumann."

Matt slapped the top of the desk. "Hehehe! Bad blood? I'll say. You couldn't put the two of them in the same room, that's for sure. A project McClurg did for Neumann ten years ago got his goat and didn't let go. You know, Neumann tried to ban him from the project."

"Thanks. That confirms the information I had."

"You think McClurg had something to do with what happened?"

"I don't know, just something I'm following up on."

Matt fiddled with his keyboard while I considered that Bryce had access to the roof and construction drawings. He could review the design of the sign supports, examine the weak points. Police! Yes, I needed to get them up to speed. Perhaps I could trade some information. "Let me ask you about Bryce McClurg."

Matt nodded.

"This is a little out of school, but I have to ask you about a celebrity memorabilia that passed hands from Bryce, to you, to Jerome Neumann."

"Hehehe...did Bryce tell you about that? What a

hoot! That Bryce, such a ladies man. Makes an old codger like me jealous, you know? I suspect it had the same effect on old Neumann. To hold that piece just for a few days and pretend she's written that note to him..."

"You won the item in a poker game with Bryce?" I said.

"Yeah, we play poker twice a month. Thursday nights. When Bryce is in town we meet at his office. I had good fun that night and Bryce was out of cash."

"When was that?"

"Let me see, yeah, that would have been the 15th. September 15th."

"Then later you passed it to Neumann, at his insistence?"

"Yeah, that's about the way it happened. You should have seen his eyes bug out when he first saw it! He must have had the hots for Bailey Justine himself. But I never thought Jerome would hold on to it. I was drunk. He kept on. 'Only one night,' he said. He's got his problems you know, but something like that I figured I could trust him. He told me he'd give it back to Bryce. Finally I gave it to him just to shut him up. After he got his jollies for a while, he would have given it back."

"But it the meantime, when Bryce found out you no longer had it, and had in fact given it to Neumann, Bryce yelled at you."

Matt waved both hands in front of him, like he was pushing away a pile of dirty socks. "No stock, he had it wrong. Why did he get so excited? I'll tell you why. He was afraid the word would get out. So why was he flaunting it around to begin with? He's a sinner, and it will catch up to him."

"Now, here's a new question. I heard something about an invention. You designed some pneumatic destruction equipment?"

A broad smile crossed Matt's face. The kind of smile

that crosses a grandfather's puss when he talks about his grandchildren. "Hehehe. Yeah, that was a good one. In doing our research—you know about our facility right? Research labs, auto bays. We tend to take things apart more than we put them together. I've got some of the sharpest minds in the industry working for me."

I nodded. "Yes, I've heard you have quite an operation out there."

"You should come take a look. I'll give you the grand tour." He paused. "Well, maybe not so grand. Some areas are restricted. You know. You wouldn't believe how industrial espionage has picked up in the last few years. Technology is advancing so fast, there's always one more thing to watch out for. We have controls in place that weren't conceived even two years ago. One of the reasons cars are becoming so doggone expensive."

I tried to get Matt back on track. "And in the process of doing this research, you stumbled upon—"

"Propellant devices, like airbags. You know how airbags work right? An impact causes an igniter to burn the solid propellant, usually sodium azide, which creates an awful lot of nitrogen that explodes the bag practically instantly, in one twenty-fifth of a second. You've seen the tests where the force of the airbag opening can actually cause injury to a child. What if that force were used, were directed, were controlled so that the force itself could be used for good?"

"Uh-huh."

"Look, basically it works like this. You get a number of deflated bags, you insert them between two materials you want to separate. The bags are hooked up to hoses from the propellant sources. Could be one bag, could be multiple bags which can be deployed simultaneously. With my accelerator, the nitrogen is dumped into the bag like an explosion, causing instant demolition."

"And this—what do you call it?"

"It's new desk."

"Excuse me?"

"N-E-U-D-E-S-Q.   It   stands   for   pneumatic destruction equipment."

"And that's available here?"

"Some of the local demolition equipment houses carry it, for purchase or for rent. The process is hard on the bags, but the construction is strong: neoprene materials reinforced with Aramide." I must have looked blank, for he inserted an explanation. "It's a heat resistant, synthetic fiber, stronger than steel in which the chain molecules are oriented along the fiber axis. Much of the strength comes from harnessing the chemical bond. The army uses it for apparel and equipment. It's a cousin to Kevlar. Hehehe, this air bag: the whole shebang is less than an inch thick. And they are made in various sizes up to four feet square. You need compressors, hoses and accelerators. There's a place downriver that carries them."

"Sounds like a great innovation."

"Believe me, it is. Now, don't get this confused with those lifting bags the fire and rescue departments use."

"Excuse me?"

"They have bags, too, made of similar materials, use them to raise heavy materials for rescuing victims pinned by cement trucks, busses and stuff like that. Hook them up to compressed air. But that takes a few minutes. Mine. BAM!" He slammed the palm of his hand on the desk. "It's done."

He gave me the address. I would inquire about this new desk.

I walked out to my car, climbed in and punched my phone.

"Boyd."

"Hi John, Ken Knoll here, I have a question I hope

you can answer."

"Yes, Ken. This is a switch. Usually I'm the one asking you questions. By the way, have you taken a look at my den? Any ideas?"

Inwardly, I winced. I should have anticipated his question and prepared a response before I dialed his number. A-B-C, *always be closing,* as Dennis Miller says. "Mediterranean. Do you care for the Mediterranean look: high ceiling, expanse of windows, large columns? Textured walls, rich sky blue with warm terra cotta accents. Perhaps some mosaic tile around the fire place?"

"You've got my ear...Do you have examples?"

"Yeah, yeah, I was pulling some illustrations together for you last night. Perhaps we could meet later in the week."

"Perfect, but not Thursday night. Poker, you know."

"Right. So, John, the doors to the city offices, are they electronically monitored?"

Boyd chuckled. "You've seen the building. We have some remodeling to do before we think about electronics. No, they are not tagged. Why do you ask?"

"Someone was in those offices Saturday night, before the accident. I've been trying to find out who, but no one seems to have seen anything."

"Sorry, there's no way electronically to know who used the office. No camera, nothing"

I thanked him and hung up.

Chapter 25

I reached Nicole's cobblestone driveway and parked next to the empty stone fountain as before. Sad. *Ok, Ken, let's make this a mutually beneficial meeting.*

Nicole opened the door. She was all smiles, her Tootsie Roll hair pulled back in a French twist. She met me with a brief hug, and I smelled the faint wisp of *Opium* dancing in the air. She led me into the dining room. "Oh, I was in the mood to do something special," she said.

The polished oak table was decked out in a German lace coverlet and Blue Danube dishes, with a plate of triangular pastries and a teapot matching the plates.

"The tea is kava, good for stress—and sex too, by the way—and I baked chocolate scones."

"You baked these?" I said. "How can I resist?" I took two.

We munched as I filled her in on the talk with Molly and Rusty.

She furrowed her brow. "They're an odd pair for sure, but hardly seem like the type that would cause destruction, let alone kill someone. I did always think Molly peculiar when I attended a board meeting. She speaks funny, if you know what I mean, off kilter. But violence? I hardly think so."

"Uh-huh."

"Her agent, Rusty, I only met him once. It was an afternoon strategy meeting, and he arrived before we were finished. Apparently he was driving her to a speaking engagement that evening."

"Well, something seems off, but I can't put my finger on it." I took another scone.

"It's a waste of time, Ken. Why didn't you talk to Julianne again? She's hiding something, I just know it. The way she slithers around, peeking around corners, wearing those big sunglasses. It's not natural." Her hands were fists on the table.

"Now, Nicole," I said, stroking the back of her hands. "You leave this to me. I'll get to the bottom of it. I spoke with Bryce this morning and he admitted to taking that framed memorabilia from Jerome's office."

"I told you!"

"Apparently it belonged to him. It wasn't your husband's," I explained.

"Are you sure? He wasn't just saying that?"

"He told me the full story."

"Oh, well, that's a relief at least. But why did he have to break in here? Scared me to death. I would have given it to him."

"Yeah. He was worried you would find it and think the worst. Believe it or not, he wanted to spare you."

"Well, that's something." She paused. "Oh, Ken."

I was determined not to let my feelings stop me from making progress. "Nicole." I caught her sweet doe eyes. "I've been curious about something. Do you mind talking about Jerome?"

"No." She straightened up. "Of course not. What is it?"

"What was it that drew you to him? I mean, he was..."

"Older? Yes, of course, but in the long run it didn't make much difference. I was swept away by his charm. He'd seen me on the shaving commercial—the one you mentioned last time—and weaseled an introduction through a mutual friend. Of course, I was put off by his age—we're...were...twenty-nine years apart—but he was so worldly. I admired the business circles he traveled in. His associates. Took me to the finest dinners. It was all so exciting. But beyond the entrapments, he was a conversationalist. We could talk for hours. When we were together, time flew by. Those early days were really sublime, romantic. Don't know if I'll ever—" A lump caught in her throat and I felt my emotions going out to her.

I waited.

"When he proposed, I was caught by surprise. I mean, for someone like that to be taken with *me*. We had fun for sure but, someone like that. Hmmm. We married in 1999. I remember we joked about having Prince's song at our wedding. And we did."

"No, seriously?"

"Yes, at the reception."

I smiled. "Nicole, I have to ask you something else. And I need you to tell me the honest truth." I took her hands.

She slowly raised her eyes to meet mine. "Did I have a crush on you when you were dating my sister? You know I did."

"No," I said evenly. "Something else...Did you kill your husband?"

Sadness crossed her eyes, but they continued to hold mine. "No."

"Did you blow the sign?"

She looked down and let out a breath. "No, Ken, no." Her voice was stronger, and she pulled her hands away. "I *told* you before, I had nothing to do with this."

"Sorry," I said quietly. "I had to be sure."

She wrinkled her lips like she'd sucked on a lemon.

"Oh, let me tell you, I talked to Matt Lance this afternoon. This could be a promising lead. It seems he designed some demolition equipment that uses pneumatics to accurately pinpoint the destruction. It's light weight and..." Nicole had a sudden far-away look in her eyes. "What?"

She cleared her throat. "Matt Lance didn't design that equipment; Jerome did."

"What do you mean? Your husband?"

Nicole nodded. "As a matter of fact, he and Matt were in a patent dispute. Lawyered up and threatening legal action. I don't know much about demolition, but as I understand it, the patent was worth millions."

I was stunned. "Tell me about it."

"Well, six years ago, Jerome was in a creative period. He was constantly watching MacGyver re-runs—you know he was fascinated by that show. And he studied da Vinci's journals. Well, in the middle of a MacGyver episode one day he jumped out of his chair and headed over to his office, started jabbering away, playing loud music—Alice Cooper for crying out loud—and, well, I had to go to bed. But the next morning he told me he had the nucleus of a new product. Revolutionary, he called it."

A fourth scone filled me up and I made my good byes. Nicole certainly was a sweet one, much more pleasant than Dani, and less melodramatic. In another time, under other circumstances, perhaps she would capture my senses. But for right now, my heart was slowly, surely, being engulfed by one Kristen Blume. Things were working really well right now. Despite the actress factor.

I called Julianne to set up a time to talk about the will, and she agreed to meet for breakfast before school the next day. My waistline was growing on this assignment.

A heavy sigh left me. The emotion of these conversations was unraveling me. I needed to push through. Get to the end. But who would be at the finish line?

Chapter 26

The comfortable confines of Nicole's Cotswold Cottage behind me, I entered the chilly atmosphere. It was the first week of October. In Michigan that meant anything from 30s to 80s. While it had been relatively mild over the weekend, a cold front had moved in the day before and temperatures were dropping. I was now officially chilly as I entered the car, the dress shirt and T-shirt inadequate.

Ella's radio program emanated from the Travelers' Tower in Southfield, a half-mile up Evergreen from the murder scene. I had agreed to meet Kristy at the studio for the live broadcast. Ella had requested that Kristen and I arrive thirty minutes before the five pm show time so that we could get comfortable and Ella could meet her beforehand. I worried something would come up and Kristy would be late.

I had been to the WKAC studios on a couple of occasions previously: in 1998 to pick up my winning tickets to a Dixie Chicks concert at the Palace, and second to congratulate my sister when she won a Marconi award for Personality of the Year a couple of years ago. Ella's daily program on "Politics and Pop Culture" was widely received in Metro Detroit, and Sunday mornings she hosted a weekly roundtable featuring local politicians and community leaders.

It turned out that I didn't have anything to worry about. Kristy called me as I was exiting the freeway onto Evergreen. "Are you on your way, Mr. Architect? Your sister's a scream!"

They started without me. I was hoping to make the introduction and smooth things along. I pulled into the lot, parked, grabbed my briefcase, slung it over my shoulder, and hustled into the building and up the elevator to the 10ᵗʰ floor. The doors opened onto a dimly lit lobby, cast in glass shelves and velvet draperies. As I made my way across, barely seeing my feet in front of me, I heard the program, broadcast on the overhead speakers and recognized the voice of Ted Nash.

Traffic has slowed to a crawl on I-696 westbound at Orchard Lake following that mattress dumping incident we reported earlier. Alternate routes of 12 Mile or...

A tall, highly polished desk piled with radio knick-knacks (read: junk) stood at the other end of the space and I made my way to the reception desk, where a young woman with a nose diamond greeted me with big eyes. "May I help you?"

"Ken Knoll. I'm here for the 5 o'clock interview with Ella. I'm her brother."

"Of course, she told me to expect you." She smiled. "I understand you're an architect. Through those doors to your right." She pointed to a pair of glass doors. "She's in the third studio."

I entered a hallway with no more light that the lobby. After a short section of wall, there appeared a long stretch of floor-to-ceiling glass, and I could make out the first two darkened studios: seats, knobs, microphones, the first one set up with a three-tiered stage for musical guests. I imagined Detroit natives Bob Seger or Madonna having a jam session there, back in the day, the same stage now perhaps frequented by Kid Rock.

The third studio was lit, Ella at the microphone, a skinny youth at the console and two guest chairs waiting. A red light in the corridor ceiling was illuminated, announcing the studio was on-live. The glass made a turn at the end of Ella's studio, and I pivoted into another hallway. I circled around 180 degrees to where I was behind the action and found a solid door with a sign "ON AIR—WAIT" illuminated. Ella had seen me arrive. I stood at the door, awaiting admittance. I hadn't coached Kristy on exactly what words to use, but she knew the gist of what we were after. I felt it was best to be natural, although I was now having second thoughts. Of course, she was an actress and could have made any script appear natural, right? My sister was unaware of my ulterior motive, and this gave me pause. Had I told her Kristy and I had started going out? I couldn't remember.

"Ken!" I heard Kristy's voice. She waved at me, standing by an open door on the other side of the hallway.

I went sideways through the doorway, too close to Kristy, who was attired in a red knit dress with a belt that hugged her body. The structure gave her small breasts a pointed shape and created tender cleavage at the V of her neckline.

"Hey Kristy. Sorry I'm late."

"No problem. Ella boosted me in here." We stood in a small room, perhaps nine by ten, a small couch across one side, an upholstered chair against the other. "She's so nice and friendly. And has a high regard for you too, by the way."

That was a surprise. Not that I presumed Ella didn't, but I was taken aback that she thought to point it out to anyone else. We sat on the green couch and Kristy crossed her legs, revealing those magnificent legs.

"Up here, big boy. Are you ready for this?"

What did I have to be ready for? "No, I'm not going on."

"Right, but are you ready for the move we prompt?

What are you going to watch for? Who's going to do what?"

She made a good point. Who did I need to keep an eye on, and what was I expecting to happen? My cards came to mind.

The door opened suddenly, straight black hair flying into the opening. Ella's crinkled eyes poked in. "Ok, weather, traffic, commercials. We have eight minutes. Hi, Ken."

I stood and gave my sister a hug. "Hello, Ella. Wonderful to see you. How are Neil and the kids?"

"Great, great. Melinda's teenage horns are sprouting. Lately we're going toe to toe over all the social media manifestations. It's dangerous out there, you know. A kid gets a few flattering messages and falls head over heels, without knowing who the hell is on the other side of the conversation. Damn! We'll have to catch up later. Let's get set up. Come on, Kristen." She reached down and grabbed Kristen's hand, pulling her off the couch as if leading a child. "Ken, are you going to sit in the studio with us?"

I looked at Kristy, and she was blank-faced. "No, you go ahead. I'll probably go into the hallway and take a peek at you while you're talking, if you don't mind."

Ella said, "I don't mind at all. I don't give any attention to what goes on outside."

The comment had been intended for Kristy, not my sister. Kristy shrugged her shoulders. She didn't care either. When they had left the room, I pulled my index cards out of the briefcase and began my routine of running through the suspects and adding notes. The overhead speaker broadcast the announcer as he went through the news, weather and traffic. Then commercials. I began adding cards for today's talks with Bryce, Molly, Rusty, Nicole and Matt.

The lusty memorabilia of famous anchorwoman

Bailey Justine was evidence of a relationship with Bryce. As proud as he was of the artifact, he was angry that it fell into Neumann's hands—shouting at Matt, "I'm gonna kill you!" for giving it to Neumann. He went to great lengths to retrieve it after Neumann's death, breaking into Nicole's house. Is it possible Neumann was blackmailing Bryce over it? Threatening to tell Bryce's wife? And why were they poker buddies, given that Neumann had tried to have Bryce removed from the auditorium project? Motive? Opportunity: Bryce, as subcontractor, had access to the project plans.

Molly remained an enigma. Fitzgerald's granddaughter, who was "not so much concerned with right and wrong, but with the truth within us." What was the truth within *her*?

Two people disappeared from their seats during intermission: Julianne, the other woman, due to a headache which is an excuse that stinks of a lie; and Rusty, Molly's agent. Was Julianne's five million dollar inheritance cause for motive? Get the cash before Neumann changed his will?

What about Matt Lance, whose claim to design the pneumatic destruction equipment was disputed by Neumann? A kill to shut him up? A heavy motive, when viewed in concert with his old grudge regarding a business deal in the 80's which lost him money and a wife.

And sweet Nicole, the widow who was due to receive the bulk of Neumann's estate. Had Neumann made another decision? A decision to leave his wife for Julianne? I had only the two women's word that it was the other way around. If he had changed his mind, he would certainly then alter the will, and Nicole's loss of millions would be weighty motive.

Ella's voice came over the speaker: *All right, we have a special guest in studio with us today, actress and*

196 Civic Center Corpse

local talent made good, our very own hometown girl Kristen Blume. Welcome to the program, Kristen. Delighted you could be with us today.

Thank you, Ella, it's my pleasure to be here. I've heard good things about your show. Kristy sounded upbeat, chipper.

Well, let's get right down to it. I understand you are in town with us to film a portion of your new movie, A Mother's Dilemma. *What's the movie about?*

As Kristy summarized the film, I gathered my cards and returned them to the briefcase. I wanted to see these two as they spoke to each other. I got up and opened the green room door.

So it's really this exploration of a mother and her child, half-brother, and their getting to know one another.

Oh my, Kristen. I can't wait to see that one. Now, you're not really from Port Huron, are you? I understand you are from this area.

Yes, I was raised in Huntington Woods, went to Royal Oak High School—class of '04.

Laughter from Ella.

I used to work at the Fresh and Tastee Yogurt Shoppe in Royal Oak.

They said in unison, *When it's fresher it's tastier!*

More laughter from Ella.

Do you get back here often? Are you enjoying the old haunts?

I had wandered into the corridor, and from my perspective I could see animated Kristy, talking with her hands, apple cheeks smiling, blue eyes open wide as she went on.

Well, I must say, I'm a bit nervous about that murder at the civic center, just down the road from here.

Murder? Ella quizzed.

Yes, where someone caused the building sign to

plummet from the roof, killing that poor man.

Oh, you're referring to that accident that happened Saturday night.

Oh, no, Ella, it wasn't an accident. I've talked to the architect. He's doing an amazing job with it. He found that the supports were unbolted. Now how would that happen? That man was killed.

At that moment, I saw movement out of my peripheral vision. I turned to see a woman's form crossing along the other side of the studio. Shirley.

Well, I'm sure the police will figure that one out. Kristen, thank you so much for dropping by today. I am so looking forward to seeing that movie in the fall. A Mother's Dilemma. *Indeed, it will be a shocker. Folks, thank you for tuning in and we'll see you tomorrow on* Ella Polaris Pop Culture and Politics. *Until then, think quick and turn slow.*

An investment commercial came on, and I watched Ella rise and storm across the studio in my direction. She opened the heavy glass door at my end and started in on me.

"Ken, what on earth are you thinking? What was that? Planting this woman in here with that garbage about the auditorium sign being done by a murderer?"

"That's what he does," Shirley said.

Ella looked blank. "And who are you? I wasn't talking to you. Ken, what is this? Did you think you could use me?"

Kristy poked her head through the door and raised her eyebrows at me like Groucho Marx. "Ella, don't blame him. It was my idea." She came over and put her arm around me.

"Kristen! You letting this guy talk you into things?" Shirley glared at her while she spoke.

"I gotta get back in there," Ella said. She raised her hand and pointed in my face. "Don't think this is over.

How *dare* you use my program!" She pivoted on her heels, powered back through the glass door and was gone.

Kristy looked at me with *is it ok?* doe eyes.

Shirley stared at Kristy for a moment, her expression empty, eyes darting across Kristen's face. She stuck out her hand. "Shirley Hanson. I love your work."

"And what are you doing here, Shirley?" I said

"Just taking a stroll in the neighborhood; you know, I love these radio stations. All the gizmos and whatchawhozits."

I slid my arm around Kristy's waist and squeezed closer. "Watch what you say to her. She's a reporter who specializes in—what would you say, Shirl, dirt?"

Shirley crossed her arms and tapped her toe. I turned to Kristy and whispered in her ear. "Let's go."

"So long, Shirley," I said over my shoulder. "Enjoy your stroll through the neighborhood." I guided Kristy toward the green room.

"Not so fast, Ken, wait," Shirley said. "I have something to tell you."

Movement at the other end of the corridor caught my attention. Four teenage guys in jeans, sneakers and jerseys approached. "There she is!" one of them called out, and they rushed toward us.

I pushed Kristy toward the green room. She struggled free. "It's ok," she said, whispering, "Don't be so mean." Then to the group of guys, who had caught up to us, "Hey, guys. What's up?"

The dark-haired one in the back studied the ground, flicked his eyes up at us. The freckled one beside him poked the one in front, the tall skinny one who spoke first. "Kristen Blume! We just heard you on the radio," he said, his Adam's apple bobbing.

"Yeah, wow, can we get your picture?" said the blonde with the broad shoulders who stood next to him.

He fished a camera out of his shirt pocket.

"Sure, how about we do this one at a time?" Kristen said.

The guys nodded and grinned. She took turns hugging each one of them while another took pictures. Shirley put her hands on her hips and looked on. Jealous, I bet.

"Hey," said the blonde. "We're heading over to Friday's. Want to catch a beer with us?"

Kristen grinned. "Sounds great, but we have plans." She threw a glance in my direction. "Maybe another time."

I was happy to be *plans*. Altogether, she handled the ruckus beautifully I thought.

The boys retreated down the hallway as we stepped into the green room to collect my briefcase. "Shirley, I'll have to talk to you later," I said.

"But—"

The door shut in Shirley's face, I gave Kristy a full body hug. I enjoyed the feel of her against my chest, though her rose perfume pricked at my nostrils. "You were amazing with the fans."

"I don't mind the attention."

When I opened the door, there was no sight of Shirley. As we walked past the booth, I gazed at Ella at her console. She was studying the screen like it was a David Copperfield magic trick. We took the elevator down and traversed the office lobby to the parking lot. The wind had picked up. It was downright chilly. Kristy looked cold so I put my arm around her to share some warmth. As we walked side-by-side, my phone rang. *Mighty Mouse.*

"Hi, Edison, what's up?"

"Hey Ken, I heard the show. That was pretty cool. Kristy hit the right words."

"Yeah, she's something else." I looked at her. She

smiled.

"Hey listen, Ken, I have some news for you. I learned something about Molly's *Extreme Honesty* book. I don't trust that woman."

"What did you find?"

"Well, one of the gentlemen you have been talking to, one of the board members, Matt Lance, has a son named Mortimer. He's a keyboard player, and a good one. Mortimer plays the organ at Jeanelle's church. It's one of those modern churches, you know where the minister comes on stage in his blue jeans and they do little morality plays and like that."

"What does that have to do with the price of beans?"

"Jeanelle has been practicing this play, and working with the music director, who turns out to be Mortimer Lance."

"Yeah, Edison, can we pick this up later? I'm about to grab some dinner with Kristy." I made some hand gestures to Kristy, asking if that was ok. She nodded, and held her stomach like she was starving.

"Ken, here, ok, I'll tell you quick. Mortimer doesn't talk to his dad anymore. They had a big argument, explosive, and now he's dead to Mortimer. From what I gather, Matt is so angry he could spit."

"Umm, ok, so they had a falling out."

"It's about Molly Gross. That book *Extreme Honesty*. It was when Matt read the book and started implementing its ideas to talk to Mortimer, that his son stopped talking to him."

Chapter 27

I hung up and we climbed into Kristy's Saturn.

"Where's the Mustang?"

"Got to keep the paparazzi guessing."

"But you don't mind the fans?"

"Of course not. Fans are great. I love connecting with them. But those cameras get nasty sometimes."

As she started the car, my phone chimed again, this time playing the *Darth Vader theme*. Robert.

"Hey Chief, what's the buzz?"

"You have Edison fact finding for you? He's an intern, not your personal assistant."

"I can explain."

"Just watch it. You can't order him around. We don't need an HR issue here."

Huh. Kristy pulled out of the lot, apparently having decided where we were going for dinner.

"By the way, did you get Sue Watts settled down? I haven't heard from her today," Robert said.

"Sure, yes; everything is taken care of. I emailed the report to her earlier. No news is good news, right?"

"I certainly hope so." On that note, he hung up.

"What's wrong?" Kristy said as she stopped at a red light. She glanced over at me, her eyebrows were knit, and her eyes danced around my face.

"I never heard anything from Sue Watts after I sent the report. I hope everything is ok."

"I'm sure it's fine, Ken," she said as the light changed and she started rolling again. We were on Ten Mile, heading into Novi.

"Sure. That interview went well. You are quite the personality."

"Meaning?"

"Meaning I like the way you worked the whole murder sign thing in, very natural."

"This is what I do, make it sound natural."

I looked at those dazzling diamond eyes. And something went *ping*. "My biggest question is, what was the deal with Shirley? What brought her there in the first place?"

"You don't think she just stumbled on the place? Checking out her favorite radio station?"

"Shirley doesn't do anything spontaneously. Everything with her is cold and calculated."

"Oh." Kristy glanced in the rear view mirror.

There was a chill in the air, a mood, something. "Do you still want to do this?" I said. "Are you expecting the paparazzi?"

"Yeah, yeah. It seems to be fine right now."

We drove for a while and our conversation stopped. I needed a rest. All I wanted to do was enjoy the evening with Kristy and not think about the case. Did I leave my cards behind? I looked in the back seat. Yes, my briefcase was squeezed between the seats.

We pulled into a restaurant called "Hacienda Miguel." Sandstone accent walls, barrel tile roof, stucco exterior with brightly colored ceramic tile in red and yellow. Kristy pulled a cloth bag from the back seat and extracted a brunette wig. She tugged it on, stuffing her blonde locks underneath. She pulled out a pair of dark-framed eyeglasses and when she slid them onto her face, viola! Transformation.

"Hey, that reminds me of the episode of *Marley's Crew* where you played the computer geek."

"Very good, Mr. Architect."

"It doesn't disguise you very well."

"Pshaw. A little diversion, that's all. In case there's any photographers waiting for us."

As I slid into the booth, Kristy changed her position and scooted in next to me. "You don't mind, do you?"

"Oh no, lovely to be next to you."

She said, "Have you been here before?"

I shook my head.

"I used to come here as a kid. Well, teenager."

As if that was a long time ago.

"I don't know what they make better, chicken enchiladas or fajitas. I may get both."

We ordered Margaritas. Dinner went uneventfully. I shared the information from the day's round of interviews and proddings. And then the conversation circled to Julianne.

"Turns out Neumann left her a considerable sum of money," I said. "Of course the bulk went to Nicole, but five million dollars is nothing to sneeze at."

"Sounds like motive to me."

"But is it enough to plan and commit an elaborate murder? I don't know; that's not really my department. I only know what I learned in Sue Grafton and Michael Connelly books."

She smiled. "The butler with the candlestick in the library."

My face remained fixed. "Something like that."

Kristy put her hand on my knee and leaned against me. "When was the last time," she drew out the word *time*, almost singing it, "you went go-cart racing?"

"Go carts? Ha ha ha, I don't...well..."

"Ok, it's been too long. Let's do it."

She paid the check, and we raced to her car— literally. Out the door, she took off in a sprint. "Last one to the car is a rotten egg!"

She beat me there, only because she had led off with a head start. We climbed in and she drove a couple of miles to a cascading asphalt course along a bare stretch of road. There were a few cars on the track—black, yellow and red—making a hell of a lot of noise with their engines roaring. Kristy grabbed her sunglasses as we left the car.

We walked up to a little nondescript booth. Kristy bought two tickets and we were instructed to wait by the chain link fence encircling the track. A young man—perhaps eighteen— in a brown T-shirt and blue jeans stood by a gate, as well as another couple, I assumed also waiting for a car.

The black car raced around the course, taking the inside lane, cutting close to the center on the turn and then swinging wide afterward as he revved his engine and picked up speed on the straight away. It looked like fun, but how did these cars operate? With a gas pedal and brake like a car?

A yellow light went on at the stoplight above the gate, and a voice came on a speaker overhead, *All right, please head back to the starting position...please head back.*

I saw that they had an area set off to the side where there were perhaps ten cars lined up, ready to go. Business must have been slow. The red and yellow drivers pulled in, but the black car didn't stop at the pit and raced past. The voice came back over the speaker, *Black, pull off the track NOW. Black, pull off the track NOW.*

We waited as the black car made another lap around the track, careening around the hairpin turns, then pulled in. The driver got out—a ten year old girl!

The man opened the gate and took our tickets. When we walked to the pit area, I was surprised how small the cars were. Kristy picked the black one that had just come in, saying, "This one's fast!"

I took the red one next to her. The other couple was

in cars ahead of us, and a worker told us how to operate it—gas pedal on the floor, brake at my hand. *Fasten seatbelts, please!* We were allowed eight laps, and they would announce when to return.

The moment the car in front of her took off, Kristy peeled out. Not to be outdone, I gassed off with a jerk, then stopped and started again in a choppy motion. *What an amateur.* In a moment, I got the hang of it and drove out onto the track. The others were already halfway around. The steering wheel was tiny, I was close to the ground and the turns were sharp. Much sharper than I imagined, watching the others before my race. Black passed me on the left—Kristy! I had to get rolling. I pushed down on the accelerator and started whizzing along, holding on to the wheel to make those tight turns. The chilly air felt good on my face, and my hair flew back with the wind. It was exhilarating. With each pass around, the fun grew. I didn't even mind the other woman passing me in her blue car.

Finally, they announced it was over, and we returned to the pit. Kristy bounced out of her car. "Wow," I said. "That was fantastic. Why haven't I done this before? Wow!"

"Because you were waiting to experience it with me, silly." Kristy smiled at my delirium.

As we walked back to the car, she slipped her hand into mine. It felt good. Real good. The sun beamed low in the sky, shadows long in the parking lot.

"I'm bushed," Kristy said. "Do you mind if we call it a night?"

My face must have registered disappointment, because she clarified, "Together, of course. Would that be ok?"

It was only a little past eight o-clock, but the thought of another night with Kristy was heady. "Sounds great."

"Good," she said as we climbed into her Saturn. She

started the engine and we roared off the lot.

I debated about locations. My client's home in Grosse Pointe was far off, but my Ferndale fixer-upper was not suitable for entertaining. Not only had I left my bed a mess, but there were pieces of removed trim in the hallway, and the house reeked of urban renovation. I was relieved when Kristy had her own suggestion.

"Let's stay at my hotel," she said. "It's a bit pretentious, but it's close by. I can drop you back at your car. You can meet me there."

"Where's that?"

"The Belmont, on Maple in Birmingham."

I whistled. "Who-hoo! That's a classy accommodation." I was glad I'd repacked my bag.

Both hands on the steering wheel, she shrugged her shoulders. "What can I say?"

As we pulled back into the lot at the radio station, Kristy's phone buzzed. "Let me check this text message. Oh, no! Paparazzi at the hotel. Well, I'm not going there. The management is real cool about making it easy to get in and out without being seen, elevators from the basement parking garage and all, but sounds like somebody tipped them off and they're camped out in the garage."

"So..."

"So, it's plan B. Can we stay at your place?" Her smile was captivating.

Mine was forced. "Well, I'm not really set up for company, and—"

"Come on, I'm not company. It'll be an adventure, right?"

"Maybe we should stay at the Grosse Pointe house."

"That's so far, and I'm about ready to crash. See, I'll have my eyes closed soon, and won't even notice anything."

I nodded.

"You're going to have to show me your dirty laundry sometime, Cannoli."

"Yep. Ok." I gave her directions and got out of her car.

"All right, I'll see you there, Mr. Architect."

"K."

This would be bad. All I could think about was Mary constantly berating me for my living conditions. I had not done her well. The moment I had completed my house renovation so we could enjoy the lively new place, I bought another fixer-upper and moved into that one. Wally had given me the advice as well, *Women don't want to live in a construction zone. Get yourself a grand old place, great room, fireplace.* Why hadn't I listened? My refrigerator was bare, too. I would have to arrive first and do a quick cleaning before she arrived.

But her Saturn was parked in the driveway before I pulled in. I stopped the car behind hers and got out, to find her at the back of the house examining my tiny yard. The paint on the garage was peeling, with a litter of white paint chips on the grass.

"I just bought this house last month, and it's barely started. I'm beginning on the inside—the garage and back porch will have to wait."

"No need to explain. It's wonderful that you're working to improve the neighborhood."

I led the way through the side door, up the three steps into the kitchen, where I did my Vanna routine, pointing out the vinyl seated booth, old checkerboard kitchen floor tile. It was embarrassing.

"This is so cool!" she said, and I thought she was mocking me. "Before my family moved to Huntington Woods in the ninth grade, we had a little house in Clawson. The kitchen was just like this! Same floor tile. We didn't have the vinyl booth though. It would have been awesome. Do you have black and white ceramic tile in the bathroom too?"

I led her down the bedroom hallway. "Watch your feet. I took all the door trim off last week and haven't had a chance to dump them yet. I think they are all turned with the nails facing down, but watch your step just in case."

"You know, you're supposed to take the nails out as you go."

"Yeah, well, some of them were stubborn and wouldn't come out. It's all trash anyway, I just need to get them to a dumpster."

I was glad I had cleaned the bathroom at least, but it was a simple porcelain sink, water closet and tub. The wall covering was silver foil with pink and purple psychedelic swirls. "I'll take down this gawdawful wallpaper, put in new fixtures, paint. Your house in Clawson didn't have hippie wall paper like this, did it?"

She shook her head. "If it had, I'm pretty sure I would have had nightmares."

Finally, we got to the bedrooms. The larger one was crammed with ladders, drop clothes, tools and equipment. The smaller one opposite the bathroom was where I stayed and it wasn't pretty.

"This is it, but let me look first and clean up a couple of things."

"Ok," she said. "I'll wait in the kitchen."

My housekeeping skills were shameful. And this was truly madness. I picked up the clothes that were strewn across the floor and dumped them into a basket in the closet. My mattress was on the floor. On these remodel projects, I never took the time to make a bed frame. Why bother? The queen size mattresses were stacked, the head pushed up against the long wall opposite the closet. A sheet was hung over the window. The two end tables with lamps were relatively cleaned off. There was a TV at the foot of the bed, on top of a small junior desk I'd purchased from the thrift store for five dollars. It doubled as the place where I kept bills and placed my laptop when I wasn't working in the kitchen.

I peeled the sheets off the bed and pillowcases and found a fresh set in the closet. They were the red, white, and blue striped set I received for a birthday gift from Ella. I had never used them. From the bathroom I picked up a shaker of baby powder from the shelf over the toilet I had purchased when I had some issues with my feet. I dusted the mattresses with the powder and then unfolded the fitted sheet and shook it so that it billowed out above the mattresses. Kristy came in at just that moment, weaving in next to the other side and helping me fit the sheet on. I grabbed the other one and we unfolded it and put it on top.

"Fresh sheet, clean scent. What more could a girl want?" she smiled at me.

The sun poking through the gap on the side of the sheet covering the window created odd shadows on the wall. Kristy turned to me, wrapped her arms around my waist and laid her head on my chest.

"I like that you're helping the community. Doing all this, risking the critics to live in an awkward mess like this. You're an honorable man."

I half-smiled. She was special indeed.

She raised her head, turning her eyes to my face. "Would it be terribly rude of me to hit the sack? It smells so good, and I'm bushed. I was up at three this morning, remember?"

"Not rude at all. That's fine with me, I have an early breakfast."

She set her bag down and raised her eyebrows. "Sleuthing again?"

"Yep, meeting Julianne."

"Ah, the other woman."

"Right."

She pouted. "I know, this is serious. But...never mind."

I tilted my head, "Something more you want to share?"

"No...no. Let's get to bed ok?"

"Ok."

Kristy had set her bag near the door. I pulled out a towel from the bedroom closet for her. She pulled off her top, stripped down to her panties and slipped under the covers.

"I don't have a call tomorrow. Do you mind if I sleep in?" she said.

The thought brought a smile to my lips as I stripped down to my underwear. "Sure, I'll try to be quiet when I leave. Make yourself at home and stay as long as you like. I don't have much here for breakfast, but you should find some coffee in the cupboard." I slipped into the sheets next to her.

She snuggled closer to me and placed her hand on my chest. "What time is your breakfast meeting with that hussy?"

Stroking her hair, I spread my fingers and let the silkiness slip through. "Six o'clock, but it's not exactly breakfast, I'm meeting her at her house. She's a high school vice principal and needs to get to work."

"Huh, high school authority figure, in an affair with a married man and suspect in a murder charge." Kristy played with my nipples, and tugged at the hair on my chest.

"Huh. Yeah."

"Ken? Will you come back to me after?"

Leaning toward her, her breasts brushed against my chest. My mouth found hers. I felt the curve of her waist and caressed my way around to the small of her back. Her breath grew heavy and her soft hands on my back pulled me in. Our lips separated and she moved her head to place her lips near my ear, "How do you expect me to sleep now?"

I had the same problem, and I took her question as an invitation, but she said she was too tired. "I'll make it up to you soon, I promise."

How would I wait?

Chapter 28

I kept waking up, feeling Kristy's warm body next to me, the sweet scent of coconut, and the smooth skin on her back taunting me to touch, explore. One more minute of restraint, one more. Just as I let go and fell into nothingness, the *bleip bleip bleip* alarm on my phone chided me to rise. And greet the day. Rubbing sleep from my eyes, I curbed the urge to touch her and slipped out of bed. I reflected what a nice time we had, before dropping into bed. I took a shower and prepared for the day. Kristy hadn't seemed to mind the accommodations, or at least had been gracious about it. Either way, kudos to her.

What a nice sunshine day it was going to be.

I set up the coffee maker and sat down at the kitchen table to check Shirley's blog.

Blah blah blah. Ok here we go:

...and isn't it interesting that 18 months ago, after her book tour, Molly Gross changed her trademarked phrase "Extreme Honesty" to "Personal Honesty." This was the same period of time she joined the city's planning board, which governed the library building where her grandfather built the reading room.

...also of note is that Molly's literary agent Rusty Wagner was employed by Molly's grandfather Ralph 'Jazz' Fitzgerald for five years in the early 1970s while Wagner attended college on the GI Bill.

This reporter has also learned on good authority that the dead man left $5 million to his mistress.

She wasn't going to quit, was she? That bitch! Niggling, niggling until she wore everyone out and weaseled her way to success. What was wrong with her? How did she find out about Julianne's inheritance? I only myself discovered it the day before. This bit about Rusty was interesting. Molly was Fitzgerald's granddaughter; Rusty was Fitzgerald's ex-employee. What was significant was that they were now working together, Rusty about thirty years Molly's senior. Who was keeping tabs on who?

I quietly let myself out the side door, went into the back yard where I had spied some blue wild flowers a couple of days prior. Ah, there they were. I snipped four stems off with my pocket knife.

Back in the house, I grabbed an olive oil bottle from the recycle bin—nice, square, clear glass—rinsed it out and peeled off the label. I filled in water from the tap, stuck in the stems and left the vessel on the kitchen table. I wrote a note on a white paper napkin, "Blooms for my favorite Blume."

Corny, I know.

Laptop packed, I headed out the door. I needed to find out what Julianne knew, and I hoped she hadn't seen Shirley's morning blog.

Her residence was a twenty minute drive, up I-696 to Lahser. Traffic was light, though I noticed drive-thru lanes at Burger King and McDonald's were backed up. As I entered the subdivision, the houses immediately garnered my attention, not only in size but in rich detail. Lumbering homes of stone and slate. Landscaping designed with élan. Trees were beginning to bare their bark. Virtually all the homes exhibited lawns clear of clutter, neatly edged. It was the middle of the week. Who had time to rake?

I parked my Taurus in the grey cobblestone drive constructed not of true cobblestone, but concrete that had been colored and stamped. It was professionally done, though, not the hack job I'd seen on some restaurant parking lots.

Her house was a colonial, with richly carved pediments over the lower windows on either side of the entrance, and natural slate roofing. Warm grey brick with keystone detailing faced the street, with quoins fortifying the building's corners. Two brick steps up to the porch, and I rang the bell as the wood door opened before me.

Hunched over, she pushed the storm door toward me and said, "I saw you approaching."

I took the door, and as she retreated I noticed she had one hand on a dog's collar. The alert golden retriever was a handsome dog, with long hair the color of spun honey. It maintained its curious gaze on me as I entered and her owner tugged at the thick band around her neck.

"Come on in. Let me put the dog away."

My feet stepped onto the oversized porcelain tile floor, in buckskin. An oak console sat beneath a mirror framed in silver, with a small Paul Klee on the opposing wall: geometric forms against a warm red and gold backdrop. It was small and appeared to be an original, but the size didn't quite work in the space. A brass chandelier dangled above, which I took to be just a bit cliché, and beyond it, I noted the sweeping curve of a stairway.

She returned, brushing the front of her beige suit skirt. She wore a sheer ivory blouse with a simple neckline—no frilly scarf to hide her neck—and three thin silver necklaces.

They didn't have vice principals like this when I attended high school.

"Thanks for seeing me at this hour," I said.

"It's fine, but I'm not sure how much help I can be.

Follow me into the kitchen. I need to finish preparing for the day while we talk."

We strode through a barrel vaulted hallway, trimmed in dark rough sawn wood from the wainscot up, including the curve. I found its unique character pleasing.

"What's your dog's name?"

"Bosco. I've had him since he was a pup, four years ago. My sister's dog, Mango, had a litter."

She cleared breakfast dishes one by one, dropped crumbs into the waste can under the sink, rinsed off invisible dirt, and filed them one-by-one into the dishwasher. She shuffled back to the glass table, cleared away the tapestry placemat, and wiped down the surface. She seemed peppy enough. I was certain she hadn't seen Shirley's blog.

"I hate coming home to a dirty house," she said.

She'd risk a rash if she stepped into my kitchen.

I stood in the doorway, hands clasped. Finally she looked up, the signal it was ok to sit down. I wondered if this is what her students went through, lingering in the hallway while waiting for an appointment with her.

"Now, how can I help you, Mr. Knoll?"

"Ken, please."

"Ken?"

I noted her blue eyes, rimmed in brown, like Kristy's. I wondered if Neumann saw in her what I saw in Kristy. Which was what exactly? Passion, understanding, sweetness; definitely sweetness.

"Mr.—ah, Ken?"

I looked down at my hands. There was no easy way to do this. "Julianne—if I may call you that—"

She nodded.

"Julianne, I'm sorry to bring this up. I know this is a trying time—"

"Look, I know why you're here, Ken, and the

subject we're going to talk about. But no, you *don't* know what kind of time this is for me."

I thought for a moment her eyes moistened, but the chill in them sent a shiver up my back.

"On the night, ah, on Saturday night, at the poetry reading...You mentioned on that particular evening you spoke to Jerome."

"Yes, you asked me about that previously, and we discussed it."

"And this was before the event started? About what time?"

She exhaled. "It was shortly after seven. I remember because Jerome had arrived alone and we had to hurry because Nicole was to join him there, and he expected her to show up any minute."

I paused. She was doing a good job of hiding the pain in her face, relaxing the lines around her mouth. "Where did you talk? You must have found a quiet place, where no one would bother you, overhear you?"

She looked down at her fingers. Long fingers, soft. Probably used tons of hand lotion. Pinkish nails, polished with dark purple, almost oxblood, tips. A combination I would have thought garish, but the effect was stunning.

"He insisted that we not be seen at the auditorium itself. He met me in the parking lot behind the library, down by the golf course."

"That's a long way to walk from—"

"Oh, we didn't walk. We each drove down to the other end. Jerome got out of his car and into mine. We talked in my back seat."

"Your back seat?"

A slight bit of color rose in her cheeks. "It's not what you think. There's just more room back there, without the console. Anyway, we had the conversation I told you about. It was finally..." moisture appeared in her eyes, "over."

Sadness fell over me, like storm clouds crossing a lake.

"He grabbed my hand in his, squeezed, like he was giving me a last handshake, got out of the car and into his and drove away. That was the last I saw of him."

"And do you ever take your dog in your car?"

"My dog? Funny you mention that. Bosco had a styling appointment just that afternoon, and my van was in the shop so I had to take him in the car and he got hair all over the seat. I only had time to do a quick Dustbuster number on it before the event. Later, I did some real cleaning on it. Why do you ask?"

I shrugged. "Where did Neumann go after your conversation?"

"To meet his wife in the lobby. I remained parked for a couple of minutes after he pulled off. When I arrived back at the front entrance, Michelle was waiting for me." She started fiddling, pulling her purse off the back of the chair, fussing with its contents.

It was time to go. I stood. "Thank you for meeting me. I'm sorry to interrupt your routine."

She smiled. Forced. "It's ok. Anything to help."

Back through the barrel vaulted hallway and into the foyer, I paused and looked back. Julianne was standing up from the table, and smacking her lips like she'd just applied lipstick.

I walked out. As I backed down the driveway, a familiar blue Grand Am turned into the drive. Shirley waved at me as she passed.

As I accelerated onto the street, Avril's *Complicated* sounded.

"Hey, Lover."

I broke out in a grin. "Not yet."

"Soon, Mr. Architect, soon. Listen, I've been called into work. We have to redo a shoot. So don't bother coming back to bed. I won't be here."

"I can't anyway. I have to see Nicole."

"Always another woman with you, isn't it?"

"Uh-huh."

"How about some afternoon company?"

"Ah, wish I could, but I have to get some work done."

"Well, what are you up to, Mr. Architect? Or is it Mr. Detective this afternoon?"

"Just work."

* * *

Something was wrong and I needed figure it out. I made a mental note to ask Nicole how she traveled to the auditorium that night. I pulled into Kerby's Coney on Northwestern, and took my pile of detecting cards with me. I'd have some coffee and eggs, and lay out my index cards like the Tarot.

I set out small piles of suspect cards in front of me, right to left:

Nicole,   Bryce,   Julianne,   Boyd,   Scofield, Molly/Rusty.

The waitress came and I ordered coffee, cheese omelet, wheat toast. I had to have *something* healthy.

On a blank card for each suspect, I wrote that suspect's motive.

Nicole: Angry over cheating husband. $17M

Julianne: Angry over staying with wife. $5M

Bryce: Blackmail? Expose tryst to wife? Neumann tried to have removed from project.

Matt: old grudge

My order came. I fixed my coffee and chowed down while I flipped through each suspect's deck of cards. I took bites of omelet in between rifling through the notes.

There was a persistent prickling at the back of my head. Like a feather brushing against me. I was missing something, a small thing, an idiosyncrasy.

It wasn't until I inked cards from that morning's meeting with Julianne that I realized I forgot to ask her about the will. That would have been awkward, anyway, but I had intended to nonetheless. I placed the new cards in her deck. Think, think, think. I shuffled the order, then took a card from each stack in turn, hoping the juxtaposition of the information would shake something loose.

Whoa. Of course! Why didn't I see this before?

Could it be?

Yes.

I packed up my cards, swallowed the last of my coffee. I would mull over the information in my head on the way to Nicole's.

* * *

Nicole, wearing a dark green paisley dress and pearls, greeted me warmly. She stepped in to hug me. The pressure of her fingertips on my back brought a bead of sweat to my forehead.

"Hello, Ken, would you—"

"Hold that thought," I said.

"But—"

I shook my head to quiet her. "I have a good idea who killed your husband. Here, let's sit on the couch." I took her hand. She squeezed it tightly, and didn't release it when we sat down.

She looked at me with all her attention, tilting her head. The sun caught it and the shimmer made her look even so more beautiful.

"Matt Lance."

"The board member? He never did care for Jerome. Are you sure?"

I nodded. "As sure as I can be. Here's what fits. Matt and your husband had a disagreement on board business."

"That landscape ordinance, yes. But that's just business. Jerome disagreed with lots of folks. That's not much—"

"No, listen. Back in 1987, Matt Lance invested in your husband's business. He invested every penny of his life savings and lost it all. After he was wiped out, he suffered enormous financial difficulties, and his wife left him. Matt became angry. He never forgave Jerome. Later, they had a patent dispute over the design of the destruction equipment. There's the motive."

Nicole slouched back against the couch. Her eyes were light and attentive, but behind her facade I felt exhaustion. She pulled her lowed lip into her mouth and chewed her white teeth against it.

"Matt attended the event with his date Amelia Day. Now she says Matt had irritable bowel syndrome that day and was up and down during the event. Here's what I think happened. First, he called Jerome to arrange a meeting in the office and returned to his seat. Later, he went to meet him. He killed him at the office, then dragged him onto the lawn to cover things up with the sign plunge. He returned to his date, reinforcing the alibi, then excused himself again to topple the sign on top of your husband. He constructed the perfect excuse to do those actions without attracting attention. He had an alibi, he was at the event and people saw him, but he was able to slip out and complete his actions."

Nicole narrowed her eyes. I sensed the underlying anger. "So he was the one who called and lured Jerome to the office?"

"Right, exactly. Then he overpowered your husband, put him in harm's way under the sign, and went up to the roof and finished the job."

She shook her head. "I don't know. How did he do the sign?"

"I'm still working on that. He knows a lot of people

in the construction industry. Matt is friends with Bryce McClurg."

"That son-of-a-bitch!"

"Exactly. Somehow, he devised a way to blow the sign off the roof afterward."

Nicole nodded slowly and put her hand on my arm. "Oh, Ken. I'm so grateful for your help."

I sat forward to change gears. "There's something else I need to talk to you about."

"What is it?"

"I heard you and Jerome didn't arrive to the auditorium event together."

"No, we didn't. Why?"

"I'm trying to trace Jerome's movements. Might be important to fill in some of the details. Can you tell me about it?"

She shrugged. "Not much to tell. My girlfriend Sandy called me and needed a ride. I asked Jerome if we could swing by and pick her up on the way."

"Uh-huh."

"See, he was coming from work to meet me here at home. But once we began talking, it made more sense for me to pick Sandy up and then meet Jerome at the auditorium."

"So that's what you did?"

"Yep."

"What time did you arrive, you and Sandy?"

"Oh, must have been about seven-twenty. We were almost late."

"And Jerome—"

"In the lobby waiting for us. Fuming."

I raised my eyebrows.

"Never did like to be late for anything. He took my arm and we hustled to our seats."

I made a mental note.

"What will you do now?" she said.

"I need to get this information to the police so they can take action on it. But I wanted you to know right away."

"Have a cup of coffee before you go. Oh, well, wait, Shirley is here in the kitchen. Shirley!"

"What?"

"I tried to tell you when you came in, but you—"

I moved quickly into the kitchen. "Shirley!"

Shirley was seated at the kitchen table, gnawing on a scone, half-filled coffee cup in front of her." Oh, hi, Ken. I didn't realize you were here."

Nicole brushed past me into the kitchen. "Oh, Shirley, I'm so glad you decided to have a scone."

"They're delicious," Shirley said, smiling.

I stepped over next to her. "Did you hear our discussion?"

Shirley's eyes were rimmed in long lashes, crisp eyeliner highlighting the pronounced vertical curve of her lids. "I've been sitting here the whole time."

Nicole stared back at me unemotionally. "If by chance, you did hear, Shirley, please keep it to yourself. If this got out, it could affect things, you know."

"I don't know what you're talking about."

I looked to Nicole for help, "Please" I motioned toward Shirley.

"I don't think she heard anything." she said. "Anyway, you can trust her. Shirley came by to check on me, and see how I was doing. Isn't that sweet?"

About as sweet as a white onion on a bed of sauerkraut. "Sure is. Listen, Nicole, I'm gonna run and have that discussion. I'll talk to you later."

She nodded.

"Oh, Ken," Shirley said. "Give me a ride to my car, will you? It's at the far end of the property, on the Westphalia side. I parked over there thinking it was closer, but it isn't."

"Ok, but let's get going."

Shirley rose and said, "Nicole it was nice seeing you. I'm glad you're doing well."

We walked out the front door, and Shirley settled into my car.

As I pulled down the drive she said, "You know, Ken, you have to remember Nicole's husband was killed four days ago. She hasn't even buried him yet."

"What are you talking about?"

"Long hugs, holding hands. What was that about?"

I stopped the car. Hard.

"So you did overhear our conversation?"

She looked at her nails. "You're a bit too friendly to the new widow. You should stop."

"Now you listen here. You ignore our conversation. Let the police handle this. I don't want to read any of this in your blog."

"Ken, Ken." She looked at me directly. "Yes, twenty-four hours. I'll hold on. Then, anything goes."

I shook my head. "No. You can't reveal this. Let the police do their job."

"Instead of you?"

We'd pulled around the block and Shirley got out. "Don't worry about me, Ken. Just worry about that widow."

She sauntered to her car, put her hands up behind her head, and adjusted her scarf tight around her head.

I slid down the driveway, downshifted and blew out of there.

* * *

A couple of blocks later I pulled over and dialed Officer Tallman.

"Hey, Cannoli, long time no hear from."

"Yeah, yeah. Hey listen, I have something for you."

"What chu got? Anthrax?"

"Listen, I know who killed Jerome Neumann. I need

you to get on this."

"Whoa, back off. We act on our own. But I'd love to hear your theory. I'm listening."

I explained how Matt Lance called Neumann to the office, killed him, dragged him to the spot on the grass—

"Wait. Isn't Matt Lance about seventy years old?"

"Yeah, yeah, but he's in great shape. He's one of the fittest seventy year olds I've seen. And don't forget Neumann was a little guy. Five-six, skinny. I bet he couldn't have weighed more than one-twenty."

"So, suppose he drags him to the spot. What then?"

"Then Matt runs up to the roof, and blows the sign off the roof, onto Neumann."

I explained about the pneumatic destruction equipment, and the ease of set up and tear down.

"And you think this guy could do it?"

"Absolutely."

"Well, it's an interesting theory, Cannoli."

I smiled. Of course it was "interesting"; he wished he would have thought of it.

"Only two problems. One, Neumann was alive when the sign crushed him."

"Alive? But he was dragged—"

"Uh-huh. I didn't say that part was wrong. Probably knocked out, then dragged to the location. Not far, maybe ten or twenty feet. Not the hundred and twenty feet from the office door."

"Hum. Maybe—"

"Nope, wrong. Matt Lance has an alibi. He was at the poetry reading."

"That alibi has more holes in it than a Swiss cheese sandwich."

"Yeah, the diarrhea, right, I know. But at the moment the sign came down. When all the noise was made, he was sitting right next to his date, miss....wait, it's here somewhere...like that flyer."

"Amelia Day."

"Right, that's it."

"And you believe the pair of them? I think he made up the digestive issues to cover his tracks."

"Maybe so, Cannoli, but I got three witnesses that put Matt Lance in the auditorium when the sign pulls off the roof and onto a living Neumann."

I hung up the phone. What did this mean? I needed to look at my cards again. What I was thinking, playing detective. Sounded like Tallman had the same pieces I did, only they made sense.

Crap.

My phone rang. My heart sank. "Sue Watts! How nice to hear from you!"

"Cut it, Ken. What was the one thing I told you not to do on this matter?"

"Didn't you get my report?"

"That's not what I'm talking about. The one thing I told you *not* to do?"

"Uh—"

"Press, Ken. No press. No words, no information, no nothing. Now I have it on good authority that you orchestrated your girlfriend appearing on your sister's radio show, talking about the so-called murder?"

"Well, I—"

"You what? Decided to take the investigation of this case into your own hands? And another thing. There's information all over the Internet from this woman, this investigative reporter Shirley Hanson. I understand she's a friend of yours, and—"

That was a rumor I was happy to dispel. "No, she's not a friend at all."

"Well, that makes it better, doesn't it? She's not a friend. Just someone you share information with that gets into the public arena."

"No, you don't understand."

"There is one of us who doesn't understand, and it's not me. Listen, you'd better put a silencer on all this, or it's going to hurt your firm." She hung up.

I couldn't do this. I wasn't equipped to be a detective. What was I thinking? Whose lives were at stake? Didn't I have enough to do for work, my livelihood? Was I so overwhelmed with feelings for Nicole that I let my good common sense go to waste? I needed to stop this. I would gather all the information I had collected—all my index cards—and drop them at the police station. Get them off my desk and to theirs. Nicole would have to understand. After all, I was wrong about Matt just now. I was about to—had in fact—indicted him. I exhaled. I needed to get to Sargent Gilmore.

I couldn't tell Nicole, let her down. Maybe tomorrow. Maybe the cops would have a lead, someone to look at. Damn. I hated to give up, but I wasn't doing this very well, and there were things I was good at that needed tending to.

But no. I couldn't surrender my detective notes. Not just yet. I had some pieces here. Maybe if I went over the cards one more time. Later today. I'd have to make time. There was something there, I just knew it.

The road was crowded, but I made it back to the office for the ten o'clock meeting with Wally to prepare for the Val's Market presentation. Steve was in the office reviewing projects. Wally and I hogged the small conference room and hashed out our delivery. Our ideas on the pacing of a presentation and method of nailing major points were as different as greyhounds and Greyhound buses. But we worked though it.

When we finished, I sought a diversion for lunch. Steve was released from his meetings about the same time, and we snagged Edison to head out for coneys.

Edison looked at me and said, "What's got your goat? Something wrong?"

I couldn't tell him. Not yet. "Everything's ok. Let's eat. I need a volume lunch today."

"Works for me," Edison said.

Steve agreed.

We exited the rear door of the building and hoofed it to my Taurus. We were silent through the short ride to Ray's Coney, arriving moments before noon with a handful of people waiting to be seated before us. The interior was run down, with makeshift decor. They used plywood panels—varnished and glossy—for tabletops when the old one went kaput. My phone rang the standard bell.

"Hey, guys, I have to take this. Grab a table and I'll be right there." I blew out the back door as I answered the line. "Hello?"

"Ken Knoll? Hi; this is Molly Gross. I want to talk to you."

"Oh, Molly, hi. I need to speak with you as well."

"As soon as possible. This afternoon?" She made it a question.

Fine with me. "Shall I come back up to your place? How about four o'clock?"

"Um, can you make it a bit earlier? I'd like to talk alone, and Rusty may come by later."

We settled on three-thirty.

I returned to the coney and found the guys huddled around a square table on the cruiser side, underneath a large aerial photograph of the Woodward Cruise taken from the intersection at 13 Mile Road.

"Ken, always dealing with the ladies," Steve said.

"Well, she was female, but it was business," I said.

Knowing smiles passed between them.

A waiter appeared and we ordered our coneys, fries and Cokes.

"Hey did you guys see Shirley's blog today?" I asked.

Steve jumped in. "What was that piece about Molly Gross changing her phrase?"

"She's not right in her head," Edison said. "I told Ken a while back. She has this image, and it's phoney baloney. Which is really sad because her whole thing is honesty."

"I don't know, Edison," I said. "I interviewed her yesterday, and the vibe I get is true, but she's like she's on another planet. She's calibrated in Metric when the rest of us are Imperial."

"The whole thing bugs me," Steve said. "I read her first book, and I understand the whole thing—be completely honest in everything you do and it will all work out; work to your benefit. I respect that. But to change now to *personal* honesty, it's like she's hedging. It's political."

Grunts around the table.

"What's the deal with Rusty, though?" I said. "He's supposed to be her agent, but there's something incestuous about their relationship."

Steve spoke, "What?"

"You should see how he protects her, like...like they're family."

Our food appeared and we dug in.

"Well," Edison said, his mouth still stuffed with coney hot dog. "You read Shirley's piece. He worked for her grandfather early in his career. So he has some...emotional stake in her wellbeing. Also, I did some research last night on the Internet and I think maybe there's more to this Rusty character than what it appears to be."

"What did you find out?"

"I found this article. It alluded to Fitzgerald's last days, and the people around him, including this war hero with one leg—they didn't mention him by name—but they said somehow he was always by Fitz's side."

"And you think this war hero is Rusty?" I said.

"Hummm," Edison said, sliding a fry into his mouth.

"What about this other piece?" Steve said. "About Julianne inheriting five million dollars. She's really got her sources, doesn't she?"

"She's full of herself," I said.

"Who?" Steve said.

"Shirley. When I expose the murderer, that will shut her up! She is so obnoxious, I can't stand that woman. And she appears everywhere I go. Like she's got me on Lojack or something. It's not natural."

Edison laughed. "What is natural, is I think someone's got a crush here."

I looked at Edison. "What? Me? I told you, I can't stand that woman. Seriously, I'm gonna find this murderer and put her in her place. Not to mention quiet Robert and Sue Watts down."

Steve and Edison hushed.

Steve's phone buzzed. He looked down at the display and picked it up.

"Yeah. Oh, hi, Jenny. Locked down? Right. Yeah, I understand. But can you give me the highlights? ...No....Right...Wow, great. Yeah, thanks. I owe you."

Edison and I looked at him.

"MTC. They put out the preliminary report to the cops, but they wanted the info kept on the QT. We should have it in a couple of days when they say it's ok to release."

Huh.

"But," Steve said, "She gave me a teaser. The bottom horizontals have stress bends every five feet or so."

"Stress bends?" I said.

"Yeah, like they were acted on by some force, a big

weight. Crushed. A point load."

"Five feet apart? Like where the signs were connected?"

"No," Steve said. "These are in addition to the dead load of the letters, and much heavier. But here's the punch line: the stress load was caused, in-between supports, and from the bottom *up*."

Chapter 29

The new information cast a black pallor, a fog in my head. *From the bottom up.* Perhaps I had the scenario correct, but not the person. I was anxious to find out if Matt Lance had orchestrated the murder.

We finished our lunch and I dropped the guys off back at the office.

"I'm going to make a few calls and see people," I said. "Later."

Ironically, it was Matt who had given me the information on an outlet locally that carried the pneumatic destruction equipment.

Chet's Dozers was downriver, in Southgate, and this time of day the drive would take me about forty minutes. I cut east on 12 Mile Road to Southfield Road, went south until it became a freeway. From there it was clear sailing. I eyed the business sign a few blocks after Southfield freeway became a surface road again. I pulled into a deteriorating asphalt lot abutting the dumpy storefront of a metal building. Black paint peeled from the steel entry door.

I entered the warehouse and paused until my eyes adjusted to the dim light. The gabled structure was wide open up to the roof deck. The front desk and plastic laminate counter was about two decades old, which would put the old geezer behind the counter in his prime about then. Somehow, the guy's appearance— potato nose, broken blood vessels—gave me confidence in his construction knowledge. As far as I could tell, he and I were alone up front. A banging of metal on metal, coming from the back, echoed throughout the building.

I offered my card. "Ken Knoll; I'm an architect with BPW Architects. I wonder if you could give me some information about your destruction equipment."

"Hey, Ken. Glad to be of service. Tom Kiah. Hmm, destruction. What kind of demolition you got going on?"

"Well, I'm looking for something that would be gentle with my existing building. Something I can slip in like the jaws of life and rip things to shreds."

He smiled. "Ah, you're another one, right? Love to see stuff blown apart?"

"You got my number. Nothing I like more than seeing things taken apart and smashed to smithereens. The faster the better."

"I knew it. I can show you around back, which would be best."

He took me out a side door. We crunched across the gravel. The space was packed wall-to-wall with yellow and blue steel munching equipment. "Here you got your back hoes, your front end loaders. I got those in 10 yard and 20 yards pieces. Your hydraulic pincher and pulverizers, mechanical shears and pulverizers."

The hydraulic pinchers looked like giant dinosaur jaws.

"Now over here," he paused while we walked to the other side of the yard. "We got concrete processors, and your robotic hammers."

"This is all mighty impressive Tom, but I need a gentle touch."

He squinted at me. "You ever see the front end loader in the hands of a professional?"

"Well, the stuff I need moved is on a roof. I can't get that piece of equipment up there."

He scoffed. "Shit, why didn't you tell me? What you want is the air carrier. That's what I call it. Newest thing on the block. This baby will take you places. Let's go back inside."

He showed me these bags that looked like giant deflated medicine balls. "These puppies will do you." He described the action.

"Hey, I think I heard about these from a friend," I said. "A businessman; he's in the car parts business. Matt Lance."

"Matt, yeah, he designed this stuff. Figured it out while he was messing with car parts. Stumbled into it, you know."

"Does Matt use your equipment too, or does he have his own stash?"

"I don't know what he has, probably just some test equipment, beta models things like that. Working on improvements. Me, I haven't seen him in months."

"Who are your clients?" He cocked his head at me. "I mean who rents this equipment? Contractors and homeowners?"

"Mostly demolition contractors. McCarthy out of Wixom. Lunstrum out of Lansing."

"Oh, so you get business from a long way off."

"Yes, this has been a real boon to the business. There are others, too, last week we got a civilian, a girl. Shows you what the product can do."

My heart did a little dance. "Girl? Can I get a name?"

"Those records are locked up. I can't get to them."

"Hold on a minute, I'll be right back." On a hunch, I went out to the car and pulled the *Full Moon Meter* brochure out of my briefcase. I went back inside and showed him the picture on the back.

"Yes, that's her."

I noticed the yellow sticky note on the brochure, "See you there." The fan note the poet had penned to Nicole.

Chapter 30

Not Matt, but Molly rented the equipment? But she was on stage. Did she rent the equipment for a different reason? Or did she rent the equipment and someone else—her trusted associate Rusty—felled the sign? Rusty, who had left his seat at intermission and not returned at the time the sign tumbled?

I drove to work. I had an hour before leaving to meet Molly. I walked right to my office, checked email, wrote replies, and then consulted with Edison about the next day's presentation to Val's Market.

"No sweat, watch this," Edison said. He pulled up the power point and led me through the demonstration.

Slick. "Nice work, Edison. That should sell the piece."

"Speaking of which," Edison said, "What about Kristen? Have you given up yet?"

"Edison." I shook my head. "We're supposed to meet for dinner tonight. I still can't believe this is happening."

Wally walked in just then.

"All what is happening?"

"Me, Kristy Blume. It's like I'm in a dream."

"Cannoli," Wally said, "Watch your back. You don't know who you can trust. Don't let Robert get too close. He'll steal her away from you like he did Gwen."

I gave Wally a scowl and Edison said, "Kristy could be playing you."

"For what? You guys! Just because I've had a bad track record with women doesn't mean something good can't happen."

"Track record?" Wally said. "Bad judge of character is more like it."

"Enough. Wally, are you ready for tomorrow?"

"Yeah, yeah. Edison finished the graphics. We can do a run-through in the morning."

"Good." I said. "I gotta hustle."

Just as I was zipping up my briefcase, ready to make tracks, Sally came over the PA and announced I had a call. I picked up the line next to Edison's desk. It was Walter Gruen—owner of the shopping centers that Val's Market was hoping to become part of—asking us to include a couple items in our presentation: our demolition approach and maintaining their integrity of the existing buildings. These were items we had discussed in developing our proposal, but not explicitly covered in the presentation.

I tasked Edison, "Hey, buddy. You think you can add this to the presentation?"

He scrunched his nose. "Crap. That means re-doing slides 37 through 45."

"And?"

"Yeah, it's doable. I just wish they would have told us before."

You and me both, Edison. "Thanks. Knew you could handle it."

I hustled out, got in the car and pointed the Taurus toward Molly's residence. Reviewing my mental file, I selected a few high points to discuss, then zeroed in on what I really wanted to know.

A few minutes late, I hustled up the sidewalk, admiring the blooming red roses. Knocked.

The door opened and Molly stood before me, long hair loose over her bare shoulders, white tank top hanging to her thighs, purple bra strap showing. Her eyes, though devoid of make-up, were bright and alive, in contrast to the dull peepers I had seen the day before.

"Hello Mr. Knoll. I'm glad you came."

"Please, call me Ken. You make me feel like an old man."

"I can't make you *feel* anything. You do that on your own. But I will honor your request, Ken. You can sit on the couch or a chair if you like."

I moved through the room and made myself comfortable on the sofa.

"Are you thirsty? I can offer you a soda or a glass of water."

"No, thank you." I found myself watching the precision of my words, trying to match her passion for truth. "You're alone?"

"There's no one else present here now."

"When you called earlier, you expressed the desire to meet with me. Is there something you wish to talk about now?"

She shook her head. "You also mentioned the request to speak with me. I'd prefer to answer your questions first. Then there may not be a need for me to express what I had in mind."

"Ok, I'll be blunt, Molly, since that's apparently what you prefer."

An edge of a smile.

"Back in February when the construction of the auditorium began, there were a series of protests. Groups that opposed the tearing down of the Fitzgerald Reading Room picketed the project. Mothers for Historic Preservation and fans of architect Arne T. Fehn protested peacefully. But the group Talbot X apparently was behind damaging the contractor's equipment and job trailer. Do you know these protesters?"

"They wanted to stop the project."

"Do you know them personally? Were you involved in engaging the protesters? Organizing them?"

"Everyone speaks and acts from their own heart, Ken. Did I guide a channel for people to express the displeasure with the project? Yes. Did I pay anyone, no."

"No, I'm not suggesting you paid anyone to protest, but you were responsible for organizing and inciting?"

"I would not use the word inciting, I—"

"Removed."

"I provided a meeting place, where others who shared my passion for the Fitzgerald Reading Room could convene and talk about steps of action."

Pursuing this farther wouldn't get me any more information so I changed the subject.

"It came to my attention that a year and a half ago you stopped using the phrase 'extreme' in reference to your stand on honesty, and replaced it instead with the word 'personal'. Why?"

"You asked me about my philosophy the last time you were here."

"Would you mind answering my question?"

"Yes, I would. I'm irritated by reviewing the same information multiple times. It bothers me that you can't understand it the first time."

"Oh."

"The point of my work is to be true to yourself and your family and friends. Your personal relationships will benefit from a complete exchange of feelings. The same does not hold true in dealing with corporate or governmental entities. Your relationship with the United States government, for example, will not improve by being honest. On the contrary, it may— depending on circumstances—deteriorate. The focus of my books and talks is interpersonal relationships."

"I see."

"Do you? The point being, improved relationships through complete exchange of feelings. Not absolute baring of facts to government, police. There's a liability factor there I had previously missed. My work has to do with improving relationships, not disclosing illegal actions. The goal is to remove the barriers that incapacitate our ability to act honestly. Do you understand the significance?"

"I think I do, Molly. When you joined the board, was it to oppose this project? You never revealed your relationship to Jazz Fitzgerald."

She smiled. "I sought service on the board because public service is an honorable profession, and I aspired to lend my sensibilities to the community. To my good fortune, Mayor Sternberg agreed when she appointed me. The auditorium project was not envisioned."

"But you held back the information about your relationship with your grandfather. It was a conflict of interest and should have been noted."

"Should? When something is in the public interest, it needs to be done, regardless of personal preferences." She studied my face. "How are your relationships, Ken?"

"How are they?"

"Describe them to me."

"Well, I don't know, I..."

"Do you tell the truth?"

"Well, of course."

"The truth that's in your gut? Your true feelings? Without reservation? Do you tell the other person when they anger you, when they sadden you? Do you express your feelings of admiration or expectation or love when they enter your mind?"

"I don't know, I haven't thought about that."

"Think about it, and do it, Ken. It may save you. Now, what other questions do you have for me?"

I studied her face. "I was at a place called Chet's Dozers this afternoon. They rent equipment for demolition of property. The man there recognized your photo and told me you rented some pneumatic destruction equipment last week."

Molly sat back in her chair. "Yes." She hung her head and stared at the back of her hands. "Yesterday I listened to Ella Polaris's radio show, and heard her guest—an actress—mention that you were investigating the death and had learned that the sign supports had been unbolted. I realized it was only a matter of time before someone questioned me. I feel regret that the man died. I have sadness. Fear, for the loss his wife must be feeling."

"So you admit to destroying the sign, making it plunge from the roof?"

She nodded.

"But you were on stage."

"I had an assistant, who shall remain nameless. I'll tell you, but I ask you not to inform the police. I cannot console myself about the man's death, but I won't impugn another. I planned the detachment and falling of the sign. On an unused side of the building, during a public event. That man's name! On my dear grandfather's building! My goal was to remove the sign, not commit murder. I had help, but I won't implicate anyone."

"Your partner, did he see anyone?"

"No, he says he didn't. No, no one uses that side of the building."

"Did anyone know you were doing this?"

"Just my partner."

"You never told anyone, not any of the other protesters, no one to gloat about this? Members of Talbot X?"

She shook her head.

"Plunging the sign is a big deal. It must have taken a lot of planning."

"Yes, planning, checking and re-checking. Arrangements."

"You must have been proud. Most people can't keep something like that inside. Maybe you told someone, casually."

Something flashed across her eyes. An idea, a thought. "That person," I said. "Who just crossed your mind?"

"Well, there is someone," she said slowly. "But I don't know if it matters."

"Who, Molly? Who did you tell?"

She giggled and put her hand over her mouth. "This is so unlike me." She sat back against the couch, composing herself. "I met a man. Handsome, chivalrous. I met him at a book signing. He was so...frank. Well. Forthright. Told me he found me attractive. Went right out and told me he wanted to sleep with me."

I watched her eyes liven as she remembered.

"You know, I found that honesty refreshing. He even told me he was married, but it didn't matter to him."

"Uh-huh."

"It only lasted two days. We were intimate, in spirit first. You know, we told each other everything. Do you know how rare that is? The physical and emotional intimacy came next. I was enthralled. That's the kind of relationship I'm referring to, the kind we all can have, if we just open up to each other and tell the truth. Personal honesty."

"Who was this, Molly, who did you tell?"

"In a weird twist of fate, he is one of the contractors on the auditorium project. That's why I particularly thought it was relevant for him. He knew the roof, could relate to the details I shared. His name is Bryce McClurg."

Chapter 31

I punched Kristy's number and waited while the ringer cycled through and went to voice mail.

It's me. You know what to do.

I disconnected and punched up Bryce's number. He answered on the second ring.

"Hey Bryce, I have some more questions. Can we talk tonight?"

"No can do. I'm booked today. How about in the morning?"

It was only four-thirty, and I hoped he could spare a few minutes, wedged in between work phone calls, but I didn't want to push him too hard. "That's fine. Breakfast?"

"Sure. I'll be doing some patching on the auditorium roof tomorrow. Why don't you meet me at the Kerby's around the corner? Say, six am?"

A feeling gnawed at me. I really needed answers from him tonight. As in *right now*. But I agreed.

Worries nagged at me, too, that Shirley would broadcast my suspicions about Matt's guilt to the world in tomorrow morning's blog. She had to be cautioned. Firmly.

But first, I was compelled to see Nicole and fill her in. So many fronts needed tending to, I felt like a five-wok chef.

Once in the Taurus I tried Kristy again. No answer.

I made good time and pulled up to the dry fountain in front of Nicole's otherwise charming estate. Today's visit would tend toward the social call side, leaving out the detecting information. Building bridges was a constant activity. Plus, I was not ready yet to share what I'd learned from Molly.

The sun was lowering itself in the sky. As I walked by, I noticed motion in the bottom of the fountain. Barely able to move, a baby bird wobbled to one side, then the other. How did it get in there? The walk was swept and free of debris. Shrubs were trimmed and beds clean. No loose pieces of anything I could use. I strode back to the car and looked through my briefcase. Ha! A file folder. I slid the contents onto the seat and walked back to the fountain. The bird looked up at me. Silently, I slipped the folder in front of the bird. "Come on, get on." I said. Magically, the bird wobbled forward, onto the flat stock. With both hands to steady the flimsy cardboard, I picked it up. Holding it in front of me, I walked carefully to the edge of the flower bed and bent down, laying the folder flat on the ground. I stepped back and watched as the bird hobbled forward, into the green.

"Nice job." I turned to see Nicole watching from the doorway. She greeted me warmly, her Kimono-like red dress slipping against me with the electricity of her hug.

"I baked some cookies, still warm," she said. "Chocolate chip. Half with and half without. I wasn't sure what kind you prefer."

I didn't understand until she added "Nuts."

"Nuts, definitely nuts." She had tea ready in the dining room, in a lumbering ceramic pot decorated in pink baby roses. We took cookies on matching plates. "How are you holding up, Nicole?"

"I'll be better when the next few days are behind me. I can't believe he's gone. My mornings are empty without his wit, his patience. Thoughts and notions are poking at me, sleeping in fits and starts. And the thoughts about the act that took him down. Dear, dear man." She breathed heavily. "I don't know." She used her palms to smooth the table cloth, then squared her shoulders. "Did you talk to the police? The news didn't mention them arresting Matt Lance."

"Um, yes, I spoke to my contact at the police department this morning. Gave him all my information." Her eyes questioned mine. "I'm sure they're just checking all the facts and preparing their case."

"But you said—. I need to get this over with."

"Believe me, Nicole, I want this closed as much as you do."

Her arms were stretched out on the table, her fists balled. "Can't you follow up with them? What more information do they need? What if he gets away? Don't you see—"

"Listen, Nicole. Relax." I put my hand over hers. "They have it now."

"You listen. I've got—"

The house phone rang. I was glad for the interruption. She sighed, raised herself out of her chair and did a little shuffle to the phone, which hung from the kitchen wall.

"Yes, yes...."

As she listened, I saw her face turn quiet, then stiff, her eyes losing their focus. She said "Ok" almost inaudibly and hung up the receiver. She remained still, arms limp and tears welling up in her eyes.

I got up from my seat. "Nicole?"

"Oh, Ken." She put her arms around me and fell apart like a stack of Dominoes. I shifted to one side, put my arm around her, helped her into the living room. I set her down onto the sofa, where she began to cry.

"I'm so... this is...I can't..." She sobbed in heavy spurts, her breathing erratic.

"Shhh," I said. "Shhh."

I held her, rocking gently for several minutes. Gradually her breathing slowed to normal.

"It was the County. They're releasing...him."

"Oh, Nicole."

Shortly, I was able to decipher that the Oakland County Medical Examiner was releasing the body to the funeral home. At Nicole's request, I placed a call to the funeral director, who would send his crew to pick up Neumann yet that evening.

After arranging the business of death, Nicole calmed and I realized it was getting to be evening time. I needed to make my way out of there.

"Do you have help with all of this? Is your mother...?"

"She's keeping the kids occupied. I think that's best for them right now, though they have so many questions. Oh, and I didn't tell you. Dani's trip was delayed. She'll be here tomorrow from New York with her husband. I can't wait to see her. Lord knows I can use her support now."

I had no idea what seeing my old girlfriend, and her husband, would do for my mood.

* * *

As I was pulling out of the cobbled driveway, my phone rang. *Complicated.*

"Hey, Kristy."

"Hi Ken. I saw you phoned a couple of times. I was tied up this afternoon." Her voice was flat as a stale beer. "Meet for dinner?"

"Nothing I'd like better. Maybe in Southfield? Have an appetite for anything special?"

"Casual. I don't feel like getting dressed up." Her voice was limp too, as if it had lost its spring.

"Are you ok?"

"Fine. How about Greek? There's a Little Daddy's at Twelve and Telegraph."

We agreed to meet at eight-thirty.

I pointed my car toward Shirley's borrowed apartment. It was important to reiterate the importance of keeping quiet about Matt. I hoped Amanda would not be there. To avoid the possibility of Shirley's excuses, I didn't call ahead. Like a panther sneaking up on an unsuspecting prey, I wanted to catch her off guard.

Waiting outside a few minutes until someone approached the vestibule, I pretended to fumble for my key. A man in a suit held the door for me. We entered the elevator together and I waited for him to push five before I hit the button myself. Luckily, he was not a talker. I held my tongue until he exited and I reached my floor. I found Amanda's apartment and knocked. Twice. The door cracked open, Shirley's broad smile shining out at me.

"Ken, what a surprise."

"Hi, Shirley, I only have a few minutes but, eh, can I come in?"

"Sure." She stood back and I walked through the entry hall into the living room. I took in the panoramic view through the windows, pink sunset settling down on the city, painting the roadways with glistening life.

Shirley circled me and said, "Have a seat, they're free."

"No, I can't stay. I just wanted to make myself clear about this morning. Please don't put anything in your blog about Matt Lance. The information you overheard could be detrimental if it got out in public and—"

"You think I'm a moron? I'll hold the lid on it today. We'll see tomorrow."

I studied the sunset. When my glance returned to the room, I spotted it. A cigarette lighter on the coffee table, a familiar lighter. Shirley didn't smoke. Where had I laid eyes on it? Jack Daniels logo in brass, with raised letters. Suddenly, I became aware of a musky smell, a man's cologne. A man was in the other room.

"I...all right, then. I'm going to trust you."

"You don't have much choice, do you? Why don't you come back when you have a little time?" She grinned at me. "Meanwhile, here's a freebie. While he was in college, Rusty Wagner dated Molly's mom; Ralph 'Jazz' Fitzgerald's daughter. She broke it off after three years without promise of a ring. Now, I think he has a thing on for Molly."

As I left the building my eyes fell upon a Prime Roofing truck. Bryce McClurg. Of course, his lighter. What was he doing at Shirley's apartment? And why had she made him hide? I thought back to Sunday dinner, meeting Julianne at the restaurant when I ran into Shirley and Bryce. Was there something going on between the two of them? Bryce seemed to play fast and loose with the opposite gender. Did Shirley know he was married?

Back in the Taurus, my thoughts turned to Kristy. A twinge of dread struck me, like suddenly wondering if I turned the oven off as I'm at the airport heading out of town.

Guiding the Taurus off Northwestern into the parking lot, a waning moon hung low in the sky, tattered clouds shrouding half its face.

Once through the vestibule doors, my eyes scanned the room. I spotted her and a lump formed in my throat. She sat, staring at the tabletop. Her fingers grasped the menu, curling the corner, like a smoker trying to quit.

I strode over and tried to liven things up. "Hey, Kristy. Wonderful to see you."

"Hi, Ken." She didn't smile.

"What looks good? I haven't been here for a while, but as I recall the shish kabob was delicious. How about you?"

"I'm not very hungry."

"How about a chicken gyro? I remember that's one of your downfalls."

"Where'd you read that? Some fan magazine?"

"Kristy, what's wrong?"

"Nothing. Maybe I should eat."

The waitress came and we ordered Greek salads and Cokes.

"How was work? Did you shoot out at the lake today?"

"Why? What's so interesting about the lake?"

"Not the lake, Kristy, you. You interest me."

She swallowed hard, and brought her eyes up to meet mine. "I have to tell you something."

There was something dead in her eyes. They wouldn't hold mine. I straightened my napkin, rearranged my fork. Lifted my eyes back up at her. Those sweet blue eyes seemed so fragile in that moment. "Really? I thought it was Shirley you had to tell."

Her eyes stabbed out at me. "How long have you known?"

"Just now. I had a suspicion, but I didn't want to believe it."

Neither of us spoke for several minutes, then Kristy broke the silence. "I started this on a lark. I was there, in Amanda's apartment with Shirley, that first night. After you hung up on her, she asked me to meet you at the scene, and ask you some questions, find out what was going on. I thought it would be fun, you know, going undercover, doing a little spy gig. Then you invited me to dinner at Emerald's. Well—"

"So it was my fault."

"No, no. That's not what I'm saying. Shirley, when I told her about our dinner, her little wheels spun and she asked me if I'd meet you some more, and keep her updated on how your investigation was going. I have a lot of respect for Shirley—"

"You do?"

"Well, yes. She exposes some really bad things. Out in California—"

We paused as the waitress returned with our food, then I said, "This isn't California."

"No, no. Listen, you're a great guy, a normal guy with high morals. I could really fall—"

"Please. Stop. Well, that explains why you didn't want to..."

"Yeah, well, actually at that point I was confused. You were different than I expected, unlike what Shirley told me. I thought I could go through with the charade, play it like a game, but then I was starting to fall for you and didn't want to begin that under false assumptions."

I stared at my plate.

"Maybe I should go." She threw her napkin on the plate, pushed back her chair and got up. She moved away from the table.

I watched her walk away, thought of her smile. This was a girl I could really be with. Not because she's an actress, but because she's a really good person.

Shirley, that bitch! Sending in this spy? Following my every move. Was there any level of mistrust, any devious deed that was not in her arsenal?

I drove home.

My legs faltered as I pulled myself into the booth in the kitchen and tossed the cards on the table. My thoughts returned to Kristen. Our rapport seemed so full, like finding a new friend. It felt really good. Never mind the actress thing. We worked well together. We were 'on the same page.'

But were we really? How much of it had been real?

Damn that Shirley! Who did she think she was? So much of her professional life was devoted to exposing cheaters, liars and thieves; shining her high and mighty light on unscrupulous people who use sex to get the things they're after. She'd gone overboard, sending Kristen in to aid her. Still, despite her methods, I always credited Shirley with morals higher than the norm. I mean, she was about exposing bad actions, not doing them. I wondered if she knew about Bryce. She couldn't possibly, otherwise she wouldn't be with him. Shirley wouldn't knowingly commit adultery.

But how could she *not* know?

The cards ran through my hands; suspects flipping through from beginning to end. Again. My mind was unfocused. My thoughts and heart were with Kristen, with our shared time, and with her generous heart. How could this not be real?

I stormed into the bedroom and threw myself into bed. Of course, it had been hopeless from the beginning. My eyes stabbed at the darkness. My body twitched this way and that, seeking a comfortable spot. There wasn't one.

There wouldn't be one for a long time.

Chapter 32

Thursday morning I checked my phone. Nothing.

Shirley's blog contained the following nugget:

Comrades, buddies! What do Nicole Neumann and poet Molly Gross have in common? Aside from Nicole's husband being murdered while Molly was on stage at the auditorium that bore his name...The two of them were on Cranbrook's "Serious Moonlight" committee together. Coincidence?

My arms and legs were heavy as lead as I showered and prepared to hit the road and high tail it to the coney to meet Bryce. I had more than a question or two.

At the car, I hoped for a note, a word, something—anything—from Kristen. Nothing. I backed out of the drive. Perhaps she was gone for good.

Powering along I-696, I took the Evergreen exit, turning south toward 10 Mile. When I passed Shirley's building, my eyes wandered to the parking lot. His truck was still there. Damn.

The coney was packed. Once a month they hosted a meeting of a geocaching group that filled every available parking space. I had to park in the empty lot next door, where an old pet store had been torn down. The resulting vacant lot was part old foundations and crumbled asphalt, but predominantly overgrown weeds. Luckily it hadn't rained in the last two days and the ground was dry. Unluckily, the area boasted no parking lot lights.

Once inside, I found a booth and situated myself with an eye on the door. Ordered coffee. It was six-oh-five.

Bryce arrived ten minutes later, apologizing for his tardiness. I struggled to keep it together; I wanted to blurt it all out without reservation. *How could you do that to Shirley? Do you get off on seducing unsuspecting women? How can you do that to your wife?*

"Thanks for meeting me. A few questions have come up."

"Yeah, yeah. No problem. I was in the area anyway."

Right, slime ball. "I know you saw Shirley last night." He looked up at the mention of her name. I couldn't contain myself. "Keep your mouth shut. Just listen. Don't hurt her, ok? She obviously doesn't know you're married, and would have a fit if she found out. It's not fair to take advantage of her like that."

"Sorry, buddy, I didn't know you cared about her." He drew a breath. "But she's a big girl and can decide for herself what, or who, she wants."

I studied his mussed-up hair. Less than an hour earlier he had rolled out of her bed. "You're not listening. It's not about me. It's about her. She makes a business out of exposing people who cheat and lie. Adulterers. She can't be made out to be one herself. Just step away."

He held his eyes on me for a moment, then he slammed his palms on the table and got up.

"Hold on," I said. "Tell me about Molly Gross."

"That's over. Shit, Cannoli, why the sudden interest in all my relationships? Gonna tell me who I can and can't sleep with?" He began walking.

"It isn't about that," I said. *But thank you for confirming it.* "Molly told you about her plans to blow the sign."

That stopped him. "What?"

"She told you about the plan to take the sign down." I waited.

Bryce took a few steps back toward me. "Is this some kind of trick? Cannoli you're trying me."

"No trick. Molly told me about your, uh, relationship. I want to know what you did with that information."

He lowered himself back into the booth, scoffed. "Yes, Molly told me she was going to blow the sign. I didn't think she'd go through with it. A quirky little story. She sure boasted about it—it lit her up like sparklers on the 4th of July."

"Do you know how it went down? What happened that night? Molly swears she didn't know Neumann would be underneath the sign at the time."

"I don't know who killed Neumann."

I considered the butter melting on my toast. "Who did you tell about Molly's plan?"

"Tell? I didn't tell anyone. I just thought it was funny."

"She engineered this crazy scheme. Molly is one-of-a-kind, a little unstable woman, always interesting. You were close to her, probably know a little more about her idiosyncrasies than most folks. You find out she's preparing to drop a three foot tall sign off a rooftop; you thought it was comical and you didn't tell anyone?"

"Wait. Maybe I told Matt." He looked up, as if considering the condition of the ceiling tile. "Yes, I did. We were coming out of a Toastmasters' meeting at the Community House and stopped a couple blocks over for coffee. We shot the breeze—little stuff like the new Denzel Washington movie, and the best chili recipe. I let loose with that little nugget. He thought it was hilarious."

Chapter 33

I thanked Bryce, curtly, for the information and walked out. I dialed Matt's cell phone. No answer. I felt the noose tightening. It was almost time, however, to meet with Wally about Gaylord back at the office.

My phone went off. Robert.

"There's been another accident. Matt Lance is dead."

"What? I just talked to him last night."

"That was then, this is now. What the hell is going on, Cannoli? Sue Watts is gonna kill me! Get over there, will you?"

"Right away. Where am I going?"

"Southfield's new office building project. The railing gave way. Seven floors. Broke his neck. Can't you guys get anything right?"

"There wasn't anything wrong with that railing, Robert. We were just there yesterday."

"I don't care. Get there now."

I crossed the lot to my car, stepping to avoid the weeds. I clicked on my seatbelt, put the key in the ignition and turned. A flash of heat across my face, my head snapped back, my shoulders pressed into the seat. Smoke stung my eyes. Slo-mo. Thursday. My hands— worked. My chest—ok. Seatbelt tight around my lap. Cold air blew in from the open passenger door. I needed to close the window...the door...Where was the damn door? My eyes scratched. Crap.

I undid my seatbelt. Walked around the car. There. In the weeds. My car door. Glass shattered. I looked at the side of the car. Along the front panel, where the hinges used to be, there were brown burnt spots. I leaned in. The passenger seat was singed.

Damn. I called Tallman. Two people in the Kerby's lot looked over at me.

"Cannoli, you must have heard we got a fresh one."

"Yeah, I did, actually. But someone just blew the door off my car."

"Where are you?"

"In the Kerby's parking lot, at Northwestern and Evergreen. Well, next door in the lot. I'm leaving the car. I'm gonna hoof it over to the scene."

"Hold on. You need to stay with the evidence. I'm on my way. I'll give you a ride over to the auditorium after."

I agreed to wait only because the police station was four blocks away and I figured they would arrive quickly. I grabbed my briefcase out of the back seat. On the floor was a note, a white piece of copy paper on which were written two words with a fat marker: "BACK OFF."

I had angered someone. To the point of trying to injure me. This was a murderer, and an explosives expert. Why would I stay on? Why wouldn't I give this up and let the cops do their thing? I was only doing this for Nicole. I had done my duty. Satisfying the fair Nicole was not something I was willing to get maimed for. Or killed.

But inside, I was high-fiving myself. I was on to something. I had made someone nervous.

It took the cops half an hour. I was hustled into the back of a patrol car for a statement, while a couple of cops put tape around the crime scene.

"Did you see anything?"

"No, it was dark. I came out of the restaurant. Crossed, watched my feet, slid into my car, pulled on my seat belt, and put in the key. Next thing, the door was toast."

He nodded. "Uh-huh. Did you see anyone?"

"Lots of people in the restaurant."

"Ha, funny guy. I guess that's a wrap here. When this gets typed up I'll need your signature."

"Can I get my ride now?"

Officer Tallman drove me back to the station. I crossed the lot to the building next door. I admired the building's simulated granite sandwich panels. It was a sophisticated look. Three cop cars were in the lot by the door.

As I entered the lobby, my stride grew stronger and my resolve solidified. This murderer was not going to get away with this.

Steve was waiting for me by the drinking fountain, a silver disk that brought a smile to my lips.

We shook hands.

"You ready for this?" he asked.

I nodded and pushed the elevator button.

"I can't believe there's been another accident at one of our projects."

"Steve, don't believe it. I was here yesterday and the railings were fine."

We rode up and stepped onto the eighth floor. Sargent Gilmore recognized me as I approached.

"Hi, Ken. You designed this building right?"

"Yes, it's a BPW project. Steve is the structural engineer on this one too. So you got us all. What did you find here?"

"Let me show you." He walked to the edge of the corridor in front of Matt's office. There was a gap in the railings. "As you can see, a portion of the railing is missing. We found the victim and the railing section down below. If you—careful don't touch the railing—but if you lean over here, you can see the tarp. We have the body identified as Matt Lance. From all appearances, he leaned against the railing, it gave way and he plunged to his death."

Steve bent down to examine the post. "Did you find the bolts?"

"Yeah, we retrieved them down below." Sargent Gilmore pointed toward Matt's office. "Looks like he was moving in." There were a couple of boxes sitting outside the office. The door was ajar and I could see others piled up inside. "But what I don't understand is, there are construction tools and packages down the hall. It wasn't complete."

I nodded. "Yes, the city signed off on this floor yesterday afternoon with a temporary Certificate of Occupancy. Matt was anxious to move in. Someone must have called him."

"Is it possible the contractor left out the bolts, or didn't tighten them all the way? The railing was unstable and only—"

"No," Steve and I said at the same time.

"The railing was fine when I reviewed the project on Monday," Steve said.

"That agrees with what I know, Sargent Gilmore. I brought a few people, including Matt, up here to tour the office yesterday, and there was nothing wrong with it then."

"How do you know?"

"I stood there, leaned against it." I shook my head. "No, this was deliberate."

Sargent Gilmore started thumbing through his notebook.

My phone chirped. Robert. I excused myself and turned away. "Hey, boss."

"Did you get a look at that railing? Are we liable here?"

"No, not at all. It was perfect yesterday."

Huge sigh. "Great. Nice work. This will keep Sue

Watts off my case. Get some pictures will you?"

"Well, the pics won't—"

"Just do it, Cannoli, and don't give me your lip."

"Yes, boss. It's done." I turned to Steve. "Hey, hand me your camera, will you?"

He obliged and I snapped a few pics. Railing, blank space, railing. I decided to do a 360. Corridor. Matt's office door. Boxes. Cordless drill.

I walked over to the drill, lying next to the door frame. "Have you seen this?" I asked the cop.

"Yeah, we took note of it and photographed it."

Taking a closer look at the tool, an orange sticker caught my eye. "Prime Roofing." What would a roofer be doing inside, in this corridor?

A couple of bays down, I examined the railing. The panel was fastened to the post with stainless steel bolts, the kind with a hex nut end that would sort of disappear when the assembly was complete. Looked like 5/16 to me. I went back to the drill, which was set up for a matching 5/16" hex attachment.

My phone chirped. Sue Watts. "Ken, another accident? On your watch?"

"Yes, hi, Sue. No accident. The railing was deliberately taken apart."

"You better get lots of pictures. And I want your report A-S-A-P."

"Yep."

"And Ken, no press this time."

"Yes ma'am." I leaned against the railing, three supports down from the blocked off police section, gazing down at the atrium. Landscapers had been going to town, setting natural vegetation: Indian grass and a variety of purple and yellow wildflowers. I hated the trend toward putting in weeds. The pavers, a tumbled brick in smoky grey without grout, had been set the week before. Michigan granite boulders popped up at the ends of the building and at doorways.

While I gazed at the view below, I noticed Shirley striding in, looking around this way and that—trying to get a bead on the murder I was certain—then she plowed right into a line of bagged wood chips and landed square on her face.

Oh crap. Not now. There was no way to avoid the confrontation I needed to have with her.

"Steve, I gotta talk to her."

"I have to run anyway. See ya!" Steve walked away and I said my good byes to the cop. He said he would have more questions for me later. I ran for the elevator, pushed the button. I tapped my foot, as if it would speed the cab reaching my floor. Jumped in, rode down. When the doors opened I was staring right at my nemesis.

"Ken, lovely to see you."

I strode out, grabbed her shoulder and pulled her aside before she could get into the elevator. "Are you ok? I saw you take the fall."

"Fine. But I need to get upstairs. Let me—"

"Not now. What were you thinking?"

She raised her arms in a 'who me' signal, and put them back down again. "Oh, you're miffed I see."

"I thought we were friends."

"Huh, I thought so too. Did you sleep with her?"

"Isn't that what you sent her to do?"

"No, not at all. I just sent her to spy. I never thought... a-hem...You fell in with her pretty quick, didn't you?"

"Don't make this about me. *You* sent a spy after me."

"A spy? Hardly. I just asked Kristen to let me know a few things about what you were doing. I thought you'd enjoy meeting a star. And apparently you did."

"Shirley." Humpf. "You don't ask people to spy on

your friends."

"No, I suppose not. But you can see why, can't you? You didn't give me any information, and lord knows you were collecting plenty. I didn't think you'd fall for her. Hollywood and everything."

"Jealous?"

"No, hey. I need to find the cops. Are they upstairs?"

I stared at her.

"Of course they are. Excuse me." She walked to the elevator and pushed the button.

Chapter 34

I stepped across the lobby after her. "Hold the phone, Shirley. We need to talk about a couple of other things.

She put her hands on her hips.

"Did you share my suspicions about Matt?"

"No, of course not."

"Yesterday I made a pretty strong argument that he killed Neumann, now he's dead."

"And I'm responsible?"

"I know you, Shirley; you probably traded that information, just as you used Kristen and me to further your career."

"Umpf. You're wrong, Ken. Like you were wrong about the door that was blown off your car."

"Huh? What do you know about that?"

"It must have scared you silly."

"Yeah, well. Obviously someone is getting nervous. Wonder what button I pushed."

"You're not the only one pushing buttons, are you?"

"Hey, listen," I said. "I have something else. This is rather heavy, let's go sit down; there's a break room back here."

She stalled for a moment, then gave me an 'all right, let's just get this over with' sigh. I led the way behind the elevators, to an area with tables and outside windows.

Shirley looked at me expectantly. I hated to break her heart, but I felt she had to know the truth.

"How was your night last night?" I said.

"Fine." She looked around. "What?"

"I saw Bryce's truck was in your parking lot all night long."

"Is that what this is about? You're jealous? After what you said about Kristen, seems you should be the last person to be jealous."

"I think you may be into something you shouldn't be."

"Come again?"

"You spent the night with Bryce, right?"

"Come on. You don't have to pry into my life just because I accidently tread on yours. Now if you'll excuse me." She rose.

"Bryce is married."

She stopped short. Turned, looked at me.

I held her gaze. In her dark eyes framed in thick lashes I saw a dull mass eclipse the sparkle, I saw the light fade, saw the hardening of her spirit.

She spoke firmly. "Yeah, I know."

But she didn't. As usual, she was trying to hide things, keep control on her side. She wasn't as tough as she made out to be. Her eyes had betrayed her. "Yeah," I said. "Ok."

"Look," she said. "I gotta run. I'm actually late for an appointment. Catch you later."

And she walked out of the building. I sat there, looking through the glass. I saw her stride to her car, jerk the door open and slide in and slam it shut.

A moment later an explosion shook the glass next to me. Her passenger door tumbled across the lot in a puff of white smoke. I jumped out of my seat like a lightning bolt, shot out the front door, and dashed over to her. I jerked her driver's door open.

"Shirl! Shirl! Are you ok?"

She turned her head, looked at me and raised her hand to her forehead. She glanced around, paused at the view of the passenger side, and mumbled, "Hey, matching cars."

Chapter 35

I helped Shirley out of her car. She was wobbly, so I did the fingers in front of your face trick. "How many—"

"Unless you're going to put one of those fingers where I'm going to like it, get them out of my face."

She was ok.

"This is too much," I said. "What say we get lunch and figure this out?"

"We'll have to talk to them first." She pointed behind me. Sargent Gilmore and Officer Tallman were hustling toward us.

"Hey, hey, would you look at that," Tallman said. To me, "She's got one just like yours. What have you two been up to now?"

I shook my head.

"I need to get places. Are you gonna wanna hold on to my car?" Shirley said.

"Yes, ma'am. And we need your statement. Cannoli, did you witness the explosion?"

A group of people were gathered near the building entrance. "Looks to me like a lot of people witnessed this thing."

Grunt. "Well, I'll need your statement too. Let me get this young lady's first."

When the two of them went back inside, *Mighty Mouse* broke through the dry air. "Hey, Edison, what's up?"

"Ken, what are you doing for lunch? I've been working this presentation since four a.m. and I need a break."

"Jesus, is it lunch time? Shirley and I had the crap scared out of us this morning."

"You and Shirley?"

"No, not like that, Edison. I'll explain later. You got time? Aren't you finishing the presentation?"

"It's done. Wally's looking it over. I have to take a break before I go nuts."

"Ok, great. You don't mind if Shirley joins us, do you?"

* * *

Edison showed up before the police finished their questioning and walked over to where they were talking to Shirley. They carried on some kind of exchange through the glass. I ambled over. When the police were done, we went inside.

Shirley said, "They said they'd need to keep my car for a couple of days."

Edison had a happy puppy dog look on his face. "Nothing exciting like that ever happens to me."

"Be glad it doesn't," Shirley and I said in unison.

Shirley reached Edison's Camaro first and opened the passenger door. I made the sacrifice and climbed into the back seat, no easy task with my six foot three inch frame. I sat cross wise in the compartment. Tight squeeze. Shirley sat next to Edison. When we walked through the back door of Ray's Coney, Shirley wrinkled her nose.

"God, you guys, can't you think of a better place to have lunch?"

Before I could utter a word, Edison said, "Hey, Shirley. You're going to change your mind before you walk out of here."

"I doubt it," she said.

We took a table. I sat next to Shirley.

Edison said, "I can't believe you guys both had your

car doors blown off."

We couldn't either.

"What have you been doing? You've gotten to somebody."

"Yeah. I've been thinking the same thing." I looked at Shirley. "I think we should put down the rapiers and work together. You know, throw in, combine resources and get this guy."

"Or girl," Shirley said.

"Or girl," Edison agreed.

I jerked my thumb at him. To Shirley I said, "He thinks Nicole may be involved."

Shirley said, "I've been wondering that too. But she seems genuinely distraught."

I shook my head. "She *is* genuinely distraught. I can't imagine she had anything to do with it. Killing Neumann and then Matt Lance."

Shirley flashed her lashes at me. "You think the murders are connected?"

"Hell, yes." Edison said.

"Yes," I agreed. "Yesterday, I figured a connection between Matt and Neumann. You still didn't tell anyone, right?"

"No, I swear. Today would have been a different story, though. But what about access to this building? What do you think happened? Matt was working late, someone jury-rigged the rail, then tossed him into it?"

"Wouldn't take much. The guy was old. Strong, but old nonetheless."

Edison said, "Remember the night the sign fell? Didn't you overhear Bryce McClurg tell Matt, 'I'm gonna kill you.'"

I flashed a look at Shirley. "But Bryce didn't have access to the office here. Maybe Matt's murder is unrelated? Wait, Bryce is a contractor. Contractors have access to the offices."

"Good point," Shirley said, "But what about Rusty? He has an office in the new building too, so he would have keys."

She smiled, aware that she was showing off information I didn't possess. "This is why we have to work together now. I have an idea that will smoke him out."

Edison suddenly brightened up. "Wait! I found something else out. I have to tell you. This might make it make sense. Neumann came on to Bryce's wife."

"What?" I said. "She lives in Dayton."

"Yeah, yeah. Jeanelle's girlfriend Emile—she's a model, too—has a boyfriend who owns a four-star night club in Dayton: Jewel's. They bring in semi-big entertainment, like Sinatra impersonators and dance acts based on popular movies. From what I heard, Neumann's auto parts business supplies an auto plant in Dayton. He goes—went—down there regularly. Well, apparently he met Mrs. Bryce McClurg at Jewel's. Word I have is that she was dining with girlfriends and he walked right up to the group and weaseled himself into the evening."

I noticed Shirley starting to play with her hands. I tried to give her an *it's ok* glance, but she wasn't looking. I felt sorry for her. It was a lot to take.

Edison continued. "So apparently he made some moves on her, which she didn't accept. She told Bryce, who confronted Neumann."

"When did all this happen?" I said.

"Just last month. So it's fresh motive."

It certainly was. There were plenty of motives and grudges to go around.

Shirley, head down, suddenly mumbled, "Excuse me," pushed out her chair and ran off to the bathroom. I didn't know she had this tender side.

Edison said, "What's up with Shirley?"

"Nothing," I said.

"Is she gonna finish her fries?"

I shook my head. "No, I think she's done."

Who was doing this? Something was irritating my mind, like the pea under the princess's mattress. Something I had seen during the day was off, out of place. Some connection I couldn't place.

With Shirley's help I believed we could get to the bottom of it.

* * *

Edison went back to the office while Shirley and I ventured next door to the Enterprise Car Rental for temporary vehicles. Shirley had some things to do and I needed to check on Nicole before the evening's event.

"Are you going to the poetry reading tonight, Ken?" Shirley asked.

The organizers of the poetry reading from Saturday night were staging this event—not even a week later. Tonight's program was originally designed as a less-exclusive companion affair to Saturday's exclusive evening, but after the interruption a few days prior, they had added a few readings to this evening's program which had gone unheard on Saturday. At the same location. Personally, I thought it was in bad taste to proceed with it, but I suppose returning to normalcy had its own benefit.

"I wouldn't miss it. After what happened at the last one? Forgetaboutit."

"I'll meet you there, ok?" she said.

I nodded.

We were assigned our cars. For me, a Dodge Charger. For Shirley a Kia Sorrento. I checked my watch. One-thirty. Yikes, I needed to get a move on.

* * *

Nicole was dressed in a simple button up blouse, rose, and a knee length black skirt. She greeted me with a warm hug. I asked her how she was doing.

"Oh, well, I feel like this is dragging on so long. At least the funeral arrangements are in the works now. Visitation will be tomorrow afternoon and Saturday morning, with the funeral directly after."

I took down the information on the funeral home to share with the office.

"The kids are still with Mother. She'll bring them by in the morning and we'll all get ready."

"You're being strong, Nicole."

She forced a smile. "It's what I do." She smoothed the fabric of her skirt. "Dani's coming in tonight, late. Chad had a consultation he couldn't postpone, so he'll follow tomorrow evening. I'm glad she'll be here for emotional support."

Dani. I could still see her. Brush in hand, stroking a canvas. Color seemed to flow from her instrument. No, more than color. Shapes, figures. People. Emotion. She breathed fire and sizzle into the core of human sinew, like she breathed fire and sizzle into my life, turning a cold and rainy autumn day into a bright experience of leaves and pumpkins. And in the end, she left me with nothing but the frost.

I raised my head and saw Dani's eyes looking back at me. Of course, I smiled at Nicole and she clasped her hands together. "So what's new with the investigation?"

"Have you," I looked around the room. No TV. "seen the news today, Nicole?"

"I don't watch it anymore. Not after Jerome."

I shared the morning's events with her.

"Matt Lance is dead?" She sat down on the sofa. "I can't believe it. First Jerome, now this." She put her hand to her mouth. "What on earth?"

"There's more." I told her about my car and Shirley's having exploded.

"What! Are you all right?"

I assured her I was.

"Ken, stop this. You're in danger. I never wanted this for you. Never wanted you to be risking your life."

"It was a warning. If they intended to hurt me—or Shirley—they would have. It means we're getting close. This thing should be wrapped up soon."

The phone rang. A traditional ring. Nicole picked up the receiver in the kitchen.

"Yes, yes, Molly, I'll be ready. It's so kind of you to accompany me. You are a sweetheart. Yes, I mean it. Hahaha."

I raised my eyebrows at her when she hung up.

"Molly Gross. She's going to pick me up for the event tonight. Very nice of her."

I blanched. "You're going?"

"Well, yes, I have to keep myself occupied, don't I? Keeps me from going crazy."

"I didn't realize you knew Molly Gross personally. I found a sticky-note on your brochure for the event, but I thought it was a fan signing. But you *know* her."

Nicole said, "Yes, why?"

"Did you tell Molly that Matt was a suspect?"

"I don't like the tone of your voice. What are you implying?"

"Yesterday, when I came over here and told you I had figured out that I thought Matt killed your husband. Did you tell Molly?"

"Yes, well, she's been calling to keep tabs on me. Make sure I was ok. Yes, she was curious about the investigation you were doing. She called yesterday shortly after you and Shirley left. I told her you had narrowed down a suspect."

Chapter 36

Nicole and Molly? I wondered what this meant. Before lunch yesterday, Molly had the information. What did she do with it?

To make the presentation to the client, I zoomed through traffic. My thoughts were on the case, not on work. It would make me less effective, but I took heart in the fact that Wally was prepared.

"Cannoli. About time you got here," he said.

"Yeah, sorry, Wally. I ran into some trouble this morning, but it's ok now. We can get this."

"If it weren't for Edison, we wouldn't be good here."

"I know. He's a lifesaver, isn't he?"

Edison came bouncing around the corner. "Who's a life saver?"

Wally and I exchanged glances. No need to explode Edison's head. Wally mumbled, "Nothing. What you got?"

Edison ran through the presentation materials. We sat in the conference room—Wally, Robert and I—and talked through the slides, logic and economics. We were solid. Edison had done a bang up job. We finished our rehearsal and the clients arrived.

Two men, one woman. We all shook hands. Of course I'd met them before. We did the talk, worked the patter, showed how the Dizzy's stores could be converted to the Val's stores. Wally presented data on energy efficiency and how the firm would address green issues. No one thought the projects would seek LEED certification, but we convinced them we were set up to count the points and make it happen if they were interested.

It was a concrete performance.

And all I could think about was getting out of there, meeting Shirley and talking strategy for our murder case.

* * *

I left work drained; all the internal figuring was wearing me out. I went home to change for the event. It was four-thirty, so I had a comfortable amount of time. Shower, dress. Clean shirt. Pressed suit. Fresh. I would meet Shirley at the auditorium. Nicole would ride with Molly. Huh, wasn't that an interesting combo? Their friendship intrigued me; they seemed such different people. I wondered what attracted them to each other in the first place.

* * *

I pulled into the parking lot precisely at six-thirty, comfortably early for the seven-thirty curtain, and parked along the west curb where there were plenty of spots open. My eyes drifted across the lot, to see Shirley climbing out of her Kia Sorrento the next aisle toward the building. She wore a flaming red cocktail dress that made her legs look suitable for a Rockettes performance, and her ass tight as a snare drum.

As I crossed into the next aisle, I head the screeching of tires and looked up to see a monster pick-up truck speed my way in a blaze of blue. As this information registered, I felt a tug at my elbow. Off balance, a flash of red passed before me, and I crashed to the sidewalk, Shirley on top of me. I turned my head to see the truck blink away, my nose right up next to Shirley's. As I took in a breath to speak, she lowered her mouth onto mine. My body pulsed and I circled my arms around her and pulled her tighter.

I dropped my head back. "Umm. That was

something."

She looked sideways and raised an eye brow.

"Saving my life. That was definitely something."

"Uh huh."

I struggled against her. A little. "We should get... "

She scrambled herself to sitting. "Right. Right; time to get off to go."

"Is that bubblegum I taste?" I said.

"Just my lipstick."

"Tangy."

She grinned wide, raised herself to standing.

I followed and asked, "What was that for?"

"We definitely got somebody nervous."

"Yeah. Get an ID on that truck?"

"Nothing."

I hadn't either. She examined her dress, and I checked out my clothes. No problem. "Turn around," I said. She obliged. I reviewed her backside, pausing at the view.

"Ken, are there any smudges, tears?"

"No," I said, bending closer. "Looks good from here."

She turned and gave me a light slap, which only served to invigorate my senses.

We entered through the glass lobby doors. The place was crammed. Folks stood in small groups, chatting earnestly. Earrings dangled, dark suits backdropped lively fall outfits in red, yellow and chestnut.

I searched for familiar faces. Rusty, Molly and Nicole stood in a tight group at the auditorium doors, Molly's A-line dress, sky blue, showed off her features—and her hair appeared brushed, held back with a tortoise shell clip and matching teardrop earrings. Rusty wore his grumpy thin-lipped expression and a herringbone suit. Nicole didn't disappoint in a black skirt suit with white pinstriping, with a sheer black blouse beneath, a bit daring given her state of mourning.

Edison and his model girlfriend Jeanelle stood nearby, Edison in a cinnamon corduroy suit and his customary hiking boots, At least they were brown. Jeanelle was ravishing in a short amber skirt and matching jacket, white top and sparkly gold pumps. While their colors coordinated—Jeanelle's doing, I'm sure—I remained mystified by Edison's ability to attract high value women. Shirley and I ambled over in their direction. On the way, I noted a suited Bryce, uncharacteristically standing alone, and Julianne Bodary with her girlfriend Michelle.

Walter Scofield and John Boyd stood in the corner talking with elevated voices and vigorous hand movements.

As we made our way across, the lobby was filling up, and I noted Steve Dickerson entering from the opposite side.

Everyone was keenly aware of what had happened just a few days before. The murmurs filled the space with a ghostly presence.

So when two uniforms, led by Sergeant Gilmore, appeared at the glass doors, the crowd hushed. I exchanged nods with Office Tallman. The trio stepped inside the doors, Gilmore taking in the faces around the room. He stopped when his eyes fell upon Bryce, then motioned with a flat, pointed hand to the others. The police crossed the floor.

As they grew near, it became clear that they intended to arrest Bryce. My mind stilled and mentally I gasped, as they announced "for the murder of Matt Lance."

My thoughts raced. Bryce had spent the night with Shirley the evening of the murder, but I could not—would not—reveal Shirley's dalliance with a married man. I gave Officer Tallman the evil eye, and the cop shrugged. Didn't he realize that Bryce had an alibi? Couldn't have done it? But in order to say so out loud, I would have to expose Shirley's indiscretion, or Bryce would.

"Wait; hold on there, before you arrest the wrong person," I said.

Sergeant Gilmore, who had stepped next to Bryce, stopped and glared at me.

"I think we can settle this," I said. "I believe Shirley Hanson has some information that can reveal the killer." Shirley looked intrigued, but not amused. "I'm sure you want an explanation. Why don't we move to the Huron Room, where we can have a conversation. It's getting a little crowded in here."

The cops looked around; Gilmore and Tallman exchanged glances. Office Tallman said, "Hey, Sarge, maybe it'd be a good idea to go somewhere more private."

Sergeant Gilmore placed his hand on Bryce's arm—Bryce stiffened, but he didn't say anything—and said, "Very well."

A row of four conference rooms and a small kitchen were arranged on the left side of the auditorium in a conference center arrangement. With a little cajoling, we secured the consent of all the parties involved to be included: Nicole, Bryce, Boyd, Scofield, Julianne, Molly, Rusty. Whether they agreed as a matter of pride or a point of curiosity, I don't know to this day, but we all moved into one of the meeting rooms.

As we settled into the room, I waved at Shirley, who took the lead.

"Molly, tell us how you blew up the sign."

Molly straightened, held her head up, and looked slowly around. "Yes," she said, "It was I who rented the equipment, those blow up bags that were placed under the sign to tip it off the roof. Once the bolts were removed, it was a simple matter of connecting the hoses and throwing the switch. The thrust from the bags lifted the sign, tipped it over the edge, and off the roof. With finality, that blemish was removed."

"Molly!" Rusty snapped.

"Rusty, I love you, and I appreciate you, but the truth must be revealed."

Rusty hung his head, and for a moment I thought he would fold. But then he jerked around and bolted for the door. Into the arms of the cops.

"Just cool your heels," Officer Tallman said.

Shirley said, "Who was it that actually did the work on the roof, Molly? Did you?"

Rusty struggled against Office Tallman's hold as Molly went on. "I was on stage when the sign was blown. But I have to take credit for the idea, and the planning of the occurrence."

"Molly, you don't know what you've done!" Rusty said. "Shut up, now. Shut up!"

Shirley took the hint. "So it was you, Rusty, responsible for the sign demolition."

Rusty said nothing. But Molly went on. "I'm responsible. You will have to take me in as well."

"We will, miss, you can be certain of that," Sergeant Gilmore said.

I said, "Rusty, did you look over the roof's edge before you triggered the device? Or did you mean to commit murder?"

His eyes grew wild like a bull on the rampage. "What do you take me for? Some kind of moron? Of course, I checked it. The coast was clear."

"You had a clear view the very moment you triggered it?" Shirley said.

"Well, no. I looked over the edge, made sure everything was perfect, and then got myself into place. You don't know how these things are going to work. I went to the other end of the roof over by the parking lot and hit the release."

"So someone could have laid Neumann on the ground while you were getting ready," Shirley said. "And then the sign killed him when you blew it off the roof."

Rusty didn't say anything.

Shirley spoke to Sergeant Gilmore, "Didn't Matt Lance admit to punching Neumann and knocking him out during an argument just prior to the sign's toppling?"

"Yes," the Sergeant said. "He said it was just an argument and nothing unusual; they kidded each other all the time. But there were plenty of arguments to go around."

"Yes," Shirley said. "Like Julianne was dumped by Neumann."

Julianne raised her fingertips to her mouth.

"You did talk with Neumann the night in question," Shirley said.

"Yes."

"He was dumping you and you were begging for him to stay."

I glanced at Nicole. Her arms were folded, her mouth tight.

"Yes, but you don't understand! He loved me! And I loved him."

"Yes," Shirley said. "The dog hair on his clothes showed that he was with you, in a place where your dog also was, shortly before his death."

"My car."

"And you didn't kill him."

She shook her head.

"You didn't summon him to the office."

"No." She shook her head. "No, that wasn't me."

I spoke. "I think we know that it was Matt Lance

who made the call to lure Neumann to the office."

Shirley looked at Neumann's widow. "Nicole." She stopped, perhaps waiting for Nicole to give a sign she understood.

Nicole raised her head, grimaced.

"Two days ago, in the morning, Ken Knoll stopped by your house. What did he tell you?"

Nicole straightened her jacket. Spoke slowly. "That he had figured out who killed my Jerome."

"And?"

"It was Matt Lance, that's what Ken said."

"I'm sure you were relieved," Shirley said. "Ken gave you a huge piece of information. The man who killed your Jerome. You would finally have some closure."

"Yes," Nicole said. "It was so hard, waiting. I thought it was that bit–, er, that woman. After having my head in a vise all week, I felt like the pressure was lessening. He was going to go to the cops."

Shirley flashed her eyes at me, briefly. "Nicole, who did you give this information to? You must have been bursting at the seams to tell someone."

"Well, yes and no. I was trying hard not to tell anyone, because Ken told me to wait, but I trusted her and we've been friends for so long. I, well, it was good to get it out. Like taking a bandage off—"

"Who?"

"Molly. I told Molly. She was concerned about me, all along, she kept checking to see how I was doing. A few times a day. It's so good to have a friend."

Shirley turned to Molly. "So she told you Matt was under suspicion."

"Yes. Nicole told me."

Shirley turned to Molly. "And what did you do with the information?"

Molly looked down at her shoes. "I was so shocked.

Now Matt was getting a rap for something Rusty and I did. We couldn't let this stand. The truth had to come out. I talked to Rusty about it, told him we needed to bring our actions to the police but he wouldn't have it."

Rusty said, "Why did you have to admit the sign? I tried to protect you! They would have blamed everything on *him*!" Rusty said.

Shirley said, "Oh, but this was good news for you, Rusty? Isn't that how you saw it? You could let him take all the blame, and divert attention from you and Molly."

"He was a jerk anyway. And Molly does so much good for the world. Her ideas and concepts save people's lives. Couples are reunited. Estranged parents and children meet each other again. And Fitz, well," he was looking at Molly now. "I told him I would take care of you. So many years, we knew each other, and I watched you grow up. Do you know how proud he was, to have a granddaughter like you? On his deathbed, I promised. With Matt Lance dead, everyone would think that he did the murder and the focus would be off you, sweetheart, and you could continue to do your work."

Molly's expressions turned grotesque. "You killed him?"

"Here's what happened Saturday night," Shirley said. "Like Ken figured out, Matt phoned Neumann from the office, met him, and they walked back to the auditorium, Matt carrying a box of books from the used book sale. He must have made some excuse about taking them to his car or something. Then, with rage he hit him over the head with the books and dragged him under the sign above. He knew what time the sign would fall; he had that information from Bryce. Neumann was still alive when he place him there. The sign would kill him, placing the blame on Molly. Matt had a grudge against her; blamed her for turning his son against him. Two birds. He would be in the clear."

Shirley continued, "There's something else. Ken's car and mine had their doors blown off this morning. Rusty, didn't you serve in Vietnam?"

"Pride and glory. Twenty months of excellence, until those bastards took my leg."

"And what was your specialty?'

Rusty mumbled.

Molly helped him out. "Weren't you a member of the UDT, Underwater Demolition Team? The precursor of the Navy Seals." She paused and turned a lazy eye in his direction. "So you almost blew up two other people?"

"They weren't in danger. I just set it to blow the doors."

Sergeant Gilmore placed handcuffs on Rusty and read him his rights. They took Molly with them also, for questioning.

Shirley walked out of the room, as Edison, Jeanelle and I followed. She stormed away, and I called after her. "Shirley, wait up."

"Later, Ken," she said without stopping.

I moved toward the glass exit doors with Edison, who turned to me and whispered, "Why? You let her have all the glory."

I looked over at Shirley, who had sat down on a bench. She was staring into space, her face emotionless as if her world had unraveled. "Sometimes," I said, "doing right is better than being right. Look at her face, Edison. She lost something today."

Her face pale, she held her hands on her knees as if to hold herself up.

"Let's get out of here," I said. "I don't feel like the poetry event now. Want to get some coney?"

Edison looked at his girl. Jeanelle made a face, kissed him on the lips and said, "You boys and your grease. Have fun, and I'll tell you all about the lovely readings tonight, Pookie."

She crossed the lobby, and turned to wave to us as she opened the auditorium doors.

"Yeah. Let's do George's," Edison said.

As we reached the exit, Nicole walked up to me with a look that said the weight was off her shoulders. Wordlessly, she circled her arms around me and kissed my cheek. "Thank you, Ken Knoll. I can't ever repay you."

I tipped my hat, metaphorically speaking.

As she left, I turned on my heels and said to Edison, "I think I'll do some chili cheese fries today," I said.

"Chili *and* cheese?"

"It's been a rough day."

Chapter 37

From interrogating Rusty and Molly, the police learned a few more things about how the sign destruction happened. Molly had rented the destruction equipment, which Rusty took charge of. He practiced on some abandoned buildings in Detroit. He secured a key to the auditorium roof by bribing a window washer, then borrowed sheets of plywood from their stash in the penthouse to distribute the load from the blast of destruction to the roof deck. Prior to the poetry reading event, he removed the bolts which secured the sign frame to the stub columns, relying on the weight of the framework to keep it in place until intermission. He figured that if the wind took it, and it fell on its own, so much the better. But it didn't. He had placed the destruction equipment—bags and charger—in the penthouse before the evening began. At intermission, he placed the air bags on the plywood beneath the beams, checked for anyone down below—I believed him on this part, though I questioned in which order he performed these acts—then moved away and push the trigger. The force of the blow raised the sign a couple of inches, tilting it out into empty space and down it went. Afterward, he scooped up the bags and the charger, which were very light in weight, and stuffed them in garbage bags. He carried them over to the other side of the roof, where he threw them down into the dumpsters below. Early Sunday morning, when everyone was gone, he came back and took them away.

Chapter 38 Epilog

Friday morning I awoke with a sadness pallor. Two deaths, the first over an old grudge, consummated by a perceived need to honor an ancestor, the second to protect the identity of the first. Sad, very sad.

Padding to the kitchen, my shoulders hunched with an unwillingness to approach the day. I made coffee. I checked Shirley's blog.

Daddy, how easy it is to tumble, to slide, to plunge headfirst into catastrophe. The trusty shield of justice and day-lighting vindication may not forestall the suffering entanglement laid down by the hands of betrayal.

For is to succumb to betrayal not to betray?

The harsh tool of judgment, like sandpaper, wears at the bones of both the implement and object. With madness it ascribes blame, incites guilt, and extracts remorse. Interface abrasion provides no favors. Crumbs of compassion fall. Dust of charity clouds. Stink of spoilage rises, eclipsing—no reversing— victory. Heated scraping scorches, the onerous tarnish marring both the accuser and the accused.

Perhaps the shield of the just can be a bit too rough. Too biting. Too hostile. Perhaps exists an alternate order. Less harsh. Less contentious. Equally true.

Perhaps, Daddy.

I showered and dressed with sluggish motions. Perhaps work would rouse me. Driving to work, the traffic report answered my unasked question.

And that congestion along I-94 in Port Huron is gone, now that the filming of A Mother's Dilemma *wrapped yesterday afternoon. Smooth sailing once again, in time for the weekend.*

She was probably in the air, flying back to Hollywood. No word. I certainly wasn't going to call her.

I entered my office building with a nod to Sally and walked straight to my office. I fired up the computer and sat there while it chugged through the opening routine. I didn't have the stomach for any office conversation that might occur at the coffee pot. The day would be hard.

Wally had different ideas. He barged into my office shortly after nine o'clock.

"Cannoli, head's up. We're this close to a signed contract on the Val's Market deal."

I looked up. "Good job. I thought we would sell them."

"You don't sound too excited. Trouble with the honey?"

"There is no honey." I exhaled. "Just me."

"Don't let that skirt get you down, bro. She'll come around. Or someone else will."

That made me smile. "Yeah, thanks."

"Listen. We need to talk about assembling a team on this project, but we can't officially start yet. Val's needs to get a signature from the old man and then they'll kick us loose."

"Is Gruen still holding out? I just talked to him last weekend. I thought he was coming our way."

"Yeah. So it would seem. But no dice yet. Just hang tight."

I nodded. "Will do."

He left my office. Shortly thereafter, Rita entered with a cup of coffee for me. And a plate.

"I don't usually do this, but Wally said you were looking kind of down. It's German chocolate. A little early in the day, but it will perk you up."

"Thanks Rita, that's nice."

She left and I did email for a while.

About lunchtime Edison walked in. "Hey, Ken, I haven't seen you all day. Working hard?"

"No," I said. "Just un-motivated."

"Yeah, I know what you mean. It's Friday. I'm thinking about the weekend too."

I didn't have the heart to correct him.

"But, listen, Ken, I'm sorry I was right about Kristen. She's pretty cool; I mean it seemed like you were having fun."

I looked up. "Yeah, well, we're from different worlds. It probably wouldn't have worked out anyway, right?"

"Yeah, I don't know."

* * *

About five o'clock, Edison returned to my office.

"I thought you'd be leaving early, but I see you're still working," Edison said.

Truth is I was almost asleep, staring at the monitor. "I wanted to finish this paperwork."

"Chinese?"

"No, I think I need to get some air by myself."

I packed my briefcase and headed out the door. At Kroger I bought staples—eggs, waffles, potatoes, corn, bread. I'd make dinner at home. Alone.

At my Ferndale renovation house, I unpacked the groceries. Made an omelet and potatoes. Thought of Kristen's smile. Her silky hair. Her spontaneity made me laugh. We were a good combination.

Not like me and Shirley. I *did* have respect for her unabashed truth. Though I didn't always appreciate the way she laid it out, she got results and worked for good. A little too brash for me, but still there was *something* about her...

The food didn't taste right. I'd eaten alone before, but tonight it was tough. I piled the dishes in the sink, grabbed my jacket and slammed the side door on the way out.

There was a chill in the air. Just barely October, grass was still growing, I would have to cut it at least one more time. Maybe twice. Dogs barked when I walked past. Leaves were dropping. Particularly the yellow ones it seemed. I hated raking leaves. Luckily, my yard was small and it wouldn't take long. I circled the block, headed down the next street toward the middle school. The moon hung low in the sky. Waning. I thought of the night I met Kristen, not even a week ago. Could so much change in just a few days? She was here and gone so quickly. And took my breath with her.

I kicked a smashed-in soda can and sent it skittering down the sidewalk. When I reached it, I gave it another swift kick. Jerome Neumann's funeral would be tomorrow. Dani was in town, and it would be nice to see her. And difficult, too.

Funk. I returned to the dark house. Switched on the kitchen light and closed the shades. I dropped onto the bed in my clothes, and slept.

* * *

The funeral was a blur. Words were spoken. I saw Dani. We shared a brief hug and some non-committal words. I hugged Nicole and she gave me a restrained smile. Wally showed up, made some inappropriate cracks to Robert. Neumann's brothers and Dani's husband Chad picked up the casket and marched it to the hearse. We all filed out and proceeded to the cemetery. Robert and Wally offered me a ride, but I didn't feel like it.

Afterward, at home, I made a dinner of omelet and potatoes; took a walk. Kicked the can. I returned home, turned on the lights and closed the shades.

This became my routine for the next few weeks. Walk aimlessly. Sleep. I finished the hallway. Shirley moved to California. Kristen was back in California, too. Funny, both women away, and in the same state. I thought of that week in mid-September. Stood on my porch and looked up at a full moon. Sighed.

Dinner, walk, sleep. Late in October, I returned from a long walk, kicking sticks, and examining the ghosts and goblins on display around the neighborhood. I dumped myself onto the couch.

There was a light tap at the front door. *What now?*

I peeked through the small window. A vision of loveliness, beautiful femininity. The tenseness in my shoulders eased, and I let go of the breath I had been holding.

"I should have called. I hope I'm not interrupting. I've been thinking about everything—can we begin again?"

"I'm glad you're here." I tugged her through the door and into my arms. I leaned into her soft, receptive lips.

"Oh, Ken."

Suddenly uncomfortable, I said, "I need to take a shower. Would you mind waiting? I feel grungy. I'll be right out."

She smiled. "Do you mind if I join you?" She was already unbuttoning her blouse.

We began our passion in the shower, continued, damp, into the bedroom until we fell back in each other's arms, laying there until our breath slowed and I began drifting off.

"Hey, Ken," she whispered. "I'm parked behind you. You don't need to get up early do you? Do you want me to move my Mustang?"

"No," I smiled. "I'm not going anywhere anytime soon. I want to enjoy this moment."

Darth Vader's Theme shattered the air.

"Aren't you going to—?"

"No, that's Robert—I'm ignoring that. I don't want to let you go." I hugged her more tightly.

It stopped, then started again.

She gave me a playful shove and lay back, "Maybe you'd better."

"Jeez," I said, and picked up the phone. "Robert, it's Saturday night. Can't a guy—"

"You have to get to Gaylord! Walter Gruen is dead. That damn house you designed collapsed on him. Take Steve Dickerson with you. Cripes, Sue Watts is gonna have my ass."

THE END

ABOUT THE AUTHOR

 Christian Belz has been a practicing architect in Metro Detroit for 29 years, with experience in retail, educational, and industrial projects. He is Vice President of Detroit Working Writers. He won the Grand Prize in Aquarius Press's 2011 Bright Harvest Prize for his short story *Chambers*. Christian's fiction has appeared in *Writers' Journal, The Story Teller Magazine*, and Wicked East Press's anthology: *Short Sips, Coffee House Flash Fiction Collection 2*. His poetry has been published in *WestWard Quarterly* and *Yes, Poetry*.

Christian is one of the co-authors of *The 28-Day Thought Diet*.

Civic Center Corpse is the second of the Ken Knoll Architectural Mysteries. Find out more at KenKnollMystery.com

www.ingramcontent.com/pod-product-compliance
Lightning Source LLC
Chambersburg PA
CBHW050353260626
47156CB00003B/716